THE
NIGHT
BELL

OTHER HAZEL MICALLEF MYSTERIES
BY INGER ASH WOLFE

The Calling
The Taken
A Door in the River

THE
NIGHT
BELL

INGER ASH WOLFE

PEGASUS CRIME
NEW YORK LONDON

THE NIGHT BELL

Pegasus Crime is an Imprint of
Pegasus Books Ltd.
148 West 37th Street, 13th Floor
New York, NY 10018

American copyright © 2016 by Inger Ash Wolfe

First Pegasus Books hardcover edition August 2016

ISBN: 978-1-68177-165-6

10 9 8 7 6 5 4 3 2 1

Printed in the United States of America
Distributed by W. W. Norton & Company, Inc.

For my brother, who likes a good yarn.

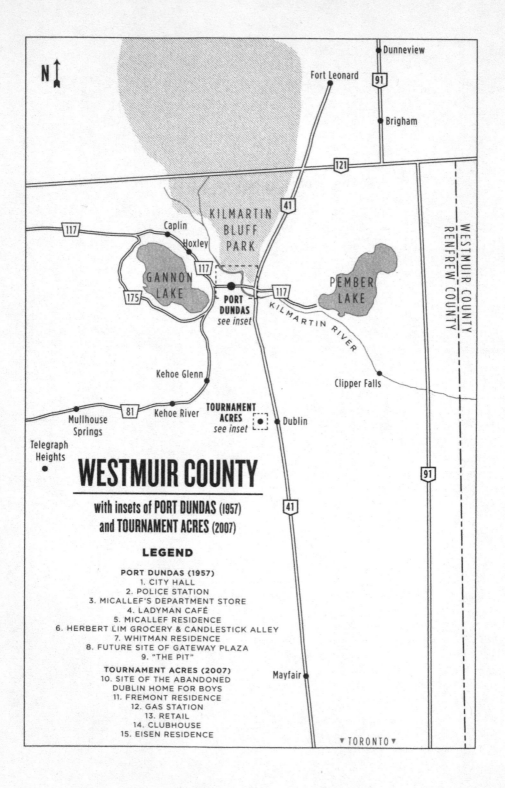

N

Dunneview

Fort Leonard

91

Brigham

121

KILMARTIN
BLUFF
PARK

41

Caplin

117

Hoxley

117

117

GANNON
LAKE

175

PEMBER
LAKE

PORT
DUNDAS
see inset

117

KILMARTIN RIVER

Clipper Falls

Kehoe Glenn

WESTMUIR COUNTY
RENFREW COUNTY

TOURNAMENT
ACRES
see inset

81

Kehoe River

Dublin

Mullhouse
Springs

Telegraph
Heights

91

WESTMUIR COUNTY

with insets of PORT DUNDAS (1957)
and TOURNAMENT ACRES (2007)

41

LEGEND

PORT DUNDAS (1957)
1. CITY HALL
2. POLICE STATION
3. MICALLEF'S DEPARTMENT STORE
4. LADYMAN CAFÉ
5. MICALLEF RESIDENCE
6. HERBERT LIM GROCERY & CANDLESTICK ALLEY
7. WHITMAN RESIDENCE
8. FUTURE SITE OF GATEWAY PLAZA
9. "THE PIT"

TOURNAMENT ACRES (2007)
10. SITE OF THE ABANDONED
DUBLIN HOME FOR BOYS
11. FREMONT RESIDENCE
12. GAS STATION
13. RETAIL
14. CLUBHOUSE
15. EISEN RESIDENCE

Mayfair

▼ TORONTO ▼

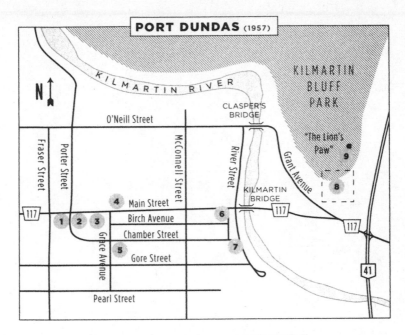

PORT DUNDAS (1957)

KILMARTIN RIVER

KILMARTIN BLUFF PARK

CLASPER'S BRIDGE

O'Neill Street

"The Lion's Paw" 9

Fraser Street

Porter Street

McConnell Street

River Street

Grant Avenue

KILMARTIN BRIDGE

8

4 Main Street

117

6

117

117

1 2 3 Birch Avenue

Grace Avenue

Chamber Street

7

5 Gore Street

41

Pearl Street

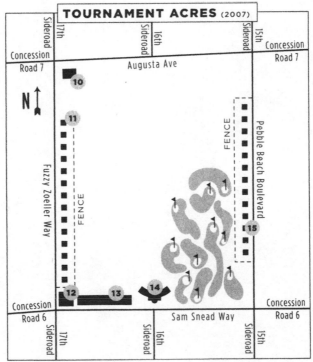

TOURNAMENT ACRES (2007)

17th Sideroad

16th Sideroad

15th Sideroad

Concession Road 7

Concession Road 7

Augusta Ave

10

11

FENCE

FENCE

Fuzzy Zoeller Way

Pebble Beach Boulevard

15

12

13

14

Concession Road 6

Concession Road 6

17th Sideroad

16th Sideroad

15th Sideroad

Sam Snead Way

Prologue

Hibiki Yoshida drank green tea from a blue ceramic cup. The steam hid his face. "I had been at Dublin Home for only one year when I heard it the first time," he said. "I was eight years old."

Detective Sergeant James Wingate began to write the numeral *8* in his notebook, but accidentally made a zero and crossed it out. He concentrated on his handwriting. The bareness of Yoshida's walls was distracting. The tea smelled like burning leaves. Wingate shook the pen. "What year was this?" he asked.

"Nineteen fifty-one. There were four dormitories on the second floor, two in front and two in back, all connected by doors." He waited for Wingate to write it down. "There were no hallways, so if you were in one of the two front rooms, there were always people walking through. I was in the back at the beginning." Wingate saw the room taking form in Yoshida's eyes. "Our dormitory had two stone walls. It was cold. But we were away from the stairs, farther away than the rest of the boys, and if someone came in the night, they would find what they were looking for *before* they got to us. That's what we believed.

"I only had a few friends because my English was so poor, and I tried to spend time among boys who seemed at least as hopeless as me. We kept each other company. Being in a group, we thought we'd be protected from the orderlies, the nurses, the older boys, and the teachers. But of course we weren't. We were like herring in a school, hiding from barracudas. The barracudas still ate.

"The first night I heard the bell jingle, I wasn't sure what I was hearing. Some of the older boys tried to scare us with stories of someone who came in the night and stole children to eat them. They called him Old Father Crumb. He had a key to the basement door made out of human bone, and when he opened it it rang a bell. That's how you'd know it was him."

Yoshida raised his cup to his mouth, and drank from it slowly, his hand trembling. Wingate waited for him to regain his composure. "Take your time," he said.

"I closed my eyes and lay very still," Yoshida said, putting the cup down. "I heard nothing, and after a while the restless feeling that had taken hold of me ebbed away and I went back to sleep."

The man stopped speaking, but it felt to Wingate that there was more. "Go on."

"It happened one other time. When I was sixteen. I'd been moved into the front dorms, where the older boys slept. The sound was nearer the second time I heard it. On New Year's Eve 1958. We raised our cups of apple juice at midnight and I still wonder what was in the juice. I didn't finish mine, but I fell asleep very quickly just the same. Some of the boys were asleep on their feet when they marched us up the stairs.

"I dreamt that there was a girl standing behind my bed, and she leaned over me and dangled a little bell on a chain. Then I heard footsteps on the stairs. I woke up with a start. My heart was still pounding from the dream, and I pulled the blanket up over my face. I heard the other boys breathing shallowly, like panting dogs.

"The door opened in the room next to ours and foot-steps came closer, slow and even. The door to our room opened and he came in and shut the door behind him. A shadow fell across me and I thought I was going to start crying, but he went by. I tried to count how many beds. One . . . two . . . he stopped three beds away from me."

Yoshida's eyes reddened. "My friend Valentijn slept in that bed. He was a good kid. Only fourteen. He'd had his growth spurt, and he was bigger than the sixteen-year-olds,

but he was slow. And he'd become violent if he was upset."
He fell silent and swallowed nervously. The corners of his
mouth moved a number of times but he could not speak.

"It's OK, Hiro —"

"I heard a man's voice. He said something to Valentijn,
and Valentijn said yes, very quietly. And then . . . I heard
the footsteps go past again, but not Valentijn's voice, not
the sound of his feet. I listened to Old Father Crumb go out
the door and when they opened the curtains in the morning, Valentijn's bed was empty."

"What happened to him?" Wingate asked. He'd gone as
cold as his tea.

"They found him dead in the snow. They said he had
gone out in the night and climbed to the roof, and he'd
slipped on the icy slates."

"That's awful. I'm sorry you had to experience that."
He gave Yoshida another minute. His notes, which were
difficult even for him to read, would prove he was ready to
return to active duty. He wrote *Pushed?* in his notebook.
"What did you hear that night, Mr. Yoshida? Did you hear
what Old Father Crumb said to your friend?"

A drop of tea leapt up from Yoshida's cup. "He asked
him if he wanted to see the stars."

] I [

In 1957, there were five convenience stores in Port Dundas. The ones at either end of Main Street were robbed more frequently than the three in the middle, and consequently their insurance cost more. However, in an act of neighbourliness not uncommon in those parts at that time, the owners of the three middle stores reimbursed the other two, so that all five paid the same amount.

The store that suffered the greatest number of thefts – and to date, the only robbery at gunpoint – was Herbert Lim Grocery, right at the gateway to the town, behind the sign that numbered its population at 4,280. A bridge ferried cars and bicycles and pedestrians into Port Dundas over the rushing Kilmartin River and delivered them to his doorstep. The bridge brought him a lot of business, but it came in handy for fast getaways too.

Saturday was market day, and on the afternoon of October 26, 1957, the streets were full of shoppers and strollers, visitors and locals, among them the odd drunk, depressive, and pickpocket. Shrinkage was worst on Saturdays. Some of the larger stores in town even hired security guards on the weekends and in the weeks leading up to Christmas and Easter, because a study had shown theft *doubled* in the weeks before those holy days.

The cost of lost merchandise was the cost of business, even in a small town.

Evan Micallef, the second-generation owner of Micallef's department store, was one of the local businessmen who had hired a security guard. "This is what things have come to," he told his daughter, Hazel. "You can't trust anybody anymore."

At the urging of his insurance company, Micallef had a plainclothes guard two days a week. The fellow walked around sizing up suit jackets and trying on caps, all the while shooting dramatic, sidelong glances up and down the floor. Every week, a different guy. They caught their fair share of thieves, though; it saved Evan Micallef a lot of money.

Herbert Lim had no need of a security guard. He sold milk, bacon, butter, comic books, magazines, cigarettes, detergent, a small selection of fruits and vegetables, and dry goods of various sorts. Lim's also had higher prices than the other stores, owing to its prominent position at the gateway to Port Dundas and being the easiest place to knock off in practically all of Westmuir County. He kept a baseball bat under the counter that he called extra insurance. Some days, when Mr. Lim heard a car idling at the curb outside, he'd steal a glance at the baseball bat. The townie kids knew he had it because he'd brandished it at some of them, just to show he meant business.

Hazel Dorothy Micallef was fourteen and a half. Her mother had finally allowed her to begin saying "almost fifteen." She'd been born in Port Dundas and lived her whole life there. In her attachment to the town, she thought of it as something that she owned.

She had just finished her afternoon shift at her father's store. One of her chores was working four hours on Fridays and Saturdays. Her father gave her a little spending money at the end of each shift, never more than a dollar unless it had been particularly busy. Despite the addition of the security guards – the most twitchy-looking people in the store, she thought – her father seemed no less perturbed by the possibility that thieves were filching from him. Once you learn suspicion, he warned her, you won't unlearn it. He'd taken to locking the stockrooms during the day.

"Here's a half dollar," he told Hazel. "Go get your brother and take him for an egg malt or whatever he likes."

"Floats."

"He's a bottomless pit," her father said, smiling. He kissed her hair. "Be good."

She decided to take the long way home and smell the air. She rode her bike up Porter Street to O'Neill Street, the most northerly corner in town. The smallest houses in Port Dundas were on O'Neill. Their backyards gave on to the Kilmartin River, and beyond it, the shale bluff that had been one of its banks. There was some danger of falling rock, and the houses on the north side of O'Neill were planted as far forward on their lots as possible.

Hazel rode the dirt curve at the end of the street to the covered Clasper's Bridge. Dirt trails led up from there to the top of the bluff. One of the trails was more than two hundred years old: it started here and ran along the top of the riverbank all the way out of town.

She rode back toward Main Street and was about to cross when she heard someone calling her name: "Hey, Micallef!" There was a person waving from the mouth of Candlestick Alley. It was Gloria Whitman. She was grinning to beat the band.

"C'mere!" Gloria hollered.

Hazel rode over. She could hear her mother's voice in her head: *What in creation is that girl up to now?*

"Hi Gloria. What's the fuss?"

"I need a lookout."

"A lookout?"

"Can you stay here for *one* minute? Just stay on your bike?"

"I don't know, Gloria. I'm supposed to get Alan and take him out."

"Can't he wait one minute?"

"I guess . . ."

Gloria's eyes were red, like she'd been rubbing them. "Watch this," she said, and she darted out.

Hazel retreated farther into the alley's shadow and waited on her bike. She wasn't sure what, exactly, she was looking out for. In the October sun, people milled back and forth on the sidewalk before her like a pantomime. Their voices reached her as a dim clangour. Nothing out of the ordinary appeared to be going on.

Just as Hazel had this thought, Gloria burst back into the alley. She was out of breath, laughing in delight. "Get ready!" she cried.

"Get ready?"

She mounted Hazel's bike, pushing her forward off the seat. "Go!" she shouted. "Start pedalling!"

"Not unless you tell me what this is about!"

From the street came a female voice: "STOP THIEF!"

"Ready now, Micallef?" Gloria gripped Hazel's shoulders. "Go!"

Hazel had no choice. She bore down on the handlebars and started pedalling. Gloria had the build of a ballerina, so it was nothing to ride with her on the seat, but it didn't allay Hazel's anxiety.

"What's going on?"

"Nothing. Go across the bridge."

Hazel doubled Gloria over the Kilmartin Bridge. "What did you steal?"

Gloria held up a pack of Luckys in front of Hazel's face. "Didn't see me take 'em."

"Doesn't sound like it."

"That was Carol. We'll be clear of her another hundred yards. But the Chink had his back turned the whole time."

"That's disgusting, Gloria. Don't call him that."

"Mr. *Lim*. He was busy stacking apples. I just *slipped* my hand behind the counter and took the first pack I felt. Ruckys! Pretty rucky, huh?"

"I gotta go, Gloria. Nice to see you and everything."

"Oh god!" she said. "She's coming. Ditch the bike!" Gloria scrambled up the dirt and stone path that went serpentine to the top of the bluff. "Come on!"

Hazel dropped her bike in the leaves and ran after Gloria Whitman. Her heart was beating so hard in her chest that she could hear it squeak, and she was halfway up the path before she realized that there was actually no one behind her. "Gloria, stop!" she called. There was no answer. Hazel slowed down to catch her breath. Then she walked the rest of the way up. When she got to the top, Gloria was sitting at a picnic table under a sign that read KILMARTIN BLUFF PARK. She was smoking a cigarette.

"Took you long enough."

"What are you playing at?"

"Just trying to inject some fun into your day, Hazel. When we were kids, you were lots of fun. Full of ideas. Never a dull moment. Now what?"

"What do you mean, *now what*? I see you all day long at school, Gloria. You can't miss me that much."

Gloria blew out an elegant smoke ring. "You going to the prom with Andrew?"

"Prom's not for months."

"I know he likes you. He said something interesting to Ray Greene." She held the pack out to Hazel.

"I don't want your ill-gotten gains."

Gloria got up from the picnic table and walked away. "OK. See ya."

Hazel felt a burn on her cheek: embarrassment coupled with something else — need or hunger. Even though Gloria was apt to make stuff up, it was true that people told her things. Boys lost their composure around her and spouted all kinds of nonsense. Maybe Ray *had* talked to her about Andrew Pedersen. "Hold on!" Hazel called. "Wait up."

The leaves had started to turn at the beginning of the month and now colour rang down like a curtain, brightening the trees that lined the county's roads, its backyards. The wind pushed the dry leaves around in the branches above their heads as they walked along the path high over town. Hazel remembered the last time autumn had come so late, in '53, when they'd gone swimming at Thanksgiving. She'd turned ten the spring of that year. It struck her now that maybe something was wrong, that summer shouldn't last so long. Gloria said she could live in a climate like this – sunny, breezy, blue skies, warm enough for just a sweater – every day of the year. But Hazel said she'd miss winter and summer both.

Gloria was going to turn fifteen at the end of January, but they had always been in the same grade. They'd been friends since they were little and the difference in their ages wasn't apparent to anyone. Gloria was small and fragile-looking, not quite birdlike, but sinuous and light, like a red squirrel or a mink. Her father called his daughter Grace Kelly, but no one would have thought Grace Kelly squirrelly. Hazel was more a Rosie the Riveter type. Big hands, strong legs.

From the top of the bluff, you had a view of the town entire, its streets sitting in the middle of forest and field like stitches in a sock. "You want some of this?" Gloria offered Hazel a small, battered pewter flask.

"What is it?" Hazel said.

"Brandy. The cheap stuff – you know, VS."

"You're full-service today. Where'd you steal that from?"

"It's not stolen if it stays in the family."

"What do you know about brandy anyway?"

"I *read.*" She took a little slug of it. "Rich French people drink it. Although they drink VSOP: Very Special Old Pale. This is just Very Special."

"Too bad for us," Hazel replied. "Won't your dad smell all

this smoke and booze on you?" Out of another pocket, Gloria produced a package of peppermint Chiclets. Hazel took the flask and drank a drop out of it. She'd had sips of her father's beer or her mother's Amaretto, but not something this strong. It made her cough. She held her hand out for the gum.

They continued along the dirt path, which wound in and out of pine forest to the edge of the rock face and back again. At the bluff's most southern tip, hunks of Canadian Shield with tenacious pines growing through it formed a feature called the Lion's Paw. On one side, the rock paw towered a hundred feet over the town and, on the other, over hectares of forest.

Both girls knew the sides of the bluff had formed the original riverbanks: they'd been taught this bit of history repeatedly, from kindergarten. The Kilmartin and Fraser rivers had once met below the town, but the Fraser had dried up in the early 1900s. East of the townsite, its bed formed the foundation of Highway 41 all the way to Fort Leonard.

Many times both girls had walked in this forest with school groups and gathered pine cones or identified birds. Now they took the edgemost path – worn by generations of walkers, "back to the tribes that once wandered freely over all of this land." The lessons had been drilled into them.

There were newer legends. Gloria led Hazel to the Passion Pit on the side away from town. The Pit was a depression where people burned bonfires and drank bottles of Labatt's 50 and Carling Black Label. It was hidden by the trees, although everyone knew where it was. There, Gloria lay down on her back on one of the flat slabs of granite that lined the bottom, surrounded by vines and lichen. She knew how to lie elegantly, with one knee bent. Boys had been looking at them ever since they were eleven, but now they were really looking, although neither girl was sure if they wanted to look back yet. "What did Andrew say to Ray Greene?" Hazel asked.

"Something about a sweater you wore last week. Don't think too much about it. Men are either dogs or brutes and most of the time you don't know until it's too late." She laughed: *Hee hee hee!*

"You sound like a demented monkey," Hazel said.

They fell to a companionable silence. Hazel had been considering whether to go to the Hallowe'en dance. She hadn't brought it up with Gloria because dressing up in costume was far below Gloria's station, supposedly. She wondered if Andrew Pedersen would go. He was in grade twelve, but he talked to her. Not shy, but not very forward either. He was planning on studying law at the University of Toronto. She was going to go to teachers' college. Probably in Barrie. She was imagining her features together with Andrew's when she heard a crack from above the Pit. Footsteps. She sat up and Gloria raised her head.

"Smells nice down there," came a voice. Gloria pinched the cigarette out. A girl was coming through the cover toward the rim. "You got another one of those?"

It was Carol Lim.

"I don't know what you're talking about," said Gloria.

Carol came down anyway and waved at Hazel. "Hey."

"Hey."

"Well?" she said to Gloria. "Do you have another one? I mean, if I stole the whole pack I'd give *one* away."

"Well, you didn't steal this pack, did you?"

Gloria's audacity was breathtaking. Carol said, "At least I'm old enough to smoke."

"You're old enough to wear a muumuu," said Gloria.

"You're drunk!" Carol Lim thrust out her hand for the flask. "Gimme."

Gloria tossed her the cigarettes instead. "Empty. Too bad for you. Go back to the old folks' home."

"You're not that much younger than me, Whitman." Carol's long, pale face was momentarily obscured by smoke. She shook out the match. "But I'm a lot more experienced." She was in grade thirteen in Port Dundas's only Catholic school. She took a theatrical drag on the cigarette and exhaled perfect smoke rings.

Gloria smiled at her. "You're bad," she said. "Give me my pack."

"Go steal another one," said Carol Lim. "You two got boyfriends?"

"Not as many as you do, I'm sure," Gloria said. This time her laugh came out more like a snigger.

"*You* done it?"

"Sure," said Gloria.

"None of your business," said Hazel.

"Virgins, huh?"

"Believe what you want," said Gloria. "Better not get pregnant."

"I bet your father would have something for that."

This made Gloria Whitman spring to her feet. "Whaddya mean?"

"Never mind."

"You better get out of here!" Gloria stepped toward her, bristling. "You people are lucky he has time for you."

"Us people? I was born here. In fact, I got here before you did!"

Gloria shoved Carol hard enough to make her stumble back a couple of paces. A pendant on a silver lace swung out from her neckline. "I hope you know karate."

"Karate's Japanese, round-eye." They stared at each other. Carol shrugged her clothing straight and tucked the pendant – a heart with a rabbit emblem – back into her shirt. She took a final drag on the cigarette and flicked the glowing red butt at Gloria. "I'll leave you lesbians alone," she said.

She went back up the side of the pit and continued out of sight.

Hazel snuffed out the cigarette with her shoe. "What was *that* about?"

"Yeah. She's royalty, ain't she? She'll be begging my father for rubbers before long."

"I mean, she didn't seem to mind you'd stolen something from her father."

"She's a queer one, Carol. Hates her parents. Know why she wears a rabbit around her neck? Because she's gonna breed like one." She laughed again, but it wasn't a titter, it was a low, mean sound. Hazel didn't like this side of Gloria, this cruel, cutting side. She'd say anything. Everyone knew the Lims and everyone liked them. She changed the subject to something she knew Gloria would be happy to talk about. "So . . . have you really? You know, *done it?*"

"Don't be crazy. I don't want some sweaty pig slobbering all over me."

"Not yet," said Hazel, and they both said "*ugh.*"

They left the little depression in the woods and began walking back, heading north into the trees on the townside of Kilmartin Bluff Park, and the light there drifted down, almost material, and lay on the forest floor like scraps of coloured paper. Hazel got on her bike. She smelled her own breath. It was possible there was still brandy on it. She'd kept a piece of Gloria's gum, and she popped it into her mouth. She rode slowly over the Kilmartin Bridge and felt the air flow over her face. She went up Main Street to McConnell, where she turned left and rode down to Chamber Street. Their house was number 39. When she got home, her little brother was waiting for her.

Tuesday, October 16, 2007. Lunchtime.

"A viatical settlement is a wonderful new option for a late-life infusion of capital! At a time when so many of Canada's elderly are struggling on reduced pensions and investments that no longer earn double-digit returns, a viatical settlement can take the pressure off, converting your life insurance into immediate cash!"

Hazel held the phone to her ear, trying to figure out what the cheery man on the other end was saying. "What the hell are you selling?" she said.

"Well, Mrs. Micallef, we're not selling, we're buying!" He pronounced it *Mickeleff.*

"Mrs. Who? Buying what?"

"Life insurance."

"Uh-huh. And how does this work?"

"We purchase your life insurance – and the payouts, Mrs. Mickeleff, are very generous, up to eighty per cent of the benefit –"

"What benefit?"

"The, uh, death benefit."

"You goddamned vultures," she rasped. Her mother was moving her spoon around in a bowl of soup, a shawl over her shoulders. "You invest in my death for a twenty per cent return?"

"That's not how –"

"I'm sixty-four. You call me at *lunch* and ask to buy my life ins –"

"Sixty-four? Is this Mrs. Emily Mikay . . . leff?"

"This is her daughter, Hazel Micallef."

"Oh. Oh . . . well, Mrs. Micallef, have you yourself thought abou –"

She hung up on him and returned to the table. "Who was that?" asked Emily.

"Someone who wanted to buy shares in you, Mother."

"A rather unwise investment."

"I communicated that to him. Have some bread and butter." Emily was looking at the simple spread – home-made vegetable soup and a sourdough loaf – with no interest. Hazel wasn't sure what was keeping the old woman alive anymore. She didn't eat, didn't leave the house, rarely watched television except sometimes at night, when she couldn't sleep, and then, only movies. She liked the strong female leads and the unbreakable men. Steve McQueen, Jane Fonda. Susan Sarandon and Sigourney Weaver and Clint Eastwood. There'd come a moment in any movie Emily watched when she'd say, "Here comes the hammer." If Hazel was watching with her, she'd add, "I love it when the hammer comes."

Otherwise, Emily spent most of her time in a fugue state between naps of varying lengths. Hazel had calculated that her mother was sleeping sixteen hours a day now. She rarely saw her before noon, and Emily used her strange new sleep habits as an excuse to miss both breakfast and lunch. She claimed she ate at four in the morning – tea and two Coffee Break cookies – but Hazel wasn't so sure. She'd taken to counting the Coffee Breaks. Her mother ate them in spirals, snapping off the sugared edges and nibbling them like a rabbit. Her remaining identifying habits were listening to CBC Radio One and making acid commentary in her diminished but still ferocious voice.

"Wheat is bad for you now," she said.

"So have a spoonful of butter. Get some calories down you. You look like a pair of chopsticks with a head."

"I have to be careful how oily I let my insides get, dear. I don't want things sliding out."

"God," said Hazel, slicing herself a second thick hunk of bread.

Tuesday was her day off. The plan had been to stay home, get the leaves raked up and put into paper bags, spend some time with her mother. Hazel had tried to engage her in a game of cards, but Emily would have none of it. She didn't want tea and neither did she want whiskey. She didn't want to watch *Bullitt*, said she was too tired. "Tired from what?" Hazel asked her.

"Everything. I don't want to see *Bullitt* again."

"But Steve McQueen —"

"Is dead."

She had a certain perspective on things these days. Hazel watched her stirring the soup in her bowl and the phone rang again. She snatched it up. "Good lord! Since when do you people call in the middle of the day?"

"Hazel?" It was Ray Greene, her old friend, occasional nemesis, and the new commander of the Port Dundas Police Department. His voice was tight. "Have you heard from Sean Macdonald?"

"I'm off today. What's wrong?"

"He's not answering his radio. He went out on a call at eleven and MacTier hasn't been able to raise him since noon."

"You're kidding me. Not his —"

"Not answering his cell. Goes straight to voicemail. It's like he's vanished into thin air."

"What was the call?"

"A woman named Honey Eisen, on that new development outside of Dublin. He went down to take a statement from her. She teed off on someone's knee with a granite pen holder."

"Ouch. You want me to go down?"

"You're closer and we're on skeleton crew because I'm in Mayfair on a 'sensitivity training' seminar. The PD down here is sending a car, but they'll wait for you unless, you know, there's trouble."

"Sensitivity training."

Behind her, her mother said, "I'm just going to pour what's left back into the pot," and her spoon clinked against the bowl as she sloshed it out. "Are you staying home this afternoon?"

"Apparently not," Hazel said.

Hazel Micallef drove the eighty-eight kilometres to Tournament Acres in thirty-five minutes. There was no Mayfair OPS officers present – she'd beaten them.

Tournament Acres took up twenty hectares between the 15th and 17th sideroads to the west of Highway 41. Its north–south boundaries were Concession Roads 6 and 7. The land enclosed in that box of roads had till recently produced nothing but crops of corn and soy, just like most any other field in the area. But the land was much more valuable when you planted cheap, prefab bungalows and gave the fields a fancy name. Just the same, twenty per cent of the bungalows already built around the perimeter remained unsold: they were still available "from" $299,999. The Ascot Group – an American corporation that specialized in large-scale, pop-up communities complete with malls or golf courses or spas — had left half a dozen houses incomplete and made those people who had bought in antsy about the safety of their investments.

Tournament Acres had been advertised and sold on the promise of its sumptuous country-club living and its two eighteen-hole courses. Now there was talk of building more bungalows where the second course was supposed to go — currently a sodden field of rotting corn stalks. People were incensed, and the *Westmuir Record* had been chewing the scenery over the debacle. The fact that most of the owners were from the Golden Horseshoe — Toronto, the 905, Hamilton — lent an air of *schadenfreude* to the talk about the ugly development, but Hazel felt for the investors. Retirees, mostly. People had spent their life-savings.

Hazel drove to Honey Eisen's address on Pebble Beach Boulevard, the new name for the 15th Sideroad, and found Macdonald's cruiser outside the house. Hazel parked behind it and tried the driver's door. She looked through the window, her hands cupped over her eyes, and inspected the inside of the cruiser. She found nothing abnormal about it, except that Macdonald wasn't in the car. All the doors were locked.

She looked around the area, over the fields to the east and at the discordant cottage-bungalows built on identical frames that lined the west side of the road. Around where

Eisen lived, the houses and gardens were complete, but farther north, they were less finished, and a couple were still
being framed. The development stopped altogether less
than halfway up Pebble Beach Boulevard.

She considered Mrs. Eisen's dwelling. It had been done
up in the same white wood as the clubhouse, with stuccoed columns in front. The front room throbbed white
and blue with television light. Maybe Macdonald was in
there watching reruns with the old lady. He'd always
take a cup of tea if offered, and he was a tireless conver-
sationalist, in both French and English. But three hours
of chatting?

She went up the walk and rang the doorbell. The flick-
ering in the front window stopped. She rang again. The
woman who answered wore a shapeless, pale-green dress
over her bony frame. "Did you get it back?" she asked.

"Did I get what back?"

"Baby Jesus, do you people even talk to each other? My
bone!"

"May I come in, please?" Honey Eisen swept her arm
out in mock welcome and Hazel entered. "Did a police officer named Macdonald come to —"

"Well, that's why you're here, aren't you? To *arrest* me."

"So he was here?"

"You should arrest the people who are building this
place. They don't know *what* they're doing. And Schnozzola
covers for them every step of the way. You speak Jewish?"

"No. Be quiet. Don't say anything else because I'm not following most of it. Sergeant Macdonald was here, yes?"

"Yes."

"When?"

"He left a . . . an hour ago at least."

"Do you know his cruiser is still parked outside of your house? He's not in it."

Eisen went to the window of her front room. "He went to talk to Givens. It's a two-minute drive!"

"Who's Givens?"

"Brendan Givens. The property manager of this whole schmazzle. Do you golf?"

"I don't. Is Givens the person you struck with the pen holder?"

"Oh, and they never built the wave pool either. It was supposed to be finished before anyone took possession. They're cancelling the second course to build more bungalows, and they've presold – signed and sealed – so our protests are pointless. Why are they selling more parcels when they can't finish the houses they've already sold?"

"You smashed his knee because the golf courses aren't finished?"

"No. I . . . bonked him because he locked my bone in his desk."

"He locked your bone?"

"Your sergeant was going to go over there and get it back. I want to show it to you people anyway."

"You don't think it strange that he didn't come back?"

"I thought maybe he had to take it to a lab or something. I mean, it's not *my* bone! I just found it. I was planting some bulbs out back yesterday morning and my trowel went along something hard and scrapey. I thought it was a stone and I dug it out and it was a *spine* bone. Whatever you call it. I went right away to him, showed it to him. 'What's this?' I said. He said it was probably from a horse, there were farms here with horses and sheeps and cows, but then he didn't give it back. He locked it in his desk and said he'd look into it. But he'll do what he does with *all* the complaints in this place: ignore it."

"Why didn't you call the police *first*?"

"I shoulda! You know, you people should be looking into him and the people he works for. You should nail them for whatever scam they're working here on us poor old people and young couples. They advertised this place as paradise. It's not. It's a cesspool."

Hazel drove to the clubhouse, and was taken aback to find that the stretch of Concession Road 6 along the southern end of the development was now named Sam Snead Way. Whoever he was, she doubted he had ever stepped foot in Westmuir County. She drove through a pair of wrought-iron gates and parked behind a two-storey building stuccoed to look like white adobe. The woman in the rental office had no idea that a police officer's car had been parked since about 1:00 p.m., with no one in it, on Pebble Beach Boulevard. She'd taken one look at Hazel's cap and her whole face had shut down.

Hazel showed her badge at the inner gate to the club-house itself, and was let through. A path led around the side of the building to a long, porticoed verandah facing the first tee. A sign explained that the clubhouse was mod-elled on the famous Pinehurst clubhouse in North Carolina, except this one had been built at one-quarter scale. It looked chintzy. Hazel guessed a well-placed spark would burn it down in less than two hours.

The main concourse was done up in style, with marble floors and chandeliers in the foyer. Young, smiling women were stationed there to hand you a towel to take into the weight room or the indoor pool. She knocked on the door labelled *Corporate Operations* and a man in security uniform answered. "Do you have any ID?" he asked her.

She showed him her badge. "Do *you* have any ID?" He looked put out, but then produced his security guard's photo card. "Gaston Bellefeuille," she said, pronouncing it the French way.

"Gastin Bellfoil," he corrected her. "Maybe you'd like to leave a message for Mr. Givens."

"Maybe you'd like to be a crossing guard."

He let her in and invited her to make herself comfortable in the suite lounge while he told his boss she was there. He disappeared into the office with the name B. GIVENS on its door.

From the lounge there was no view of the undeveloped development, but she'd seen it driving in, as well as the old Dublin Home for Boys, an old, grey, stone nightmare still standing on the corner of Augusta Avenue and Fuzzy Zoeller Way. It was slated to become the northern clubhouse. For a golf course that didn't sound like it was going to be built.

After what seemed like an extended wait, the door to Givens's office opened and Bellefeuille came out. She went in. A man with a pronounced nose and a red, unhappy face rose from a desk and came to greet her. His left knee was braced and he walked on one crutch. "Oh, *god*," he said. "You people again!" He stabbed the end of the crutch at her. "I said I'm not going to press charges!"

"I'm Detective Inspector Hazel Micallef. I'm not here about that. Did one of my officers – a Sergeant Sean Macdonald – visit you earlier today?"

The man retreated to his desk with much effort, huffing and puffing the whole way. He had a very tastefully appointed office. Signed pictures of political celebrities. A baseball in a Plexiglas case. He had excellent hair and was tanning-bed orange, but his spoonbilled nose spoiled the effect. It hung down like a glob of raw dough in the middle of his face, and it was spidery with small red veins.

"Who did *that* to you?" she asked, meaning his leg.

"I fell down some stairs."

"I heard an old lady tried to drive your knee three hundred yards with a granite pen holder."

"Oh, no no no," he said, suddenly laughing. He was going to try being affable. "It was just some heated words. I understand why people are frustrated, Detective. A development like Tournament Acres, you can't predict all the challenges in advance."

"What did you tell Sergeant Macdonald? The same thing?" The man nodded. "Did he buy it?"

"Buy it?"

"Where did he go when he was done with you?"

"He, you know, he went to talk to her."

"Honey Eisen. She said he was coming to see you."

"Oh no, he's already been and gone." There was a knock at the door. "What now?" Givens muttered, but Hazel got up to answer it. It was a woman in an OPS uniform, rail thin with sprigs of red hair sticking out from under her cap. The veins on her arms seemed to be keeping her muscles lashed to her body.

"DC Torrance," she said. "You must be the legendary Detective Inspector Micallef."

"You pronounced it right, at least."

"Have you gone over to see Eisen?"

"Yes. She's in a panic." Hazel brought her attention back to Givens. He shrank under her gaze.

"Getting the second course started is taking longer than we thought," he said. "She wants us to move her."

"I don't really care about that. I only want to know two things: what is this bone Mrs. Eisen is talking about, and where is my sergeant?"

"I gave him the bone," Givens said, pushing the whole mess away with his palms. "You people have what you need. But I just wanna say . . ." His eyes flicked back and forth between the two women.

"What?"

"Honey Eisen signed a *contract*." He fixed her with a conspiratorial look. "You know what people are like. One person panics, then there's the stampede. I've seen this before, people threatening lawsuits, people making stuff up, anything to get out of an investment if someone starts whispering things to them. But we're going to do everything we said we're going to do here. This is going to be a very desirable address." He stopped to catch his breath and read her face. He decided not to say anything else.

Hazel said, "We may want to talk to you again." She nodded at DC Torrance to show she could leave first.

"Oh sure! Come on back anytime!" His voice was moist with false bonhomie.

It was funny what people told you by not telling you anything. It took a chessmaster's intelligence to lie, and most people had already revealed themselves before a word was out of their mouths. You didn't look at faces, you looked at eyes, mouths, teeth, ears. Anything that might give you a clue to what a person was really feeling. You had to use this knowledge against people. To keep them off balance or on their toes, to see what they'd do. Givens's eyelids had not stopped ticcing the whole time Hazel was in his office. Through his face, he'd told her something was up. He'd pooched his lips out from time to time in a gesture that was supposed to look like he was thinking. But he was hiding something.

Torrance was going to do a slow crawl around the development to see if anything seemed out of order. Hazel had barely had a chance to take a read of her Mayfair partner, but the woman looked like she could bend metal. She had a buzzy alertness that came from too many power smoothies.

Hazel drove back to Eisen's house and had to blink a couple of times: Macdonald's cruiser was gone. What the hell? "Torrance," she said over her radio.

"Inspector?"

"You haven't seen another OPS cruiser have you?"

"Hold on . . . yeah! There's one coming toward me right now."

"Flag 'im down, would you?"

"Whoops! He blew right past me."

Hazel thanked her and tried Macdonald. He answered right away.

"Sean?"

"Skip?"

"I'm not your skip. Where were you?"

"When?"

"Just now. MacTier said you vanished off the radar."

Macdonald made a dismissive sound. "He asks me to come down here over my lunch and then starts panicking when I don't check in with him. He's a mother hen."

"Where were you, though?"

"I went for lunch."

"Without your cruiser?"

"Ah," Macdonald said, clearly disappointed. "Well, I know someone down here. I just went over for lunch."

"What about your radio? MacTier said he tried to raise you for an hour."

"Listen, Hazel. It's nothing."

She saw him now, half a kilometre in front of her on the 41. "You sound weird to me, Sean. Where are you now?"

"Heading north on the 41," he said. "I'm taking this thing back to Greene. I think it's from a cow or something. It's old and smooth."

"I saw the old lady. She told me she thought she was getting it back. But then she also said she just wanted to turn it over to the police."

"She spent a long time tryna change the subject with me, like I wasn't down there to talk to her about whacking the guy in the office."

"Givens."

"Him. He smells good and fishy to me, that guy."

"Me too. I'll see you back in town."

He was still on the highway, heading exactly where he said he was. "OK, Hazel."

"What were you doing over lunch, Sean?"

"Jesus," he said, laughing. "You're a bloodhound! I'm selling guns to retirees."

"Come on."

"I know a girl. Remember Alison Freemey?" Hazel didn't. "From the academy? Anyway. She lives up here. I come and say hello from time to time."

"How does Mrs. Macdonald feel about that?"

"Mrs. Macdonald wouldn't notice if I came home in a dress. Am I done being interrogated? What d'you think I was doing?"

"I understand now. None of my business, you're right. See you at HQ."

] 3 [

At thirty-eight, Charles S. Willan was the youngest deputy commissioner of the Ontario Police Services ever appointed. He was some kind of a whiz kid, a visionary who knew how to keep departments lean and clean. His pet project since he'd been installed was amalgamating OPS Central. He was going to combine a number of smaller detachments into one; make the scattered and distant outposts of OPS North–Central into a gathered force, and build it an HQ in the middle of a new shopping mall. It was going to save the OPS forty million a year. He was unflappable, friendly, and ruthless. Hazel had wondered at times if he was human.

He stood in the middle of the pen in a yellow hard hat and a silvery suit.

"Groundbreaking is less than two weeks away!" he enthused. "The beginning of a new era in policing in Westmuir County. With all of *you*" – his index finger did a tour of the room – "at the very centre."

There were two loud clappers and a smattering besides. Ray Greene and Gerry Costamides had been the clappers. "One because he has to," Hazel muttered to Roland Forbes, "the other because she doesn't have an unkind bone in her body."

Willan held his hands up to quiet the already quiet room. This was the guy who had come in and replaced the previous commissioner, the heartless lizard Ian Mason. Now they looked back on Mason's rule as halcyon days. When amalgamation took effect, everything was going to change, and not for the better. This was the era of organizational change and streamlined services, when efficiencies would be found and value added and everyone was a partner in change, even if they were about to lose their job. Chip Willan was only the most local instance of this ideology in human form – there was an epidemic of them. Everyone knew someone who was going to be out of a job. And those whose livelihoods depended on the survival of Main Street had plenty of their own worries. Gateway Plaza would catch fish much higher upstream. Who would come downtown to shop?

It was foolhardy, many thought. It would only increase the difficulties of policing such a large area.

] INGER ASH WOLFE [

Willan had heard it all too. "I know some of you aren't onside yet. I know some of you are worried what will happen when we open in Gateway Plaza. I'm not going to tell you that the fact that *your* jobs are safe should make you feel good. No. Change is hard, people. But it comes whether we want it or not. The old ways drop away. Next summer, when we open the North–Central Ontario Police Service Headquarters right here, in your town, all of your friends will have landed on their feet. Because that is what you people do, you people of the land, who wear so proudly the badge." He took a sip of water. "What I am trying to say, trying to impart to you, is that this is the very beginning of a great adventure. You will be the doorway to the entire region, coming or going, and every surge of growth that comes this way will hit you first. You will have the best services in the entire region. You will have the Internet in your streets. You're gonna be able to get signal *anywhere*."

"What about our colleagues who won't be able to afford a phone?" Dietrich Fraser asked. "What about them?"

"The Internet will come to their towns, too."

"No, Superintendent Willan. What is going to happen to *them*? How is the OPS going to make it right for their families?"

Willan's face morphed into a mask of concern. "There are going to be hardships. But everyone will have our support. No one will be abandoned."

] 36 [

"We have your word on that? Can I bring that to the union?"

"You can bring it home and serve it to your children, Sergeant Fraser." Willan addressed the room: "It is natural to go forward with trepidation. Things need to be proven to you. You are police; you want to see the evidence. I am here today to tell you that you will. You have my word."

He stepped forward purposefully with his hand out toward Gerry Costamides, who took it without hesitation, and then everyone had to shake the man's hand. Gerry waited until Willan was deep in the crowd before coming over to talk to Hazel.

"I think I once saw him sucking the air from a baby's mouth," Hazel said.

Costamides made a pugilistic face and cocked her fist at Hazel. Both women smiled. "He wants to do good things for our town, Skip."

"Don't call me Skip anymore, Gerry."

"But you like him, right? Hazel?"

"Sure I like him. But I don't trust him. He'll say anything."

"Make sure he doesn't hear you say *that*, Sk . . . Inspector."

Ray appeared to be skulking away, so Hazel followed him into his office. "Hello?"

"Oh, it's you. Thanks for the enthusiasm during Willan's speech."

"At least I didn't vomit. Did Macdonald bring in his find yesterday? He said he brought a bone in."

"It's already sent down to Mayfair. Deacon's looking at it. It's from a horse or a deer or a something."

"Did he tell you what he'd been doing the whole time half the local constabulary was looking for him?"

"He said he was walking the perimeter."

"Oh yeah. He was walking the perimeter."

Ray waited for her to explain her skeptical tone, but the door opened again. "In hiding?" said Chip Willan.

"Yes," said Hazel. "From you. Because you give off a light too intense for mortals."

"It's my natural bronze colour. I heard there was some unpleasantness at Tournament Acres. Someone found a bone in her garden?"

"It's gone down to Jack Deacon," Ray said.

"You see any heavy machinery while you were out there?" Willan asked.

Hazel knitted her brows at him. "What? You mean tanks?"

He withstood her jibes good-naturedly. Despite their best efforts, they had grudgingly begun to work together. "I mean construction."

"As far as I could tell, it was a giant, muddy field surrounded by unfinished houses."

"There's a limited number of earth-movers in the county. You'd be surprised." They gave him blank faces to look at. "Can I count on the two of you, who are well respected by the men and women who work here, to help foster a positive attitude toward Gateway Plaza? Even if they disagree in their hearts, surely you can see how important it is that the civic leaders of Port Dundas demonstrate *faith* in this important process, and *model acceptance* of it. For everyone."

"Well, it's coming whether they like it or not," said Hazel. "So I suppose we'll have to do our best."

"That is my baseline for you, Hazel. I expect no less. Commander Greene? Please tell your wife that I enjoyed her vegan meatballs very much. Keep 'em coming."

Hazel decided to go home for lunch. The autumn made her feel hopeless as well as nostalgic, but it was a feeling more like an ache than a wound. The leaves were already red and yellow; the yellow leaves were pocked with vegetal liver spots and about to fall. Time was in layers on the forest floor; it went down and down.

She drove over the Kilmartin Bridge out of Port Dundas and slowed to take a look at the grading machines that were preparing the roads at the base of the Lion's Paw. She hadn't participated in the town meetings or the protests that had greeted the announcement of the OPS's plan to centralize services at Port Dundas. The idea of Gateway Plaza bothered her so much that she had completely avoided all the public meetings on it to save her sanity. She knew a done deal when she saw one. Where Highway 117 became a country road, there would soon be a mammoth new retail and service development, featuring a community centre with a two-pad skating rink, a Walmart, a Sobey's, a Canadian Tire, a Shoppers Drug Mart, and the brand new North–Central OPS Headquarters, into which all the detachments north of Mayfair would be folded.

The groundbreaking was less than two weeks away, on the day before Hallowe'en, fittingly. Above the site was the bluff of Canadian Shield that marked the end of the river valley beyond. The smooth, treed rock of south-central Ontario protruded everywhere in the county, like stone fingers covered in moss, creating features of tremendous beauty such as Kilmartin Bluff Park.

Hazel was no longer surprised by the way things changed. Here the highways and not the towns would become the focus of much of the region's commercial and service activity.

Change was everywhere, even at home. Her mother had been diagnosed with myeloma more than a year ago, and Dr. Pass had explained to them both that it was a slow-moving illness. She could live five, ten more years with it and not feel much more diminished than any person of her age. "Excellent," Emily had said. "Maybe I'll start a blog now."

Her decline was gradual but, a year on, Hazel could detect the difference, not least of all in her mother's appetite. She had taken to eating as many meals with her as possible, but even supervised, Emily wouldn't eat very much. To say her mother had given up would have suggested that she had been vivacious before the diagnosis. The truth was, she had gotten old ten years ago. If she made it to next summer, she'd turn ninety-one, and the thought of it made Hazel grin and feel sad all at the same time.

Lunch was grilled cheese. Hot and fragrant. She could entice her mother with only salt or sugar now.

Emily's reminiscences of distant things were becoming more frequent. Dipping a corner of her sandwich into a small pool of ketchup, she said, "Do you remember when your brother broke his collarbone in the church parking lot?" Hazel recalled it vaguely. "I haven't thought of that in years." A lot of her memories were of Hazel's adopted brother, Alan. He'd died in the north of Ontario, a parolee and an addict, at the age of thirty-nine, in 1984, the year Hazel made detective constable.

"He drove your father to distraction," Emily said. Hazel cleared the dishes. There was a neat semi-circle cut out of one half of the sandwich, where her mother's dentures had clipped a bite. "After everything we did for him, he'd say."

"None of it was your fault."

"None of it," her mother said wistfully. "It wouldn't happen these days. Children don't find themselves in such circumstances now. Imagine living in an orphanage until the age of ten, raised like an animal on garbage. Do you remember how he used to eat? Like a wild boar. We gave him the best chance we could."

It was the only thing Emily had ever been sentimental or maudlin about, the fate of her adopted son, a broken boy by the time he'd arrived at the Boys' Industrial Home up in Fort Leonard at the age of two. Dead mother; abusive, drunken father. Born in oblivion somewhere in the north of the province, he made a beeline back there for most of his short life, as if he were magnetized to tragedy.

"He'll work it out," Emily mused from the table.

"Who?"

"Your brother," she said.

Hazel rinsed the dishes and put them in the rack. "He's dead, Mother. I don't think he's going to work it out."

Emily slapped her hand hard against the tabletop. Hazel spun around and caught the savage look on her mother's face. "I'm not demented, god damn you," she growled. "I know he's dead."

] 4 [

1957

Alan and Emily came through the door bearing paper bags of groceries. "Take those from him," their mother said to Hazel. She was holding three bags in one arm.

Hazel took possession of the two her brother held. One of them was cold at the bottom. Her mother leaned over the linoleum countertop and dropped the car keys. Then she chested her groceries forward. She began unpacking boxes of Hallowe'en candy and small paper bags. "Start putting this stuff away. Alan?"

Her brother shuffled over. He was twelve years old with permanently bent hair. There was always a shelf of it sticking straight out from one side or the other. He was what they called slow, but he wasn't dumb. A lot of the boys who came from homes were slow. He liked toy cars. He got lost in comic books. And he was sweet.

Her mother passed him a small box and he pried the lid off and removed a black eye-mask from inside. There was also a wand. Alan hadn't been able to make up his mind between Cardini or the Lone Ranger, so he was going as both. He'd been warned if he didn't have his bath as soon as they got home they weren't going for shell-out because they weren't going after dark. He replaced the lid on the box and marched immediately to the bathroom.

"Nothing for me?" Hazel asked.

Her mother tapped a cigarette out of its package. "You're too old to go trick-or-treating."

"I'm *almost* fifteen."

"Well, you can go out without a costume anyway. You're scary enough." She came around the counter and squeezed Hazel by the shoulder, blowing smoke to the side. "Stay home, help me with the door, and you can eat some of that junk."

"I know you bought candy corn and Swedish berries. I hate those things. You just don't want me to eat any."

Emily stalked away acting hurt, then took out a whole bag of Neilson chocolate rosettes, opened it, and held it out to Hazel. Hazel snatched it away, grinning. "Just a handful, piggy." Hazel chewed and her mother smoked and they listened to the sound of Alan's bum squeaking against the porcelain above their heads. "OK, that's enough." She took the bag back and closed it with a twist-tie. "Oh! I've been meaning to ask you, sweetheart – have you seen Carol Lim recently?"

"Carol Lim?" Hazel's heart started pounding. If her mother knew she'd been drinking, she'd be marched straight to her father. Her father was hardline on what was appropriate for a young woman to do. "Not a woman, not a girl," he would say. "Somewhere in between, where it is very important to make intelligent choices: What kinds of people you want to be seen with. Who you trust your feelings to. What money is."

"You know her, right?"

"Yes, I *know* her," Hazel said, flustered. Flustering was a very bad thing to do in front of Emily Micallef. It was like a scent to her. "Why are you asking?"

"Because she's missing."

"Missing?"

"Since Saturday afternoon." She gestured for Hazel to bring her the remaining bags.

Saturday was when Carol had showed up on the path. "I don't really know her, Mom. She's older than us."

"Us?"

"I mean me and my friends."

Her mother stared down at Hazel with a question in her eyes, but then she let it go. "Will you ask some of your friends if they've seen her? Mrs. Lim thinks she may have gone to visit relations in Toronto . . . or maybe even a boy. Ask around, OK?"

"Sure," Hazel said as casually as she could. "I'll ask around."

Hazel had been inside Gloria Whitman's house only a couple of times in recent years. It was a grand, old stone house that sat on a bit of property overlooking the Kilmartin River at the end of Chamber Street. She'd told Hazel it had been an inn a hundred years earlier. Her parents had made it cozy inside, but Hazel found it dark. All of the appliances were from the 1930s.

Gloria's mother had died when she was nine, but five years later she rarely spoke of her, and sometimes it was as if she had never known her. Her father doted on her, had her playing the cello, and drove her to and from her dance classes and tutors.

Hazel knocked and waited anxiously on the porch. Gloria answered and her face registered surprise. Long gone were the days when Hazel showed up out of the blue to play. "Hazel? What a nice surprise."

"Can I come in?"

"Of course."

When she closed the door, Hazel turned to her and said quietly, "Did you know that Carol Lim was missing?

"Missing? Since when? I mean, how do they know?"

"She hasn't been seen since Saturday afternoon. *We* saw her Saturday afternoon. Did you see her again?"

"I knew she was skulking off somewhere. You think she'd miss a chance to yank me down the hill to meet her dad? No, she was running away. Probably to get married. Since she's so popular with the guys."

"Are you sure she has a boyfriend?"

"Remember Tommy Landers? He's in Toronto now and I've heard from people who know that they're an item. Probably."

"Wow," Hazel said. She couldn't imagine leaving her family. For a boy. "What if someone saw us up there? And her. And then they hear she's missing?"

"What does it matter if anyone saw us? What did we do? She stole my cigarettes, and then we all said *ciao* and went our separate ways."

"I don't want to go up there again," Hazel said.

"People walk around the bluff all day and night," Gloria said. "Nothing ever happens."

"You don't know that."

"When's the last time anything happened in this town? She's probably making her new husband dinner as we speak. Moo goo wing wah with chicken. Hey, feel like a Pepsi?"

"I don't know. What did Ray say about Andrew and me? You never told me."

"I thought I did. I don't remember now." She left the room with a flounce. "I'm having a soda."

Gloria led Hazel deeper into the house. The floors were made of heavily trodden wood and there were exposed beams in the ceilings of the ground storey. It smelled like a century of pipe smoke. Hazel followed her into the kitchen. A half-wall recalled the house's previous life as an inn: the kitchen was just the right size for a bar.

"We should tell Commander Drury we saw her, Gloria. Before she went missing. We can leave out what we were doing up there."

"Sure. I don't care. We can't help, though. What can we tell them?"

"I don't know. But I think we should go anyway."

"You'll never get a boyfriend being a goody-goody."

"She lives in our town," said Hazel. "My own mother is asking where she could be. What if she turns up and says people should have asked us? Maybe she said something about where she was going and we weren't really listening."

"She didn't say where she was going. She just helped herself to my smokes and went on her merry way." She opened two bottles of Pepsi and put one down on the counter for Hazel.

"No." Hazel shook her head. "I'm going to have to tell my mom. You have to tell your dad."

Gloria shrugged. "Fine, I'll tell him." She rummaged in the fridge and came out with a carrot in her hand. She grinned at Hazel as she cleaned it by stroking it up and down. "I guess we can't be too careful," she said.

————

The conversation with her parents went as well as she could have expected. Her mother had always told her that it was better to admit to a lie than to be found out. Being caught in a lie cast a long shadow over you, but knowing you were wrong and fixing it was a commendable sign of strength, and they did commend her, after asking why she'd done it. She decided the truth – an incomplete but still damning version of it – would do. She told them they'd gone to the Pit to share a cigarette.

"You're too young to smoke," her father said, looking at his wife. "Do you not agree?"

Her mother tapped out ash into the large ceramic ashtray beside the couch. "Of course I agree. But if you didn't want a wild streak in your children, you shouldn't have married me."

"I don't really like them," Hazel said, and that was the truth as well. "Gloria smokes Luckys. She gave me one. I only smoked half of it to see what it was like."

"Uh-huh," said her father. "That was your first one ever?"

"No. I've tried before and I didn't like it then either."

"One day you'll suddenly not mind it. And then you'll want one." Her father had quit just the previous year. A lot of people believed they were bad for you.

"Well, anyway, it's good you thought about it and came to us. I'll call Dale Whitman at his clinic tomorrow and we'll just all have to go in and see Gord Drury."

———

The Port Dundas Police station was on Porter Street, south of Main. It had a parking lot out back where for three days every fall there were kiddy rides. Her mother used to take her when she was little and Alan still liked it, but she'd never been inside the station. It was a red brick building, about the size of a church, and they went up the steps into a waiting area in front of a wooden counter. There were rows of tables behind the counter. Hazel felt her stomach tighten. Gloria was already there.

"How interesting to see how the system works, huh?" Emily said to Gloria, and Gloria mutely agreed. Her face was colourless. "Where's your father?"

"He said I got myself into this by lying, and now I have to get myself out."

"It's all right, dear," Emily said, putting her hand on the girl's arm. "You were scared, but you did the right thing quickly enough. Now, I've spoken with Mrs. Lim, and they're very worried, but this isn't the first time Carol has done this. Once she took the train down to the city without telling her parents. To see a *jazz trio*. If you think you girls are trouble at fourteen . . ."

"Mayor Micallef, do you think the officers *here* will get help from the police in *Toronto*?"

"If they need it, they will. But our police are very capable, Gloria."

"I hope so. I'm scared now."

Commander Gord Drury appeared at the wooden counter.

He'd been in the job for more than two years now, and although originally from Toronto, he'd made a point of getting to know as many people in the town as possible. His thick, black, walrus moustache made his face instantly likable. He and his wife had already been to dinner a number of times at Hazel's house, and she had watched him dab his moustache meticulously after each course. Commander Drury smiled at the two frightened young women. "Come on then. We'll start with you, Miss Micallef. Your mother can join us."

"No, she's going to do this alone," said Emily, looking over at Gloria. No reason why the one should be punished over the other.

Passing through the pen, Drury introduced Hazel to the people at their desks: Constable Harry Bail, Detective Thorwald Mueller, and Miss Bollinger, the secretary. Hazel nodded to all of them. "The mayor's daughter," said Drury. "Swept up in a candy-theft ring." They all laughed good-naturedly.

Drury's desk was in a bright office at the back of the building. It had a wall-length window in it so he could see into the pen. Miss Bollinger sat on the other side of the window, and often communicated with him silently through the glass. He sent Hazel to sit behind his desk. "Like it?" he asked.

"The chair is nice." She got up to let him sit, but he told her to stay, he could take a seat on the other side. She lowered herself back into the commander's chair.

"So you and Gloria saw Carol Lim on Saturday afternoon."

Hazel lowered her eyes. "We did."

"Where did you see her?"

"We were on the trail up the bluff. We went down into the Pit —"

"Ah, the Passion Pit," Drury said.

"We . . . um. Gloria had a pack of cigarettes . . ."

Drury opened a notebook on his desk and started writing. "What time?"

"About two in the afternoon. I was supposed to go home and get my brother, but I went for a bike ride first."

"And what time did you see Carol?"

"I don't know," said Hazel. "Two-thirty?"

"And what did everyone talk about?"

"Boys." She smiled, embarrassed.

"Ah. Did Carol seem upset?"

"No."

"Was she in a hurry?"

"No."

"Did she say anything that suggested, even subtly, where she might have been going?"

"I think she was just going for a walk. Like us. She wasn't in a hurry. She wanted a smoke."

"She stayed and talked with you girls for how long?"

"Five minutes. Less."

"And what direction did she take when she left you?"

"She was walking around the Lion's Paw. Away from town."

"OK." Drury closed his notebook and put an elastic band around it. "Did Gloria tell you anything she heard or saw afterward? After the two of you parted that afternoon?"

"No. She said she went down to Grant Avenue and walked home."

He listened to her with total attention and then nodded to himself. "OK then, Hazel. If you think of anything else that might help us, you have your mother call me."

"Maybe there's one more thing," she said. "Gloria told me Carol might have a boyfriend in Toronto named Tommy Landers."

He wrote the name down and saw her out.

Miss Bollinger brought Hazel to the front again. Gloria stood up. "Your turn," Miss Bollinger said, and Gloria went through to the commander's office.

] 5 [

Wednesday afternoon

At least Detective Sergeant James Wingate was alive.

This was the mantra his colleagues at the station house had adopted when he'd been injured on a case a year ago. He was alive, but he was changed, and there would be no changing him back. He'd worked from home in May, and by July he was spending six hours a week in the station house broken up over three shifts. Now his hours had been increased to twelve a week — four hours on Mondays, Wednesdays, and Fridays — but he was working his desk in civvies and had not been cleared for active duty. Part of his therapy was to come in to the detachment and be in the workplace.

Although he had no valid credentials and he did not wear his uniform, Hazel still conferred with him as a "civilian consultant." She was used to his word slips now, his occasional stutter, his strange new walk. He was still inside that body, and he remained himself in all the ways that mattered. He walked with effort but effectively, one leg pointing off true. On the other side his pelvis ticked down in counterbalance, rising and falling and giving him the stance of a cowboy. He held his arms an inch or two farther from his body than before.

They'd given him some glorified data entry – clearance rates for the years 1999 to 2004; follow-up calls – but Hazel wanted to keep him in the case loop, and sometimes he had ideas.

When she got back to the station house after lunch, it was shift change, and he was right on time. Hazel tapped him on the shoulder. "Your twin let you out of the house?"

"Michael knows I have important work to do: returning the phone calls of disgruntled local citizens. Dog poop complaints, parking annoyances, nois . . . ances, *noise* complaints."

"Are they more gruntled after talking to you?"

"I don't know. I check them off on this list and move on."

Sean Macdonald hailed her from over a divider. "Husband and wife from Tournament Acres. They're in Ray's office."

"You stay here," she said to Wingate.

"This is Oscar and Sandy Fremont," said Ray Greene. "They live on Fuzzy . . . uh –"

"Zoeller Way," said the wife, Sandy.

"One of the roads in Tournament Acres," he finished, gesturing to his guests to seat themselves again. There was a couch along the wall inside his small office, and it was the only place left for Hazel and Macdonald to sit down. Everyone said nice to meet you. "Will you show DI Micallef what your dog was playing with?"

Sandy Fremont slipped her hand into her clutch and took out something wrapped in a paper napkin. She was a beautiful, slight woman of about forty. Her husband, fully grey at the temples, looked fifteen years her senior. "If you don't mind just putting that on the desk," suggested Hazel, and she did, handling the parcel like it contained a baby bird. Whatever was inside was bigger, though. It came down onto the desk with a clunk and the napkin opened like a white flower.

There was a piece of bone inside it. Hazel teased the napkin farther apart with a pencil. It was a portion of a short, curving bone, about four inches long and one inch wide. It was in the shape of a gentle scoop, white and grey, with marrow holes visible along one edge, tightly packed, like honeycomb. Part of a jaw bone? A rib? It was difficult to say. It was smooth, like a stone found on a riverbed, although there were faint indents stained black on its ridge. At one end it terminated in a clear, straight cut. "Is it human?"

Macdonald had joined her beside the desk. He ran his

finger along the length of the bone. "Maybe a cow or a pig bone? There's been all kind of cattle- and pig-raising in those fields."

"What part do you live on?" Hazel asked the Fremonts.

"Northwest part," said the husband. "Where the invisible golf course is."

"Is this the only thing your dog has brought back?"

"Sundancer brings all kinds of stuff back to the house," said Mrs. Fremont.

"Sundancer . . ." Hazel deadpanned.

Mr. Fremont grimaced. "I got her a dog instead of a boat. That's her revenge. I got you a bungalow, you know."

"Where the restless souls of dead natives stir in their clay," said Mrs. Fremont.

"It's not an Indian bone, sweetheart." He had a natural sneer.

"Could it be a burial ground?" Hazel looked around the room to shrugging. She wrapped the bone back up in the napkin. "We'll get this analyzed, OK? Does Sundancer just run wild everywhere?"

"He can't get into anyone's yard because of all the fences," said Mr. Fremont, "but the fence on our side ends before that old house."

"The old house?" Ray asked.

"The old boys' home," Hazel said.

"Ew," said Sandy Fremont, showing her white teeth. "Is that the bone of a person, you think?"

"People are going to want their money back over this kind of thing," fumed her husband. "I mean, do you know what is going on down there?"

"Going on?" Hazel asked.

"This Ascot Group," he said, lowering his voice, "it's like a stack of Russian dolls, one corporation folded inside another. We're on the board at the Acres. I see the financial statements. It's like reading Klingon. And there hasn't been *any* progress on construction, anywhere on the site, in three months. *Three months!*" he cried in a tragically hurt voice.

"I'm sorry for the trouble you're having with your new home," Hazel said, "but right now we need to focus on this." She closed the napkin. "If you want to make an official complaint about the situation in Tournament Acres, you can always do that through the right channels, I'm sure."

Mrs. Fremont arched an eyebrow at her husband. "See? That's exactly what they said in Mayfair."

"Mayfair?" inquired Macdonald.

"We've already tried to get the law involved," she said. "But maybe you people don't care if the folks getting ripped off are rich, huh?"

Oscar Fremont stood up. "Maybe we're not rich *enough*! Let's go."

Hazel handed them each a card as they were leaving. "If . . . Sundancer finds anything else, please don't hesitate to contact us."

Oscar Fremont said, "Ha."

———

Hazel brought cinnamon buns home for dinner. Her mother's sweet tooth was still functioning, and if that's what it took, then cinnamon buns it would be.

She bought three but asked for two bags. She hid one bag in the car and went in with the other two buns. She'd talk her mother into eating one to *save* Hazel from eating it herself. Some nights now, though, she was getting two and a half cinnamon buns.

The problem with painlessness is that it wakes your appetite, she thought. All kinds of appetites, even the ones you thought were in full abeyance. She'd gone a whole year now without so much as a twinge in her lower back. Her spinal surgery was well behind her, and the doctor had told her that with time the scarring would heal, the discs would continue to shrink – lessening the possibility of another rupture – and she'd find herself drug-free and fully operational.

There were days when she could almost touch her toes. If it weren't for her gut.

"In two more years you're going to look like a set of stacking rings," her mother said. "You know, the kind they give to babies?"

Hazel laughed. "Eat your bun."

"Stop buying two of them. I only want half, and you don't need the half I can't finish." Emily liked to slice the bun in half horizontally and spread butter on each side.

Her appetite was better in the evening, right after the sun went down, and her energy improved as well. She'd fill with a colour much improved over cadaverous. There was something unnatural about the transformation, however welcome it was.

She slept so much now that it was only between the hours of seven and eleven that there'd be more than hints of her true self.

"There's a new show I want to watch tonight," she said, pushing her plate away with some finality.

"A cop show?"

"I like my cop shows."

"My life is a cop show, Mother. For once I'd like to watch a comedy." She was looking at the second cinnamon bun. "Well, we're not going to waste all of this. I'll put the whole one in the fridge and I'll finish yours, since you seem so excited about it."

Emily Micallef made her eyes into pin lights. She picked up the half *and* the whole second bun and threw them both into the garbage over Hazel's protests. "I know you buy three of them, piggy. You don't fool me for an instant."

Hazel arrived at work at eight o'clock the next morning. Ray intercepted her at the back door.

"Jack's coming in," he said.

"A house call?"

"What do you say we get Fraser in the office with us?"

"Why?"

Ray looked around awkwardly for a moment. "Look, I appreciate that James is coming along and it's really terrific to see him doing better, but I'm down a detec –"

"Dietrich Fraser's not a detective."

"He's got SOCO training. And he's been talking about taking the exam."

"I didn't realize we were doing co-op here." He smiled tolerantly. "OK. But I'm still keeping James in the loop."

"I never said you had to stop. But I need someone else on this. I need someone with some field experience, and Fraser has good eyes."

"Where is he then?"

They went to the front to look for Fraser, but it turned out he had left the station house for ten minutes. She passed by Peter MacTier in dispatch. "You know where Kraut is?"

MacTier shook his head, but it wasn't to say no.

"What?"

"He went to buy toilet paper."

"For?"

"Here. He doesn't like our toilet paper."

"He has terrible piles," Hazel said. "Go easy on him. Don't tell anyone I told you about the piles, OK? Send him into 2 when he gets back."

Jack Deacon, coroner at Mayfair General and OPS Central's chief forensic pathologist, entered by the front door and Hazel led him into Interview 2. Ray Greene stood to greet him, but he received no response from the doc. Deacon was silent all the way in to the room.

He sat down at the head of the table. She and Ray joined him on his left and right, and the doctor pulled a resealable bag out of his coat pocket. Sundancer's bone was inside it. "The vertebra I'm not done with yet, although I am about ninety per cent sure it's human." He unzipped the bag and shook the bone out gently onto the tabletop. "*This*," he said, standing back from it as if it were radioactive, "I'm a hundred per cent sure about. It's the iliac crest of an adolescent boy. Between the ages of thirteen and sixteen."

"What is —"

"The top ridge of the pelvis bone, Commander." He showed them on his body, pulling his lab coat up and cocking a hip at them. "This. Been gnawed at by animals or hacked at, from the look of it."

"Which do you think it is? Gnawed or hacked?"

"I'd put my money on steel over teeth."

They all looked at it in grave silence.

"A boy," Greene said. "How do you know?"

"We're shaped differently." Deacon ran his finger along the outside curve of the bone. "The male pelvis is taller, thinner, the iliac curves inward more. The female is broader and deeper. This is a boy."

"Not a man."

"No."

"So is it from a grave?" Hazel asked. "Is there an old graveyard?"

"Impossible to say. But it would be strange for a single bone to turn up if it was a graveyard. Even with machines turning the dirt over, you'd think there'd be much more."

"Maybe there is more," said Hazel.

"And that's why they stopped work on the golf courses," Ray said, flashing on an idea. "Who wants to risk their well-heeled clients swatting some kid's skull out of a sand trap? That's why they're building low-rises instead."

"Cover it up, literally, with buildings," Hazel said. "But Oscar Fremont said they stopped construction three months ago. Maybe management knows it has a problem. They erected fences to keep people in their houses and not out hiking and stumbling across bits of Buddy."

Greene leaned in to get a closer look at the fragment of iliac crest. "I bet there are a lot of people involved in Tournament Acres who wouldn't want it defined as a crime scene."

"If we go," said Deacon, resuming his professorial air, "with the theory that the marks on the bone are from its being chopped, hacked, stabbed, or otherwise butchered, then we must conclude that the wounds are post-mortem and the body was broken down by accident or on purpose."

"Well, you know where it was found."

"Certainly. You also see that this amount of knife work is overkill for the purposes of murder. So the cause of death is so far a mystery." Jack Deacon was bloodlessly professional.

Hazel liked that about him, but she doubted outside of work that he was a barrel of monkeys either.

"How old is it?" Greene asked.

Deacon picked the bone up and put it back into the evidence bag. "It's not recent. I only have a UV in my lab; I have to send this down to Toronto for nitrogen and amino analysis. But it's at least . . . thirty years old? Forty? Two hundred? We'll know in a couple of days."

Constable Dietrich "Kraut" Fraser entered, out of breath. "Sorry."

"You get your toilet paper for your soft bottom?" said Hazel.

"Jack," he said. Ignoring her and offering his hand.

"Dietrich."

"It's a kid's bone," Hazel said. "Around fifteen years old. Top of his pelvis —"

"Iliac crest," said Deacon.

"A kid," she repeated. "Fourteen, fifteen. Hacked up."

Now Fraser sat. "Jesus."

"A heavy blade chopped through it here," said Jack Deacon, "and here. And these marks are hacks that didn't break bone. Could be when it got tossed through a combine maybe —"

"A combine?"

"The field, Kraut," Hazel said. She gestured impatiently at Deacon. "Continue."

"This bone could have been ploughed up any number of times and moved all over."

"Right. Is it possible it's from a buri —"

"He doesn't know," said Hazel. "But he thinks it's unlikely. We're going to need to sweep that field."

"God," said Fraser, taking the bag from the pathologist. He held the bone up to his eye. "How do we know it's human, though?"

"He knows," said Hazel. "We need a team. There's more out there."

"You're going to need a dozen people," Ray said.

"It's twenty hectares. We'll need more than a dozen."

"I'll see who I can get from Mayfair."

"Call Barrie," Hazel said. "I'm going to call Brendan Givens. How much do you want to bet Honey Eisen and the Fremonts aren't the first people to uncover a bone in that place. Maybe he's got a whole skeleton in that desk of his."

Fraser nodded sagely. "I bet that's why they stopped building the golf —"

"Get here on time, Sergeant," she said, "and you can take part in the cogitating."

] 6 [

They tasked fifteen uniforms to sweep the field. There was no use in complaining. Willan had sent six Mayfair officers, including Victoria Torrance, and two of his scene-of-crime officers. A few other bodies came in from other detachments and Hazel had two other SOCOs apart from Fraser: sergeants Gerry Costamides and Melvin Renald. Macdonald had begged to be included, but after his last appearance at Tournament Acres he didn't put up a fight when Hazel told him he was staying home. They'd be eighteen in total. They took two vans out of Port Dundas.

Over the phone, Brendan Givens had been apoplectic. Why didn't they come back on Monday, when there would be fewer people around to upset? Hazel told him they'd be there in two hours.

She rode in the van with Costamides and Renald. Costamides hated Renald's driving and spent the ride glaring at him. Hazel bounced around in the back seat. "You think you can slow down?" Gerry said. "The only unit that doesn't have to drive fast, but Heavyfoot here thinks there's no speed limit."

"I've got things to do later today," said Renald. "How big is this place?"

"Keep your eyes on the road, Mel. A number of acres."

"We don't have kliegs," he said. "We'll work to sundown, then I'm out."

"You're out when I say you're out."

"I'm out when Ray Greene says I'm out. It's a waste of resources to dig in the dark."

Hazel wasn't terribly fond of Melvin anyway, but now he was really getting on her nerves. It was no secret his marriage was ending, nor that it was probably time to reassign him, but the threat of the downsizing that was coming with amalgamation had been inspiring him to keep it all under control: the drinking, the depression, his on-duty behaviour. He'd been in the OPS for thirty years – bouncing around detachments and grinding out his days to retirement. He arrived at Port Dundas in 2002, dragging a sheaf of warnings and citations behind him, but he'd been a pretty good cop. She'd only noticed him slipping in the last couple of years.

Brendan Givens met them on the stone porch of the clubhouse. Gaston Bellefeuille stood behind him by the door, his arms crossed over his chest. "I warned you about this," Givens said to Hazel. "People are muckraking."

"Well, we're going to have to do the same now," she replied. Renald and Costamides were unloading their kits as the second van pulled up. At the sight of it, Givens blanched and looked over at his security guard, who shrugged.

"Ask 'em if they have a warrant."

"Of course we have a warrant," Hazel said. "We're rather organized about these sorts of things."

Givens, aghast, watched more vans arrive. "Why do you need so many people?"

"We need them to make a grid on your unbuilt golf course and make sure there aren't any more surprises out there."

"I've walked the land for that second course a hundred times," he protested. "It's cornstalks and good Canadian Shield, that's what it is. You'll see for yourselves."

"I guess we will. How many more bones have you locked up in your desk, Mr. Givens? I presume you've disposed of them."

"What bones?"

"Why didn't you get rid of the vertebra?"

His face coloured. "I liked it." Hazel shouldered past Bellefeuille, and he followed her in. "We're dealing with enough bad publicity as it is," Givens said urgently in her ear. "People shouldn't be taking matters into their own hands! That's why we have a shareholders' committee, a board of directors . . . there's a time and a place for everything."

"It sounds like your various committees and shareholders have no power over locals armed with office supplies."

"Forget about Honey Eisen!" He stopped her with a hand on her arm. "And you don't think the Fremonts aren't up to butchering a chicken and then claiming they found human remains on their property? Oscar Fremont fashions himself a muckety-muck."

"It's not a chicken."

"Do you *know* who Fremont is?"

"No."

The others had stopped. "Insurance," said Givens. "Home, life, car, injury, you name it. He'd insure your toenails if you wanted him to. He owns his company. They have two floors in Yorkville in Toronto. You know what these people are good at? Not paying."

"I don't see the angle, Brendan."

"They want out. They'll default, sue, and then others will follow. I know he's talking to people."

"Did he put seventy-two-year-old Honey Eisen up to cracking your kneecap with a pen holder?"

"Maybe," he said, pressing his lips together. There was one big bead of sweat forming in his right eyebrow. When his face got tight he looked like Jimmy Durante. What *was* that kind of nose called? Spoonbill? Bulb? "Just do what you have to do, and when you *don't* find anything out there, I want to talk to you again. We have as much right to your protection as anyone else."

"Who's we?" asked Fraser, coming past with a bundle of hockey-stick shafts bound up with velcro straps.

Givens ignored him. To Hazel he said, "The business-people who keep Westmuir County in the black, that's who. Those of us who are working hard to pump up the economy in a part of the province where soybeans aren't worth what they used to be!"

"I'll keep your good works and that of the Ascot Group in mind as we poke around, OK?" she said.

They were shown through the main part of the clubhouse to the restaurant, and out onto the long patio that faced what was supposed to be one of the golf courses, but which was enclosed by a slatted wood fence seven feet high. On the inside, it was hung with pretty planters, and stained a warm, dark colour. Hazel guessed the fence hadn't been in the original plans.

Patrons and guests enjoying a late lunch in the shadow of this fence looked up at the appearance of so many uniforms. Givens was instructing the waiters to busy them-selves with their customers. He led the search party to a locked gate in the fence, but Hazel stepped onto a wooden bench partway there and peered over. It was a wasteland beyond, with unstained versions of this same fence creat-ing an unbroken border around about three-quarters of the development. To her right, houses ranged up along the

15th Sideroad (now Pebble Beach Boulevard). The completed ten holes were to her right as well, and looking to the north, there was a mix of trees and bramble where the earthmovers had stopped carving out the final eight holes of the first course. From where she stood it was forty football fields of neglected land hemmed in by fences that were designed to keep it from view. "Pretty country," she said.

"If you'd rather not jump over," Brendan Givens replied dolefully, "you can come through this gate."

She stepped down and took one of Renald's cases from him. "Don't lock it behind us. No telling what might happen."

"I know what's going to happen," said Givens, downcast, but he said nothing else. They passed through the gate onto the field's verge.

"Someone's worried about his job," said Renald. Behind him, sixteen more uniforms flowed out into the afternoon sun.

They spread out, twenty metres apart, and began to sweep. Their sticks moved back and forth in front of them through the wet stubble, lifting the sodden corn stalks up and tossing them aside. Rotted corncobs were mashed underfoot. There hadn't been live corn in this field for at least two summers: they were walking on a layer of compost. It smelled like sweet, wet mould.

Every fifty metres, the SOCOs pushed a red plastic marker into the earth and looped a yellow ribbon into the open catch at the top. Each officer performed their task alone, only dimly aware of the others moving at a stately pace up the field. When they got midway, Hazel looked behind herself and saw some of the patio diners looking over the fence. She imagined Givens was drinking in his office by now. She would be.

They kept to a special channel and reported their finds. Sergeant Costamides found some broken glass. One of the Mayfair team called in a condom, another found a shoe. They trekked forward like a slow-moving wave, examining every bit of ground in front of them. In three hours, they reached where the houses on Fuzzy Zoeller Way stopped and the land went all the way up to the empty boys' home and Concession Road 7. When they got to the road, they shifted five metres to the east and started back down.

Hazel looked over her shoulder at the back of the old Dublin Home for Boys. It sat heavily on its plot, its gateless front pillars still facing Concession Road 7, aka Augusta Avenue. The orphanage was made of blocks of grey, local stone. Cheap when it had been built eighty years ago, it now had a fashionable brutalism to it that would make it an interesting building to convert into the promised second clubhouse, in front of which the world's second-largest wave pool was to be installed, also as promised.

Orphanages like Dublin Home no longer existed. There were no Victorian workhouses like the ones she'd read about in school. The places like the one her brother had spent the first decade of his life in were now demolished or abandoned, but they still bred secrets. Society doesn't like to talk about its abandoned children. Behind every orphan or homeless kid is a hard story: a dead parent, an addicted parent, a poor parent, a rape victim, an act of passion or carelessness, a story of abuse. Imagine being a child in that world, she thought, passed from hand to hand with no guarantee of kindness.

The kids often came out damaged, incapacitated in some way. Unable to love or to accept love. So often following a path their absent parents had launched them on, which led to unhappy families of their own, mental illness, drugs, wandering. So it had gone with Alan, who had been immune to his adoptive family's love, and who fell at midlife and gave up. Plenty of Hazel's cases brought Alan sadly to mind, but this one gave her a pang of grief.

They continued in their long file back down the field as the sun declined in the west. Renald was complaining two lengths over. "Two more hours!" he called out. "There's nothing here!"

"We go until we're done, Melvin. I'll buy the drinks afterward."

He changed places with one of the Mayfair reps so he could holler more directly at her. "There are a hundred fields north of here, Hazel! That dog could have found that thing anywhere!"

A couple of positions down the line, one of the officers drove a rotten corncob about fifteen yards with his hockey stick. She heard distant laughter.

"Nice to see everyone at least enjoying themselves," Sergeant Renald shouted to her.

"Radio!" a voice called.

"Use your radio," Hazel shouted back. "They think you've found something, bozo."

He reluctantly raised his radio to his mouth. "Private conversation."

The call came again, airborne from a distance: "I need a radio!" Someone near the end of the line was making a big sweeping gesture with her hand. One of the Mayfair crew. She held her radio aloft in the other hand. Hazel watched the next closest officer jog over. He traded radios with her.

"I found something," the woman said, breathless.

Detective Constable Victoria Torrance crouched over a white form, as if she was protecting it. It looked like the top of a huge, fossilized egg. But it was unmistakably part of a human skull. The officers gathered near, and a hush went over them. Some at the front went down on one knee.

Hazel knew immediately what part of the skull it was. It was a portion of the forehead. Above the eye. Hazel felt above her left eye: that ridge. The bone was white and smooth, like the one the Fremonts had brought in. Torrance passed it to Fraser, who cradled it in his hand. "Superciliary arch," he said. He ran his finger along the ridge. "The eyebrow grows over it."

"How old?" asked Hazel.

"I can't tell that. Not an adult though."

"God." She looked around them. "This isn't going to work. I knew it wouldn't. We need more bodies. We need to be closer together."

"Neither Greene nor Willan is going to send anyone else," said Renald.

"Then we get anyone we can, on a volunteer basis if needed, to help us sweep this field."

"I bet they came from there." Torrance was looking over at the boys' home. "Could've been a graveyard."

"Do they hack the skeletons of dead children apart in your town, DC Torrance?"

"Nice to meet you again, Detective Inspector. No, they don't. But who knows what a century of heavy machinery might have done to the land here, especially if there was a graveyard."

"That is a popular theory."

Some of the officers drifted away, returning to the search. They circled out from where the bone arch had been found, their hockey sticks swishing through the dead stalks. There was no more golfing. "Lots of smut," said Torrance.

"What?" Hazel asked her.

Torrance poked at something near her foot. It was a cob of corn with part of its husk still on. It had dried out on high ground. There was a foul, black protrusion poking through the husk. "Corn smut," she said. "It's a mushroom grows on corn. If you catch it quick enough, it's delicious."

"Good to know," she said. "Always a pleasure to have you fellows around."

"You fellows?" she said, laughing. "Did I do something to offend you, Detective Inspector?"

"No, I apologize. Feeling short-tempered today. You can get back to sweeping with the others."

Darkness fell, but now no one wanted to leave. They strapped flashlights to their hockey stick shafts and kept searching, slowly, and the field turned into crosses of white beams sweeping over one another. At eleven, they were still less than half done, and they'd found three other fragments of bone. They were too scattered to make a pattern. If they were old, as Deacon had surmised the pelvic fragment had to be, animals could have carried these bones from all over. Their source wasn't necessarily nearby. There could be bone all over the region, a rain of bone fallen on nearby fields. Calcium for corn.

With the moon high, their shadows took on a silvery glint, the beams of their lights sweeping through layers of dark. Many of the houses around the perimeter were lit up, and those tenants with outdoor chairs or stepladders or sturdy tables were standing on them and looking out over the slow-moving silhouettes in their giant, common backyard. At times during the sweep, Hazel looked up to see the door at the end of the clubhouse patio open and Givens standing there, picked out in shadow, his arms crossed over his chest. Things were not going to get easier for that gentleman. She had called in the situation to Greene and word was going out: to Gilchrist and Fort Leonard, to the Queesik Bay Police Department. More from Mayfair. In the morning, they'd have seventy to a hundred bodies in this field.

At midnight, she decided to call it. "Come in," she said into her walkie-talkie. "Buddy up and come in." The beams turned and what seemed like two-dozen faerie lights began to bounce back toward the clubhouse.

"Hazel?" came Costamides's voice from among the approaching beams. "I don't have Mel with me. My radio's dead and we got separated. Can you get him?"

"Mel?" Hazel called into her handset. "Sergeant Renald? We're turning in, come back."

"Maybe his batteries are dead too," Gerry offered.

"And his flashlight?" Costamides emerged into the light. Hazel spoke into her radio again. "Clear this channel of unnecessary chatter, please. Everyone quiet. Renald? Come in, Sergeant Renald." She heard an electronic gurgle and a short blurt of sound that was like a human voice, but maybe from another part of the dial – a commercial or a CB interruption – and she called out to the officers streaming past her, "Have you seen him?" They trod by apologizing, and she asked a couple of them to look for Renald inside the clubhouse. She spoke his name again: "Mel? Can you hear me? How can you be out of range?"

Then a voice she'd never heard before said, "How can you stand so still within my sights?"

"What? Mel?"

"No." She heard the gurgle again. "I have your face in my crosshairs, Detective. Your bewildered face blown up ten times in the lens. Why are you still standing there?" She heard the report of a gun and the ground leaped up in front of her. She lay on her stomach, frozen.

"Shots fired!" someone shouted. "Shots fired!"

"Shut up!" Hazel cried into her handset. "Who is this?"

"Well, I have his radio, sweetheart," said the voice.

"Where's Renald?"

"He's resting after a long day. You should go home and get your beauty sleep. Take your playmates with you." Another chunk of wet dirt exploded beside her head. "Any more questions?"

Her sweepers were surging back into the field at the sound of gunfire, and Hazel called them off. "Don't return fire! Go back!" She crawled on her elbows and knees through the stubble. Up close, the dirt smelled like sulphur, like hell was cooling off below the tangled, rotting stalks. From her elbows and knees she shouted: "Rendezvous on Concession 6 outside the clubhouse gates! All personnel off the grounds!" She heard the crack of the gun again and involuntarily jumped up and ran crouching the final hundred metres to the clubhouse. Givens held the gate open for her. "And here I thought chivalry was dead," she said to him. "Consider yourself on lockdown."

She was checked out by one of Mayfair's people and pronounced fit to go back on duty. It was twelve-thirty on Friday morning and they were down an officer.

Sandy and Oscar Fremont watched the search from their backyard picnic table. Together, they had lifted it and carried it over to the fence. They lived close to what was still called Concession Road 7, in a house done up Tudor-style, with stained wood beams laid in stucco over a wood frame. There was no real brick or stone in Tournament Acres. The houses were imitations of other times and materials.

At nine o'clock, they went in to put on extra sweaters and open a bottle of red wine. They returned from time to time to observe the progress of the search, and later it was possible to tell from their footprints in the still-wet grass that they had come out three or four more times before finally going in.

] 7 [

Sandy Fremont brushed her hair at the computer, using the internal camera as a mirror. She read an email from her sister.

> Sandy, please don't be mad, but I'm not going to make it up for Christmas this year. Carol's been invited to the Irish dancing finals right afterwards in San Antonio and David says we can't afford to come to you and then jet off to Texas, and it means a lot to her. I know you'll understand, sis. It just feels like the stars aren't going to align this year. Please forgive me!

"Oh, sweetheart," she called over her shoulder. "Miriam isn't coming!"

"Coming to what?"

"Christmas!"

She heard Oscar walking back and forth in the bedroom. "Oh, that's too bad."

Sandy put on her baby voice. "She and David have to take wittle Carol dancing in Texas instead." He laughed. She turned out the light in the office and began down the hall. "Oh god," she said, sighing. "What a dread business it must be, ferrying your spawn to and from things."

First, she heard him cough. Then his wine glass dropped onto the buttercream-coloured broadloom in their bedroom doorway, spilling wine everywhere. "Oh *Jesus*! Oscar! Did you have to take a glass in there?"

Oscar lurched out of the room into the hallway and she started screaming. Blood gushed from his neck, and his hands scratched frantically at the dark red jetting between his fingers. A man appeared behind him in the doorway. He held a long knife, dripping red.

"Whatsamatter?" the man said. Sandy stepped backward, avoiding her husband, falling toward her. The man approached her slowly and she retreated into the office, eyes averted. "Not happy here in paradise? You want to ruin it for everyone?"

Sandy Fremont found her voice. "I don't want it to be ruined for anyone. I want everyone to be happy!"

"Look at my face."

"Just take what you want and let me get my husband some help! Please!"

"Your husband doesn't need help now. Look at my face."

She didn't have to. She'd recognized his voice. She began to scream and lunged for the phone on her desk, but she never got the receiver off the hook. Two minutes after her death, however, she sent an email to Ray Greene.

Hazel woke from a dream of walking across smashed eggs, their insides slippery under her feet. She reached out for purchase and woke with one hand in the air. She stared at it against the ceiling. She'd heard a sound in her sleep.

She put on her glasses and checked the time. It was 6:15 in the morning – she'd been asleep for four and a half hours. She wasn't sure at first if it was her or her mother who'd been making a fearful, choking sound, but then she was instantly sure that it wasn't coming from her own bedroom. Emily was making a chugging noise, soft and low. Hazel threw the covers off and rushed down to her mother's room. The sound was louder now. She flung open the door.

Emily was sitting up in bed, both hands against her chest, whooping for air. Her pupils roved madly in a sea of white. Hazel rushed to her side and held her shoulders. "Try to slow it down! Mom, look at me!"

Emily turned her terrified face to her daughter. Her pupils were like huge black nailheads. "I – I – !"

"Don't talk. Look at me. Go slow, slow down your breathing!" She tried to show her what she meant, but her own breath was fast with fear. She rubbed her mother's back as if Emily were her own child waking from a nightmare. Gradually, haltingly, Emily began to breathe.

"I —"

"Just wait a minute longer —"

"I woke up. I — Hazel —"

"You're better, it's over now."

Her mother slumped forward a little, and Hazel held her up. After a silent minute, Emily finally said, "Goddammit."

"What?"

"Your father will know I've been drinking." When she raised her head she looked drunk. "Don't tell him," she said. Her eyes rolled back.

Hazel almost dropped her in shock. "Mom!" She cradled her mother's neck and head and laid her down on the bed. There was a rattling noise coming from the back of Emily's throat. "Oh no! Mom? Can you hear me? Can you open your eyes? Oh god . . ."

She rolled Emily onto her side and braced her with pillows, then ran to get her cell. It was out of power. Fucking thing. She raced downstairs and dialled 911 on the wall phone. "The Micallef house on Pember Lake! You know it?"

"Yes ma'am," answered a male voice.

"Send an ambulance."

Emily was fully awake by the time Hazel returned to the bedroom. What's more, she was lively. She'd gotten up and had even made the bed, and she was sitting at her table, writing. Hazel approached her slowly. "Mom?" She looked over Emily's shoulder. A list, in her mother's tight, steady hand, read:

money
¼ lb sultanas
¼ lb glacé cherries
oatmeal
pick up Alan

"Mother?"

Emily looked up, startled. "Oh, Hazel, I didn't see you."

"Are you all right?"

"Of course I'm all right. Why are you home from school? Are you ill?"

"No, I'm fine. I was . . . just going to make some tea."

"I'll have a cup."

"Oh, it's ready now actually. Come down before it's too steeped."

"Don't paw at me, child." Emily stood up on her own. She was grounded, steady. Hazel dashed ahead into the kitchen and ran the tap water hot and filled a teapot halfway with it. Her mother came in and sat in her regular seat. When she wasn't looking, Hazel dumped a teabag into the pot.

"Where are my cigarettes?"

"You don't smoke, Mom."

"Where'd you put them?"

"You ran out."

"The deuce I did, Hazel. Where are my cigarettes?"

"Ah! The tea." She turned back to the countertop, quivering. How long was the ambulance going to take? What was happening? Her legs were weak with fatigue and fear. She reached unsteadily for two teacups. They never drank tea anymore, only coffee, but her mother had preferred tea when Hazel was in school. She looked hard at the cups. She poured. "Milk?" she asked her mother without turning around.

"Do we have molasses?"

"In . . . in your tea, Mom?"

"No. In the cupboard, Hazel."

"Yes, I think so."

"Would you mind looking with your eyes?"

Hazel did. There was no molasses. "There's plenty," she said. She couldn't turn around or her mother would see her crying. "What are you making? What's the list for?"

"A fruitcake for the Chandlers. I'll buy the others, but I like to make the Chandlers their own."

"Just the Chandlers?"

"Well, Delia was such a dearheart that time, stepping up when your father was in hospital. She was a great help to me during my campaign. She painted some of our posters by hand."

"I didn't know," said Hazel.

"And of course Rupert and I play bridge at the same club. I see him all the time."

Rupert had been dead for decades. He'd been dead long before her father and Delia had begun their affair.

There was a knock at the door. Hazel put her mother's tea in front of her and quickly left the room, wiping her face along the arm of her dressing gown. The paramedics saw this kind of thing all the time. "In here," she said, letting them in. Two women. Behind them, standing beside his car, was James Wingate, dressed in uniform. He said something she couldn't make out. She gestured him toward her with her arms. "Get in here!"

He took his cap off and entered. "I don't want to disturb you."

"What's going on? Did they find Mel?"

"Oh . . . no, I —"

"Why are you in uniform?"

"In case you needed me here. To . . . to have an officer present."

"You can't be an officer present because you are not currently an officer of anything, you're on admin leave. And how did you —"

"I know Mira. What happened to Mel?"

"Fuck, come in. Who's Mira?"

"The paramedic with the freckles. She sent me a text when the call came in. She knows we're . . ."

"Close the door behind you." For a moment she felt dizzy and she reached out for a wall. Wingate caught her forearm in his hand, lightly, and immediately let go. She waved him toward the kitchen. "Do you even know about Renald?"

"What?"

"He's missing. Melvin Renald."

"Oh shit —"

"I spoke to someone. On *his* radio. Someone fired two shots at me."

They stood in the doorway to the kitchen. The paramedics sat at the table and Emily held a teapot aloft between them. "This tea is terrible," she said. "I didn't offer them any."

Hazel was eager to have something to do with her hands. "I'll make more," she said.

Emily sized up the paramedics with a squinty eye. "Are you two pilots?"

"No, we're from town. We came to see you. How are you feeling Ms. Micallef?"

Emily looked at them and then over at Hazel. "Hazel? These ladies are talking to you."

"Call her Mayor," Hazel told them.

"They're not calling *me* Miss Micallef?" She pinned the paramedics with an icy glare. She could hold two people still, one with each eye.

"No, ma'am, Mayor. How are you feeling?"

"A little piqued if the truth be known. I've misplaced my cigarettes."

"I have one," said the paramedic with the freckles. "Is this brand OK, Madam Mayor?"

"It's fine," said Emily.

Mira passed her the pack, and Emily took one and leaned forward to have it lit. She hadn't smoked a cigarette in over forty years. But then she took a natural, long drag and exhaled slowly.

"Do you know what day it is?" Mira asked.

"What kind of question is that? Are you *both* pilots?"

"No ma'am," she said. "We're paramedics. Your daughter called us and said you were having trouble breathing."

"She's not herself," Hazel said in a stage whisper. "She hasn't smoked since she was in her fifties."

Emily took a second drag on the cigarette. "You know I can hear you, right?"

"Mayor Micallef, how old are you?"

"What a question. Are you serious?"

"Well –"

The kettle began to whistle. "I'll make the tea," Hazel said.

Wingate rushed to turn off the stove. Emily followed him with her eyes. Hazel realized her mother was looking at what she thought was the only police officer in the room.

"Oh for the lovvah . . . What did you do now, Hazel?" she said, rounding on her daughter.

"No – no, Mayor," Wingate said, "she hasn't done anything at all. I was just dropping by."

"Since when does the constabulary *drop by*?"

"When an ambulance is dispatched to the home of the mayor, you know, people are concerned."

"This is not about that Lim girl, is it? Hazel has already —"

"No, Mom, he's not here about that." Hazel turned to the room in desperation. "Can we do something? Is there nothing we can do?"

The two paramedics seemed to be passing telepathic considerations. They exchanged one glance, then another. Hazel followed Mira out of the kitchen. They heard Emily say, "You have to wonder what the world is coming to if you can't go for a walk in broad daylight."

"Would you mind taking back your cigarettes? She's *ninety*," Hazel said.

"Of course. Do you have power of attorney over your mother?"

"Are you kidding me?"

"We can't really do anything without someone's consent. Will she consent to taking a sedative?"

"Can we trick her?"

"*I* can't," she said.

They returned to the kitchen and Mira said, "We'll be going then." She gestured to her partner. "Thank you, Madam Mayor, for having us."

"It was a great pleasure. Be careful now."

"And we hope your headache goes away. Maybe you should take something?"

"For what?"

"To help your headache."

Emily spent a moment processing what Mira meant. "It'll go away on its own," she said.

The paramedics left. *Enough*, Hazel thought. She got up — to use the washroom, she said — and went quietly to her own bathroom where she kept her Ativan. They were the blue sublinguals, the ones that got to work right away. Then she crept back downstairs, silently opened the front door, and rang her own doorbell. "I'll get it," she called. "Just a minute!" She waited there for a moment, her mind racing. "Oh, that's terrific. Thank you so much! We really do appreciate it." She closed the door loudly enough to be heard in the kitchen.

"Isn't that good service?" she said to her mother. "They sent the pills for your headache."

"My head is fine. And I'd better get a move on. Alan will be out at three." She stood, or tried to stand, and then she sat again. "Goodness," she laughed. "Can't be tired at lunchtime!"

"You'd better take one of the pills that nice lady sent over. Pep you up."

"Pep me up, eh? What is it?"

"A pep pill," Hazel said brightly. Wingate filled a glass of water. She opened her hand to show her mother the two small blue pills.

"What are they?"

"They're vitamins for your health. You haven't had them yet today, have you?"

"Oh — I don't think so."

"Good thing she remembered!" said Wingate, handing her the glass.

Emily took it from him. Then she took the pills. Just accepting them had a magical effect, as if some part of her knew she was not well. Almost before she'd finished the water, she began to look drowsy. She shrugged her shoulders up. "Where is Alan?" she asked. Then her eyes began to close.

Wingate drove back to Port Dundas. There were small blocks of wood duct-taped to his brake and accelerator pedals now, as it was hard for him to push his right foot down. And it was a task getting out of the car, as well as assembling his movements in the right order to achieve a standing position. Getting out of a car was only slightly easier than getting into one, which involved leaning away while facing front, squatting while on one leg, turning and bending, and falling backward.

Much of the time, his body felt like something he was wearing, some kind of technologically advanced suit that sometimes moved under mental command but often didn't. He had to get it properly oriented before walking across a parking lot and opening a door, for instance. Greene met him as he was coming through the pen. "I don't know what to tell you, Commander," Wingate said. "Her mother seemed really out of it."

"Should you be in your uniform?"

"I thought just in case."

Greene gave him an appraising squint. "In case of what?"

"Hazel's at home with an emergency. I thought –"

"Did they go to the hospital?"

"No. She's staying at home. To watch her. Emily." Half the pen was empty. "Is everyone back on the sweep today?"

"Most of them. I sent Fraser to the Fremonts' and Macdonald's interviewing people about Renald. So far – nothing. And there's something else." Wingate twitched involuntarily. "Are you sure you're OK?"

"I'm fine."

"When did you start wearing the uniform again?"

"What do you mean by *something else?*"

Greene held him in his gaze a beat longer. "Come look at this."

He led Wingate into his office and turned his computer screen toward him. It was an email message from Sandra Fremont, sent at 12:45 in the morning. Wingate read it. "Has Hazel seen this?"

"I only just saw it myself."

Wingate dialled Hazel's home number. "Sorry to bother you again. It's important."

"Renald?"

"Maybe. We don't know. Sandy Fremont sent Skip an email in the middle of the night. After Renald was taken."

"And?"

"*The sergeant is next*," he read.

"Next what? Sandy Fremont sent that?"

"It came from her address. But I don't think it was Sandy Fremont who sent it."

"Is that all?" she asked.

"It's signed *Please Stand By.*"

She coughed her disbelief. "Is anyone down –"

"Ray sent Fraser. And Macdonald is down there canvassing for Renald."

There was a bit of a silence at her end. "Good," said Hazel. "And where are you, James?"

"With Ray."

"You get around."

"I guess so."

"Pass me to him." He did, and Ray covered the mouthpiece until Wingate left the office. "How's he look to you?" she asked Ray.

"James? Like an irradiated boy scout."

"He came to my house at seven. With a pair of lesbian paramedics. My house was very strange this morning, Ray. Can you handle James? I've got my hands full."

"No problem. Difference between you and James is James obeys direct orders."

"Send him home."

"I will. Check in with me?"

"Thanks."

Greene disconnected. He called Wingate back into his office. "Shift's over. Go get your uniform dry-cleaned and get some sleep. Am I supposed to call your brother or something?"

"I'm not in detention, Skip. I'll go. You'll let me know if anything else turns up about . . . about Sergeant Renald?"

Ray promised his detective sergeant that he would.

] 8 [

1957

They'd eaten turkey three Sundays in a row. It was a tradition ever since she was a kid that her mother would
cook a huge turkey at Thanksgiving and then freeze the
leftovers in order to have roast dinner for as many Sundays
as it would last. Thanks to her mayoralty, Emily usually
received her turkey as a gift from someone, and no one
gave the mayor of Port Dundas a small turkey. The one
she'd cooked two Sundays ago had been a sixteen-pounder.
They'd be eating it until Christmas.

They'd invited her father's parents and Emily's father
over. Grandma Blythe lived at the Poplars and no longer
recognized anyone. She had been sick since before Hazel
was born, but the woman's stern gaze still presided over the
living room from a photograph above the mantel. "Your

mother's face should not be in a room where people are drinking Scotch," her father said to Emily, toasting the framed photograph sardonically.

His father-in-law frowned at the comment. "Blythe was not against the occasional tipple," he said.

"A shandy is not a tipple, Craig."

They all came to the table. Alan had refused to dress properly for dinner and sat in his overalls. He had been hard to "civilize." Ten years in a county orphanage could do that to a person. They tolerated his strange habits, like holding his fork in his fist as if he were going to stab someone with it.

The defrosted and reheated turkey was making its appearance this week as Turkey à la King. They said grace and then the bowls and platters were passed around and everyone filled their plate. Alan would not eat anything with a sauce on it, so a separate dish had been prepared for him with plain white meat, mashed potatoes, and Brussel sprouts sautéed with bacon, which he wouldn't touch. It didn't really matter what you put in front of Alan. Usually he just ate bread.

"So, what is happening in town?" asked Hazel's grandmother. Hazel called her Nana. She was the one who asked questions of the town's mayor with a slight catch in her voice, and that's how Hazel knew she was being polite. "What is happening with that Chinese girl? Has she turned up?"

Emily looked down the table at Hazel. "No," she said. "The girl hasn't been seen at all since last week. But we have a better idea of what might have happened. Hazel and Gloria Whitman went in to see Gord Drury."

"And?"

"Gloria gave a description of a man she encountered coming out onto Grant Street that evening. They did a sketch of the man, didn't they, sweetheart?"

Hazel was caught off guard. This was the first she'd ever heard of Gloria's encounter. "Um, I think so," she said.

"According to Gloria, the man was *also* Chinese," Emily said. "Drury's questions stirred her memory and she realized she'd seen a man at the end of the path that leads back into town behind Kilmartin Bluff Park."

Hazel's father was cutting his meat. "That seems to fit with what I've heard Herbert Lim say. That she probably ran off. Problems at home, and the first fellow who cocks his hat is reason enough to throw in her lot with him."

"Today's generation just wants to get everything done quick-quick," said Grandpa Craig. "They want to grow up quick, make their money, buy their houses and cars. Hope they don't want to live and die quick too."

"Well, I guess you just don't know how things work in other people's families, and certainly not among people like that."

"*Evan,*" said Emily. "Like *what?*"

"I mean folks who have no experience with the Canadian way. Maybe they did things differently at home."

"You mean chase their kids away because they didn't approve of them?"

"Shacking up at the age of seventeen?" Grandpa Craig hooted. "And where? In the Ward? Who would approve of that?"

Nana hushed him. Hazel wasn't sure what they were talking about now, but she was relieved to know that people who understood things better than she did were concluding that Carol was OK. If in a whole lot of hot water with her parents.

"I see the Lims in the shop all the time," her father continued. "Lovely people. But they don't join in, do they? You can't live in a place this small and keep to your ways. People talk."

"People talk anyway," said Grandpa Craig. "It's never any good being different." Here he looked at Alan, and Alan looked back, and the two of them stuck their tongues out at each other and laughed. "Then again, sometimes a person can't help it. Sometimes, if you arrive here from another planet, it's hard to hide it, isn't it?"

Alan turned his mouth into what was supposed to be a threatening-looking sneer, but the only effect it had was to reduce the table to warm giggling. "I'm from Earf," he said. "I eat all of you."

"Anyway," said Emily, trying to bring one part of the conversation to a close, "Gord Drury is sure they'll hear from her eventually. And there's no sign that foul play was involved, so what can anyone do but wait? You know what they say about the course of true love."

Her father looked at her mother, and something passed between them, an adult thing that might otherwise be expressed in words.

Once her grandparents had left and she had done her share of the cleaning up, Hazel rode her bicycle over to Gloria's house. Dr. Whitman opened the door and gave her a warm smile. "Look who's here," he said. "Miss Micallef." He shook her hand.

"Hi Dr. Whitman." He preferred to be called Dale, even by Gloria's friends, but as Hazel could not bring herself to do so, he deferred to her preference and addressed her with a warm, but comical, formality. He was a tall man with a round, bald head and a salt-and-pepper moustache somewhat like Gord Drury's, if not quite as walrussy.

Hazel admired Gloria's father, but he was a man of such high standing that he also intimidated her. He was confident and witty. He was handsome, although a bachelor since Gloria's mother – his beloved Wilma – passed away from cancer. He'd vowed he would never remarry. Whenever Hazel visited them, he would clasp her shoulders and squeeze them and look into her eyes. "You are the spitting image of your mother," he would say, and sometimes, jokingly, he'd add, "and a good thing too, since your father is nothing special to look at, am I right? Gloria! Hazel has arrived!" He ushered her in. "Come, come."

Gloria came prancing down the stairs. "Hazel. Hi!"

"Hey," Hazel said, shyly.

"You girls up to no good again?"

Gloria shushed her father. "I'm cutting pictures out of *Photoplay*. Wanna see?"

Hazel followed her friend up the stairs and they shut the door behind them. Gloria's bedroom was a teenager's paradise. She had a stereo LP player and a bed with a canopy. When they were younger, Hazel had sometimes slept in that bed, the two of them under the covers with one of her father's penlights. When they were still little, they'd read comic books together, but by the time they were eleven Hazel had begun to tire of Gloria's bragging. After a while, she stopped going over at all. There were other things of interest, like boys, by the time she turned fourteen.

"Did you really meet a Chinese guy coming down the bluff?"

"Yeah. Why?"

"You didn't tell me that."

Gloria put on a record: Doris Day singing "You made me love you (I didn't want to do it)." She mouthed the words, swaying her hips. "I saw a couple of people on the way back to my house, but you always see people. It wasn't until Commander Drury asked me if I'd noticed anything unusual that I thought maybe it was unusual that this Chinese guy was coming onto the trail just a little while after we saw Carol, and then Carol disappears. It's not like there are hundreds of Chinese people in this place."

"No, but I'm sure they still go for walks. Did you recognize this guy?"

"No."

"So what did you tell Commander Drury about him?"

Gloria shrugged. She stood beside the record player, watching the record turn. Then there was a knock at the door, and her father called from the other side. "Come in," she shouted.

He pushed the door open with his knee and came in holding a tray. There was a small pitcher of lemonade and some Hydrox cookies. "Don't let me interrupt." He put the tray down and left. Hazel's mother bought Oreos. There was no reason Dr. Whitman couldn't afford Oreos, but there had always been Hydroxes here, and Gloria claimed to prefer them.

"What did you tell Commander Drury?"

"That I'd run into this man just as I was coming off the path, and he was in a green jacket with a hat, and he nodded to me and I nodded to him."

"That's it?"

"I looked back," said Gloria, twisting a cookie open. "Just for a second. He looked back at the same time. He wasn't much older than her, either – I guess you could say he was even sort of cute. I just didn't think anything of it at the time."

"So you think he was a boyfriend? I thought you said she was going out with Tommy Landers."

"How do I know who she's going out with?" Gloria snapped. "Why do you think I'm an expert on how many boys Carol Lim sleeps with? Do you want lemonade or not?"

"Fine, yeah." She accepted a glass of lemonade from her friend. "But you think this guy knew Carol."

"Why not? I didn't know how unhappy things were for her though. My dad told me she'd threatened to run away before. She did it for real this time. Anyway, wouldn't you get away from here if you could?"

"I like it here," said Hazel. "Don't you like Port Dundas?"

"Are you kidding? I want to be where the excitement is." Gloria stretched luxuriously and her shirt rode up her belly, showing the soft undulations of muscle beneath her glowing skin. There were paper cut-outs behind her on the bed. She'd snipped the glamorous faces of film stars and entertainers out of her movie magazine. Their bodiless heads lay in rows, all smiling, some smoking cigarettes with panache. The display looked like a room full of people enjoying themselves, but you couldn't hear what they were saying. Hazel imagined that she and Gloria were standing at a window, looking into a Hollywood ballroom.

"Who cares where she went anyway?" Gloria said. "Carol

Lim? She's almost eighteen, she can do what she wants. It's not our problem."

Hazel looked along a row of faces that included Eva Marie Saint, Martin Landau, and Connie Francis. "What is all this?"

"Oh!" said Gloria, delighted to explain. "I put them in order." She came over to the bed and shooed Hazel aside. "Who's better looking? Eva Marie Saint or Angie Dickinson?"

"Oh, Angie for sure."

"Angie or Elizabeth?"

"Elizabeth."

"Which one is smarter?"

"I don't know," said Hazel. "I think Angie Dickinson is smarter. She looks smart."

Gloria Whitman considered Angie Dickinson's face, comparing it to Elizabeth Taylor's. "The ones who are both very good-looking and also very smart go into a special row," she said. "They're the best of the best. Cary Grant is in that row." She pointed to a section of her bed where Hazel also saw Katharine Hepburn, Jimmy Stewart, and Ingrid Bergman.

"Are you sending them prizes or something?"

"They *are* the prizes. I like to look at their faces and try to think how the world appears to them."

"I don't think you can know how a person feels just by looking at their face," said Hazel. Gloria had strange enthusiasms. One time, during one of their final sleepovers, she'd forced Hazel to hold her cat Dennis while she covered his nose and mouth with her hand. She wanted Hazel to feel how fast the cat's heart went when he was scared. Dennis had licked Gloria's hand afterward, as if he understood that she didn't mean, as she had explained, to do him any harm.

] 9 [

Friday, midday

Detective Sergeant James Wingate looked Oscar Fremont in the eye. He was standing on the stairs leading up to the second floor; Fremont lay on his belly, glued to the shag carpet. The lake of sticky blood beneath him had all but fastened him to the floor. A crime scene officer was cutting the carpet around him, and back in the bedroom, two attendants waited beside a gurney.

He'd come in through the back. He didn't recognize any of the SOCOs. Fraser was somewhere else at the scene, so Wingate was waiting where he wouldn't get in the way. He hadn't taken off his uniform, so it had been easy to get through the police tape, but he hadn't counted on running into Oscar Fremont. The dead man's carotid artery gaped pink on the side of his neck where it had been cut right through. There was a yawning wound at the top of his neck that extended to under his chin. It was clogged with pale, fleshy structures that were speckled with black clots. Wingate could see the underside of Fremont's tongue through the gash. He felt his own throat tightening.

Where was Melvin Renald in all of this? He had to hope Renald was still alive. He had the idea of trying to raise Sean Macdonald on his walkie-talkie, to see if he'd found anything, but he thought better of it. The fewer people who knew he was here, the better.

Wingate hadn't known at first whom Hazel had meant when she said *Mel*. No one, at least in his presence, had ever called Sergeant Renald "Mel." Or Melvin, for that matter. The man was *Renald*, through and through. Wingate had been surprised to learn he wasn't a lifer. He had the look of one: he could size you up in a tenth of a second, and get away with anything because he'd been there so long. But that wasn't the case – he was a bouncing bear. He'd been in half a dozen detachments. You learned to give guys like that a wide berth: they're just passing through. But Renald felt like a guy who'd come to settle. More than once, he'd given Wingate a careful look, and Wingate couldn't tell what worth had been determined. Bringing his eye level with Fremont's carotid again, Wingate wondered if Melvin Renald was even more tightly wound than he seemed. But who was he to the Fremonts? Or they to him?

He took another two steps up toward the body to get out of its eyeline, and nodded at the red-haired officer who was almost done cutting Oscar Fremont out of the hall carpet. She wore a surgical mask over her mouth and was ripping the broadloom with a small, curved knife. The gurney-bearers were gazing at their phones. Wingate looked to the right and saw Sandra Fremont's shoes, heels up, the toes splayed outward. The murder weapon wasn't hard to spot. It was sticking out of the back of her head. She could have run down the stairs he was on now, but she'd run into her office instead, into a cul-de-sac where the murderer had had an easy time of it. What must it be like to have your death come so unexpectedly, in a place of apparent safety?

The female officer and the attendants tore Oscar Fremont free of the wooden floor beneath him and loaded him onto the gurney. Wingate had to step up into the hall to let them past. On his stretcher of bloody carpet, Fremont looked like he'd died falling onto a fluffy cloud. Wingate watched them take him out the rear of the house. No way they could load him out the front, and he wouldn't fit into a body bag like that. They'd have to figure it out in the backyard.

The door closed below him. He jumped onto the exposed wood where Fremont's dead eyes had stared at him from the edge of the top step. Wingate was alone now, without paper booties or gloves. He looked upon the crisply imprinted bloody boot treads leading to where Sandy Fremont lay on a small circular carpet in her office. There were no such prints leading out of the room. Whoever's boots they were, they'd been taken off and removed from the scene.

Wingate crept toward the office on the tips of his shoes, taking care to avoid the bloody marks on the shag runner. Sandy Fremont bisected the colourful rag carpet she lay on. She'd struck her temple on the corner of the desk going down and left a smear of bright gore there with some hair in it. She was face down, her nose pointed to the floor. Wingate took his shoes off and kneeled beside her. There was very little blood.

"That took some force," Dietrich Fraser said from the doorway. "Getting a knife that far into someone's head." Wingate leaned over and looked straight down at the butt of the knife. A big, eight- to ten-inch chef's knife. Only two of those inches were visible. The handle was made of a hard, dark-brown wood, held together with four rivets.

"Don't touch it," Fraser said.

"Why'd Greene send you?"

"Why'd he send you?"

Wingate stood up. "You know Hazel's got her hands tied with her mother right now. I'm here in a more unofficial capacity. So there's an investigating officer present."

"Present, but on admin duty. And in uniform."

"Skip says you're taking the exam." Fraser didn't answer. "I'm sure you'll make a good detective."

"Thanks, James. Listen, there're enough people here. Three SOCOs and a photographer. You can –"

"Look at this. C'mere," Wingate said.

Fraser stood silently in the doorway a moment longer to register his continuing objection to Wingate's presence, but then he came over. "What am I looking at?" he asked.

"The angle of the knife."

Fraser tilted his head this way and that. "Sort of straight in, isn't it?"

"Almost exactly straight. The spine of the blade is pointing right at the tip of her nose. If we knew her height and we could get the angle of the knife –"

"Get out of the way," someone said. It was the SOCO from the hall and the gurney-bearers. They had a fresh gurney. The SOCO positioned herself at Sandy's feet. "You get her shoulders," she said to the attendants. Wingate came over to stand with Fraser.

The attendants leaned over to grip the dead woman's shoulders. "Just don't think about it," one of them said to the other. "OK, go."

They began to lift Sandra Fremont. It looked like her upper body weighed five hundred pounds, the way they were tugging. They struggled a moment longer, then there was a loud creak under her face and they pulled her up. The knife was closer to fourteen inches in length, and the end of it stuck out of the middle of her face. Her nose was a steel fin.

Wingate strode out of the room. Fraser began laughing. "James? What was that about the angle of the knife?"

On the way back to his car, Wingate puked twice.

Jack Deacon's report on the rest of the bone fragments came through just after 4:00 p.m. After Greene was done with it, Wingate made a photocopy and took it out to Pember Lake.

"You look awful, James," Hazel said when she opened the door.

"I had a bad egg," he said. "The bones from the field are at least forty years old." He gave her the report, which she started to read on her way back to the kitchen. He followed her. "How's your mom?"

"Asleep." In the kitchen, he drank a glass of water and she read and reread the report, flipping back and forth to tests and photographs. "God," she muttered. The Fremont bone was from the pelvis of a fifteen-year-old boy. The victim had died between 1950 and 1960, according to Deacon. Marks on — and indentations in — the bone were consistent with blows from an axe. He attributed the darkness in the grooves to scorching. The other bone, the frontal arch of a skull, had also been hacked and burned; Deacon put the age of the victim at twelve. He reckoned the vertebra didn't belong to either victim. So there were three bodies at least.

Hazel tossed the file onto the kitchen table. "Someone murdered these children more than forty years ago and got away with it." They both found themselves staring at the folder, as if it were glowing, and they were each correct about what the other was thinking. "Those poor boys," Hazel said.

"Poor boys," said Wingate.

She poured some coffee out of a fresh pot into two cups, made Wingate's the way he took it, and brought them back to the table. "You should go home after this."

"Our master gave me leave to stay on unofficial duty."

She raised an eyebrow at him. "Did he give you leave to keep wearing your stripes?"

"You've got a lot on your plate, Hazel. I'm just trying to keep an eye out. You've done it many times for me."

"This isn't the time to pay me back. If Ray or Willan sees you dressed for duty, they'll –"

"Skip saw me."

"Oh, right. You went straight back to the station house. And?" She looked at him funny.

"What?" he said.

"You're being evasive. Why?"

"Who's invasive?" came a voice from behind them, and they both swivelled in their chairs. It was Emily, in a housecoat, her hair aswirl.

"What are you doing out of bed?"

"What time is it?" She looked at the clock before Hazel could, then looked out the window at the long shadows on the lawn. "Is it six o'clock at night?" she asked, incredulous.

"Yes. You weren't feeling well."

"Hello James."

They both eyed her warily. "Hello Mrs. Mayor."

She was looking at their coffees with a confused expression. Her energy was subdued, not at all as it had been that morning after her attack.

"How are you feeling?" Hazel asked.

"I'm fine, I'm fine," Emily replied. "A little hungry. Groggy." She was looking around the kitchen now. Hazel had thrown out the cigarettes. "I think I want a sandwich," she said. Hazel rose immediately to make it.

"I'm glad you're feeling better."

"And what's happening tonight?" she asked.

"Nothing," she said.

"We're discussing a case," said Wingate. "I wonder if the criminals in your day were anything like the people we deal with now."

"Criminals are always angry," said Emily. "Whenever Evan noticed something missing in the store, he'd say, 'Better he took a shirt than punched someone in the mouth.'" She settled in one of the two free chairs, not noticing how Hazel was watching her. "That man knew the price of salt, but he'd let a person walk all over him if he thought it would make a better world. Is there more of that?" she asked, nodding at the coffee. "It feels like six a.m., but it's not, is it?"

Hazel poured her a cup and made her a sandwich out of a Kraft Single on whole-grain bread with mayonnaise and a crispy rib of romaine lettuce. This had been her own favourite lunch when she was a kid. Every family had its standby. She'd learned early on that a certain look in Andrew's eye could be wiped away with careful application of homemade meatloaf. She'd learned the recipe – beef, pork, veal, prunes, and bacon – from Andrew's mother.

"You two chat," Emily said, accepting the sandwich. Hazel had cut it in two diagonally.

"Time to get some rest, James," Hazel said.

Wingate got up and tipped his cap. "I'm glad you're feeling better, Mrs. Micallef."

"I am not feeling better, James. I am sucking wind and that is about it."

When he'd gone, Hazel asked, "Do you even remember this morning, Mom?"

"Yes," said Emily, taking a chunk out of her sandwich. "I was going on like a fool."

"You thought it was 1957."

"I smoked a cigarette. I can still taste it."

Hazel shook her head in wonder. "Did you at least enjoy it?"

"Not at all." She looked up at her daughter and smiled wanly, although there was a wisp of wickedness in it. "I don't much think about that time anymore, but there was a lot going on in our lives. Before everything happened." She picked up the other half of the sandwich. "Here we go," she said. "Down the long slide to happiness, endlessly."

She ate with gusto.

] 10 [

Friday evening

Instead of going home, Detective Sergeant James Wingate drove back to Tournament Acres. He had not slept in thirty-six hours.

There was still a team at the Fremonts', and many of the homes on the western side of the development were fully lit. When Wingate found him, Givens was watching the SOCOs go in and out of the Fremont house on his close-circuit feed from Fuzzy Zoeller. Cameras ringed the development at intervals of five hundred metres. The various feeds displayed across the fifty-inch flat screen in his office. A couple of the feeds were busy with people flowing back and forth under lights.

He sat in a huge, padded chair, his injured leg up on a rolling drinks cart. A half-empty glass decanter was at his elbow. "This is bad," he said. Wingate thought he meant his knee, but the man shook his remote at the screen. "Look at all that."

"Where were you last night, Mr. Givens? Say, after eleven o'clock?"

"I was monkeyfucking drunk. In my suite."

"Were you with anyone?"

He sneered. "Sure. I was with my harem."

"I'm sorry to have to ask. You knew the Fremonts, surely."

"Lovely people. They had me over for canapés after they moved in."

Wingate's head went *canned apes.* "Do you think anyone would have had a reason to harm them?"

"Oh, gosh no." Givens reached for a shot glass from the cart, filled it from the decanter, and drank it down. "They kept to themselves."

"Were they on any of the homeowners' committees? Did they have problems with their property, for instance?"

"How many years do you think separates them? I bet you can't guess."

"Fourteen."

"How did you know?"

"They're dead. I know how old they were." Givens reflected on this. "Can anyone vouch for your whereabouts between eleven last night and six a.m.?"

Givens clicked the monitor off with his remote and came around the front of the desk. He walked hoppingly, using

the desk for support. "Would you like to know how it works?"
His body blocked the light from the window behind. The
glow from the kliegs around the Fremont house made a
halo of gauzy light around his body. "First, you buy some
shitty land somewhere between a city and where people
really wish they could live when they retire. You can sell
them bungalows with a shopping centre or brick-veneer
semis with a mosque or fully detached, luxury living with
a golf course. In some US states you can even give them a
casino. The key is to sell forty-nine per cent. Fifty-one per
cent unsold and you're still the majority shareholder, and
you can walk away. You've made a killing on forty-nine per
cent of the cheap houses you built. Notice how only half
the houses advertised have been built."

"I noticed that. Is it all legal?"

"Yeah, it's legal. You have to insure the hell out of it. But
when the lawsuits come, if they do, you've not only got
that all-important one per cent on your side. People always
settle. They just want money anyway. You'd be amazed
what they settle for."

"Why are you telling me this? Is someone pissed off?"

"How much you want to bet I'm the next body?" He
grunted a laugh.

Wingate had left his notebook in his pocket. Being more
or less off-duty, he wasn't supposed to be taking notes, but
it would look good, he thought. "You sound like you're
looking forward to it."

"Anything to get out of this racket. Living in half-finished paradises a year at a time? Think you can meet a woman like that?"

"No?"

"No."

"And get this," he said, ready to spill. "The homeowners own their dwellings and the land they're on, but the corporation owns all the common property and runs its services. A lot of places they're the gas resellers, even."

"Gas resellers?"

"They buy natural gas in bulk and become the vendors to their own developments at higher-than-market prices. It's written into the contract. Something about the cost of new infrastructure. They make a killing."

"Do you think someone associated with this development killed the Fremonts?"

"Look at this," Givens said. He hobbled back behind his desk. He unlocked a drawer out of sight and returned with a huge hanging file folder. "I think you may find this interesting reading."

"What is this?"

"All the deals. You know the second course got sold to a consortium? They're the ones that are building the low-rise. No one wants to fucking play golf here except the homies. You know, the people who own the homes. No green fees, no events. It's a par sixty-three for chrissake. The land is worth more with people in boxes than balls in holes."

"What about with bones scattered all over it?"

"*Much* less," said Givens, raising his glass as if to give a toast. "Much less."

The following morning, the field team was back out in the stalks, sweeping. They were on rotating eight-hour shifts. Willan had signed off on it without hesitation. It took the rest of that day, and most of the next, to complete the sweep. By the end of the weekend, they had collected nine more bone fragments, bringing the total to twelve.

There had not been a word about or from Melvin Renald. Macdonald had come up empty. There were no surveillance cameras keeping track of what was happening in the northern parts of the swampy field, where Sergeant Costamides had last seen Renald; for all intents and purposes, he'd vanished without a trace. His wife, Janet, was apoplectic. She was already accusing someone of "dusting" her husband.

"How much do *you* know about the guy?" Hazel asked Ray Greene near the end of her Sunday shift. "He's your boy now."

"I've known him exactly as long as you have. Solid guy, typical stats, a sonofabitch, hard, one-quarter stupid. Effective. There are lots of people in policing like Melvin Renald. Go from one shop to another and never for the same reason. Some people are just restless."

"Meanwhile, he vanishes while on duty and a couple of hours later someone juliennes the Fremonts. To show that they're serious?"

"How sure are you that the voice on Renald's radio wasn't his?"

"A hundred per cent."

Ray Greene tapped the end of his pen against his blotter. The way you do when you're coming to a decision: fast. "Well, we've got more trouble coming than one of our own vanishing in a field: the minister of public safety is coming to see Chip Willan first thing tomorrow morning."

Hazel knit her face into a sneer. "Why?"

"I understand it might have something to do with the Fremonts."

"Ha!" she said. "Please tell me Chip Willan is a suspect."

"I don't think the Mounties get called in to investigate small-town murders."

"Are you telling me we're off the case?"

"I don't know yet."

Monday morning, Ray Greene delivered the news that the minister of public safety was putting the RCMP on the Fremont case. "It's not my decision!" he called over the heckling. News had already gone out, and off-duty personnel filled the pen. He thought he noticed a union rep or two as well. "When the minister of public safety comes to town, he gets what he wants." His eyes shuttled back and forth between Hazel Micallef – steaming mad – and all the bodies in the pen. "Now everyone get back to work."

He crooked his finger at Hazel and she followed him into his makeshift office. "We're to hand over copies of our files for both the dead children and for the Fremont murder."

"They're taking over *both* cases? I thought they were interested in the Fremonts."

"Apparently they're also interested in the poor orphans."

"And Renald?" She was boiling over quickly.

"They're leaving us with our own investigation."

"This is bullshit. Cockeyed . . . fucking bullshit. How are we supposed to hunt for the people who have taken Renald if the rest of the case is off limits to us?"

"You'll find a way. Isn't that how you like to work? I just want to be sure that you understand though – you can't set foot down there."

"Whose grip are your balls in?" He bored a hole through her with his eyes. "I understand."

"Does *I understand* mean *I won't?*"

"It means I won't. I won't go near it."

"I don't like it either," he said, relaxing some. "The union is muttering about it, too. They're saying this affects the whole membership and makes them look weak."

"If anything, it makes the minister look like he's covering something up."

"The reputation of the force is reflected in how the community sees its individual members. I'm just telling you how they see it."

"Willan must be relieved, at least. No more overtime. I guess I'll go back to my desk," she said, "to work a case or something." *Like hell*, she thought, getting into her cruiser.

The Dublin Home for Boys had been built on the corner of a plot of land that belonged to the home but was rent-farmed. From a cursory online search, Hazel learned that it had opened in 1911 and functioned as a home for neglected and abandoned boys until the mid-1960s, when it was closed. It had rarely been used since that time, although when Hazel was in her twenties it was sometimes the site of a bingo fundraiser for one of the charities in nearby Dublin, or the county rented it out for small concerts or cultural festivals. She also vaguely remembered a corn maze in that field – how old had she been then?

She'd been in the building only once in recent times, and that was for a local meeting convened in the 1980s to discuss county highway improvements – ironic (she thought now) given what was passing for improvement these days. The conversation – in when was it, 1988? – had been about how to accommodate increased traffic in the region in a way that would most benefit the businesses along such an artery. It was about local economic health, not consolidation, not cost-cutting, not bang for buck. It was about people and livelihoods. Quality of life.

They'd finally shuttered the building in 1993.

She drove her own car there and pulled off the overgrown driveway into a scatter of apple trees that hid the vehicle from the roads. The cold, stone building still dominated its square of earth like an abandoned castle. Behind it was the grey-green muck of the field and the tall, woodslat fence that kept the mess out of view for those who lived along its perimeter. The fencing behind the houses on the 17th Sideroad came only partway toward Concession Road 7 – "Augusta Avenue" – as there were no houses or tenants yet beyond the finished bungalows. The finished ten holes were in the southeastern part of the development, and she could barely see the course from where she stood.

Most of these provincial institutions – including old age homes and sanitariums – had been self-sufficient in some way. There would have been a vegetable garden here, and the apple trees had once been a small orchard, judging from the way the surviving trees were spaced.

There was no graveyard on this side of the home, and there was nothing she could see beyond it but the development's soggy fields. The home had fallen into total disrepair after fourteen years. All of the windows were boarded up, but many of the boards, over time, had come loose or fallen off. It gave the house an aura of silent chaos. The lights along the driveway and above the door had been smashed a long time ago, and none of the glass remained on the ground. She imagined a whole generation of teenagers on banana bikes testing their arms with stones until there was nothing left to bust.

A piece of plywood sealed the entryway. Warped and cracked with years of weathering, it was still tight. It wouldn't budge. She went around to the west side of the building, where she was still concealed from view, and looked for another way in. There were no ground-level windows and no doors, but around the back she encountered evidence of the home's mechanical functions: pipes poked out of the mortar in a couple of places and two steel ducts beside a chute of some kind angled down from the wall. Below the chute, a yellow patch of poisoned vegetation.

With much caution, ensuring she was not visible, even distantly, Hazel went over to take a closer look. She bent down and peered up into the chute. It was caked in black soot and smelled of decades of smoke and ash. She swept her hand around in the yellow bramble, but found nothing.

Beside the chute, a small wooden door had been nailed shut, but she was able to work a corner open and then tear the whole door off. She snapped on her penlight and stepped into the dark, musty space beyond. She passed the thin penlight beam around the room and discovered an all-purpose workshop, with a large metal box against one wall that vented to the chute she'd seen. The incinerator. Its mouth was too high up to look into, and anyway, she wasn't so sure she wanted to see what was inside it on her own.

The rest of the space was clogged with machines draped in cobwebs, and huge dustballs had gathered at the base of the few bolted to the floor: a drill press, a table saw, and a lathe. These had been stripped for parts over the years. She noted some folded tarps in a corner, and a few cans of old paint with rusted lids. There was nothing else of interest in the room. The door in the far wall was locked by a bolt, which Hazel wiggled open with a bit of effort. The door gave onto a set of tilted wooden steps that led up to the main floor.

The foyer behind the boarded front door was cavernous and intimidating. She recalled an assembly room at the rear of the building, over the workshop in fact, and started there. Wooden bleachers lined both sides of the room, but the middle was empty. The rotted stage curtain was drawn back. Her footsteps echoed crisply against the hard surface of the walls. She took the steps up to the stage carefully and stood looking out at the abandoned auditorium, imagining faces in the gloom. The faces of unwanted children at the mercy of whatever system had landed them here. Was this a place of celebration or of worship, or was it disquiet that ruled here? Or fear?

The rest of the ground level was given over to classrooms behind imposing wooden doors. They were all empty, their furniture long ago redistributed to other schools.

Chalkboards busy with pale grey lines looked blankly out over empty rooms. Layers of ground-in chalk from the hundreds of classes taught here made a diary of sorts, its pages all jumbled. In Room 103, she made out the words *to eat soap*, and in 107, down the opposite hallway, a rolling chalkboard crawled with numbers and symbols. The classrooms were drab, washed-out, as if they were old pictures that had been left in the sun. The only other rooms on this floor were the registrar's office, the dining room, and the kitchen.

The second floor was dormitories and bathrooms. Here, she pictured the throng of small bodies rushing to and fro. Voices. She imagined the dorm rooms, with their white, iron bedframes arranged higgledy-piggledy everywhere, cold from the air coming through the windows. Standing at one of them, she looked out over the fields where her colleagues had swept for bone. Why no windows in the sides of the building? Maybe it had been a cost issue. It would have been hard to heat a stone monstrosity such as this; windows would have let out much of the warmth generated.

Alan had remembered his dormitory at Fort Leonard as cold. That was all he talked about when he described what it had been like. The cold. The cold floors, the cold beds, the cold toilet seats. The cold food. She'd never been to the place where Alan spent the first ten years of his life, but she couldn't imagine it being much different than this one. This was how her little brother had lived. Crowded in with others, forced to line up to eat, to pee, to enter class. She wondered if they'd ever been let out into the fields to play.

Her brother had come into her life like a firecracker thrown through her window. He arrived when he was ten and she was twelve, and he had stayed in their home to the age of twenty. By then he was too much to handle. Drinking, petty theft, getting into fights and accidents. He confided to her later on that he'd suffered from crushing depression for as long as he could remember. She knew this about him, although he'd not spoken of it until they were both adults. She remembered how his face would change colour when a dark mood took over. It would purple, was how she saw it in her mind's eye. Like a bruise.

Dead twenty-three years. Made it to thirty-nine. He'd surprised people by making it to thirty. Standing in this empty dorm room at Dublin Home, she felt the shadow of her brother's despair laid out before her.

Outside, the air smelled clean again. Hazel leaned over, her palms braced against her thighs, and breathed in and out, slowly. After a minute she'd collected herself, and she lifted her head. Across the road, the fields went on north, with little stands of trees where stone had been deposited when the woods were first cleared. Here and there, among the scarlet and orange, a flare of pure yellow, the yellow of a lemon tart, caught her eye – maple leaves, all bursting bright at the same time. They gilded the distance, too. Patches of gold pasted to a blue sky.

So how would you get rid of a lot of bone? Flesh is nothing, it boils away in fire and sometimes leaves nothing but a slick. The bone burns too, but some of it always remains. There was bone at Hiroshima. An incinerator wouldn't do the job.

And how many bodies? Had all the unburned chunks been strewn in the fields?

She turned on her heel. Say this was the epicentre. If half as much bone lay in the nearest fields, that would be, conservatively – what? – a total of twenty fragments? Possibly upward of a dozen young men and boys, none of whom had ever been reported missing, whose bodies had been carefully disposed of under the eye of someone with total freedom of movement. A headmaster? A cook or janitor? The groundskeeper?

She'd hoped a small, hidden patch of headstones would offer her another interpretation. But she walked the periphery of the small plot, and there was nothing.

The ash would have been easy to get rid of. It would have been incorporated into the soil wherever it landed or was dumped. A dozen rainstorms and it was gone. There would have been meal once the bone fragments were sifted away, probably a lot of it. It's good mixed into garden soil.

The apple tree beside her car twisted down and in on itself, and the last of its fruit clung to the orange-leaved branches. The apples were diseased. She picked one and inspected it. Black impressions pocked its wrinkled skin — a *canker*, the farmers called it. It meant cancer. The apple felt hollow in her hand. She dropped it onto the ground where it cracked into halves.

When she looked up, she saw flashing lights streaming toward her. They came from the south and the east, along the old 17th Sideroad and Concession Road 7. They were white cars with a slash of multicoloured ribbon across their doors and a big coat of arms. The Royal Canadian Mounted Police.

] 11 [

Monday, October 22, late afternoon

The autopsy report on the Fremonts arrived at the end of the day. COURTESY, the RCMP envelope was stamped. The photographs were appalling.

Since they had the murder weapon – it remained firmly lodged in Sandra Fremont's skull – the report merely made official what they already knew: Oscar Fremont had suffered a fatal loss of blood as a result of being stabbed multiple times in the face and throat. Sandra Fremont died from a single knife wound to the head. She'd already been stabbed when she struck the desk, and the killer used extra force to drive the knife into the floor.

Hazel and Ray were still looking over the report when Melanie Cartwright advised Hazel that DC Torrance had sent a copy of her report from the crime scene. Fraser had written a report of his own on the weekend and submitted it. Neither report made any mention of Wingate. "The forensics and the reports look fine, but there's nothing to build a case out of," Ray said.

"I guess it's their problem now," Hazel said. "What about our further instructions? You know, on the case we're permitted to work?"

"There's nothing," he mumbled.

"What?"

"More cryptic gibberish. *Pronounce his name. End his line.* Came in an hour ago."

"*Pronounce his name.*"

"*End his line.*"

"Show me."

He spun his screen around toward her and she read the six words written in full caps. "What do you make of it?" Hazel asked.

"Someone thinks we're going to jump when they tell us to."

"We're not? Oh, right. Depends what direction they want us to jump in."

He looked right at her, and his expression clouded. "I swear to god, as soon as Willan unties my hands —"

She just laughed. "Good thing no one's given you a real clue yet. Then what would you do?" She didn't give him a chance to reply. The bad taste in her mouth was beginning to sour her stomach, too.

She returned to her glass-windowed office and accidentally glowered at Cartwright, who held her palms up in
questioning supplication. Hazel waved her off. Clearly,
word of her trespass hadn't arrived yet. None of the Queen's
representatives were in the lobby brandishing their gleaming crops. Let them come on their ceremonial black horses
and try to cover up one of *her* investigations. She stabbed a
key on her keyboard and her computer sputtered to life,
issuing clicky creaks from deep within its plastic shell. She
wasn't going to break her word to Ray again unless she
really, really had to. But he'd said nothing about continuing her research, so she logged on and went to the BMD
archive at gov.on.ca and looked under DEATHS. You could
search by year and sub-search by county. She typed in
1951 and *Westmuir*.

There had been eighty-six deaths in Westmuir County
in 1951. The website let you refine your search by date
of birth, sex, marital status, or date of death. If you
found something you liked, you could click through to
the detailed listing. And then, for fifteen bucks, they'd
send you an official copy of the certificate. Compared to
the olden days, when information was stored in drawers
and files and stacks, it was a snap. But it was insubstan-
tial whereas index cards were real. You could trust an
index card.

She scanned the 1951 death records, looking for males
with birthdates between 1942 and 1947. There were none.

In 1952, there were one hundred and eight deaths, none of them in her subset. One boy, born 1944, died in 1953 by lightning strike. That would be easy enough to cross-reference with medical records or obits. She felt queasy as soon as she realized she was pleased she'd found at least one record of a dead child. Kids fell afoul of gravity or speed all the time, but even in the 1950s they'd mostly survived their brushes with mortality. It struck her how unusual it was that just the bones they had already *found* had increased the yearly total of that demographic by something like seven hundred per cent.

Her math almost held. For the years 1951 to 1955 she found only two deaths in her category: the lightning strike and a drowning. There was one more in the other half of the decade: a boy had slipped off a stone roof near Mayfair and broken his neck. No doubt these tragic stories would be told in the newspaper archives. She could buy proof of their deaths for $15 apiece.

Three lives cut short by sad, tragic accidents. Boys properly buried, remembered, and grieved. Many of the people who had wept were now dead, and many who witnessed their suffering were also dead. Their dates, all of them, entered dutifully into the public record.

The bones from the fields belonged to boys whose deaths had not been officially recorded. The boys they were looking for had even lost their names. She clicked out of the database and leaned back in her chair. Melanie looked through the glass, as if willing Hazel to give her something to do, but Hazel shook her head and looked away. Then she looked back up. Melanie's attention was elsewhere, so Hazel threw a tennis ball at the window. It went *whonk*.

"Oh my god!" Cartwright shrieked. She jumped up and sped around to Hazel's door. "Please don't do that."

"How else am I going to get your attention? Did you bring something to take notes on?"

"No."

"Go get your pen, Cartwright."

Melanie took a pen and some paper off Hazel's desk. "In my heart, you'll always be the skip, but Commander Greene is getting along with no one on his front desk – he's taking his own calls – and half the time you're not even h –"

"Look up the number of the Westmuir County Archives. Tell them we would like to see the records of both the Dublin Home for –"

"Slow down."

"Boys. I want the years 1951 to 1960."

"It's almost five p.m."

"Call them first thing in the morning, tell them I'll be there at nine a.m., and just give my name as Hazel. Don't tell them why I'm interested."

"Keep it on the down low?"

"If you must keep it anywhere. You can go. And thanks. Oh!" Cartwright stopped in the doorway. "Don't tell Ray."

"Honestly, Skip?"

"Technicalities."

Hazel packed up for the night and saw that Wingate was still at his desk. He was in civvies. "What are you still doing here?"

"Cleaning up my desk. You going home?"

She looked around to check if they were alone and then pulled up a chair. "I was just looking through official records to get an idea of how common the deaths of adolescents were in the fifties. Not very. And nothing connects to Dublin Home. We need to find out where the boys went when they left there. Check them all off. When families took them. When they were transferred to another institution. When they reached majority and entered the workforce. There should be further documentation on every boy who left Dublin Home. If there isn't, maybe we have a missing boy. That would be huge."

"How're you going to do that?"

"County archives in Mayfair."

"Wish I was on."

"I'll pick you up at eight. Dress in your own clothes for god's sake. We're going in as regular citizens."

Hazel drove an ever more battered, sagging Victoria – the same cruiser she'd driven since she was named interim CO back in 1995. James Wingate sat in the passenger seat, where the upholstery was much less worn, and dozed. She was driving this shitbox American boat, but Ray Greene was driving a 2007 Toyota. It was part of the deal when Willan hired him as skip. Was that his way of ensuring Ray's support? Port Dundas needed a local cheerleader for amalgamation, and who better to lead than the chief of police? Ray couldn't be bought, she knew that. But he was a lot more co-operative with Willan than she had been, and she couldn't help but wonder if Ray had been offered incentives.

Or maybe Willan hired Ray to push me over the edge, give me a reason to really overstep. Then — bam! — I'm fired.

Wingate wasn't much for conversation at half past eight, and she was dwelling on past ills. After Ray quit under her, it took her a long time to forgive him because they had been friends. It was strained even after they patched things up, and sometimes it was still strained. She had a habit of letting people break her trust only once.

Just the same, Ray's return to the fold was clearly going as smoothly as everyone had hoped. She was already over the feelings of worry and then jealousy that had accompanied his reappearance at the station house. She wasn't made for being in charge anyway, and Ray was. Ray commanded respect without asking for it, because he was Ray Greene. But respect was overrated. The main task was to bring people over to your side. Or not. Defining positions. It did you well in your work to have a suspicious mind, and

Hazel needed to know where people stood. It didn't matter if they respected her or not.

A sign went by that said *Mayfair 33 km*.

Of course, you had to be right in the end, but that's supposed to be the talent: reading people. The habits of mind that you harnessed to detective work also led to seeing connections everywhere, including where there might be none at all. But why wasn't Ray angry? The case was being taken away from him too.

"You know, I can't stop seeing them," Wingate said. His voice jarred her back to herself.

"I'm sorry, James. Who?"

"The Fremonts. I see her . . . feet, and the handle of the knife –"

"You shouldn't have gone down there. Really. Look at you. Do you look like this every morning?"

"Michael gives me something to sleep."

"Like what?"

"Something that keeps me from thinking about girls buried alive or the blood all over the Fremonts' hall rug."

She shook her head as if to shake the images out. "I have to wonder, James . . ."

"What."

"If you're taking care of yourself."

"Michael thinks I'm ready to come back. He says I've made a lot of progress and I have to get all this energy varnished. *Harnessed*."

"Energy? You never used to talk like this."

"I know all about energy now, Skip. It's real."

"I know it's real," she said, beginning to feel irritated with him. "But vague words like *energy* make me worry you're unravelling. What detective even has the word *energy* in his vocabulary?" He shifted in his seat and she looked over at him. "I need to trust you, James. I'm vouching for you. Tell me the truth: do *you* think you're ready to come back?"

For a moment, his posture reminded her of a scolded boy. He pressed his lips together hard as if he were trying to keep from blurting the truth. Finally, he said, "No."

The Ontario Ministry of Children and Youth Services had only been established in 2003, and the scattered local and regional records pertaining to orphanages and children's aid societies in the province were still being collected from all over so they could be centralized at the ministry's head office in Toronto. Some offices and organizations had already digitized their own records; others had sent originals or copies to Toronto. Earlier, microfilmed records had all but disintegrated, and Hazel worried that the years they were looking for might no longer exist. The age of the victims tied them to the home, as no boys over the age of majority would have lived there.

"I might have been just a little girl when these boys died. Who could have imagined that such a thing could be going on in the countryside in the fifties?"

They walked down Grand Street in Mayfair. Wingate was still logy from the earliness of the hour. "Why would anything surprise you anymore?"

"Keep up," she said.

Grand had been Mayfair's main thoroughfare for almost two hundred years. Buildings of yellow brick fired in local kilns gave a wealthy look to the street, the two sides of which faced off in sometimes identical facades. The Westmuir County Archives and Licensing Centre occupied one half of an old brick warehouse back from the main road. The other half of the building was the Legion.

They were not in their uniforms, so they were asked to wait in the completely empty foyer of the records office. The features of the foyer were a row of chairs, a door, and a window with a woman behind it, tightly wound in a wool shawl, who with an air of anxiety had told them it *might* be some time before anyone *could* help them. Just as they settled in for the wait, a man came out of the door and offered his hand. "How can I help you?" he asked.

"My assistant called about county death records. Between 1951 and 1960."

"Oh, that was you."

"Were you expecting someone different?"

"No, I just didn't realize you were two people."

"Do you get many people here, Mr. – ?"

"Putchkey."

"Putchkey. Do you get many members of the public coming around to look at these records?"

"No," Putchkey said in a tight voice. He was a thin, nervous man of about sixty, with a flipper for a left arm. It had the words *Seize The Day* tattooed on it. "This is the first time in seven years anyone's asked to see children's records from Dublin Home. We were just talking about it, me and Cutter and Mrs. Hanteleh."

Wingate, seeing Hazel's lips flatten, took over. "I'm James Wingate. This is my colleague, Hazel Micallef."

"Gale Putchkey."

Hazel saw the top of the receptionist's head behind the window, bobbing in and out of the frame as if she were pecking at something. "Is everything OK here today? What's she doing?"

"The records have been set aside," Putchkey said, letting them pass through the door.

When they went behind, Hazel saw the shawled receptionist was hunched over her desk, her eye practically against a crossword book, a pen glued to her cheek. "Mrs. Hanteleh?" Putchkey said to her, and her head thrust up.

"Ha?"

"These people are here to see some records."

"Are they going in?"

"Please."

Hanteleh reached under her desk and pressed a buzzer. Putchkey opened another door onto stairs leading down. "A Hebrew pigeon," Hanteleh said. "Seven letters."

Downstairs they came to a wooden desk by another door. The person behind it, an older man in overalls, rose and offered his hand to Hazel. "Nice to meet you," he said. His grip was stronger than he looked. "Leon Cutter."

The Putchkey fellow was hovering behind them. This was a government office, but people were acting loopy. Either they were all on drugs or they were gripped by fascination. "When was the last time anyone came to this office?" Hazel asked.

Putchkey tented his fingers against his sternum. "*My* office? Mrs. Hanteleh brought me a Danish just three hours —"

"I mean to see some records."

"Last month," said Cutter. "Gale, I've got this."

Putchkey deflated. "I wanted to see this stuff."

"You can see it any time. These two, they came looking for it."

He let them into the archives.

A room was ready for them. Metal cabinets lined one wall. The contents of the drawers, to judge by the tags affixed to them, held the records of humans and services in a variety of provincial institutions, including the mental asylums, the nursing homes, the children's homes, and the TB hospitals. She opened one of the drawers. A small wooden box at the front contained index cards meticulously summarizing the files in the drawer. Perhaps it was not so different from the online records database after all. Each card had been typed, its embossed letters mainly in black but sometimes in red. The various methods of erasure practised through the decades were present, including single strips of paper glued over errors.

The hand truck used to haul these cabinets out of their dark storage was still inside the room, and the person who had done the lugging now showed them to a wooden table with a solid pine top and three chairs. The table was bowed from years of being burdened with paper.

Cutter had a strongman's body, although he wasn't thick in the limbs or the chest. He'd evidently been a wiry mongoose-type once, but the cables of muscle in his neck and arms had gone slack. "If I can be of any use," he said, "you know where to find me. The Wi-Fi code is *Beethoven*. Does everybody know how to spell —"

"How well do you know your way around these records?" Hazel asked.

"I more or less know them inside out."

"And how good a job did they do with the filing back in the fifties?"

"Painstaking. I'm sure there was some sloppiness, but the people who organized this information cared about it.

You can tell. The Internet is a dumping site. You can't really find anything. Only what wants to be found."

"Stirring words," Hazel said. "We're looking for dead ends. Individuals whose births are on record, and who are documented somewhere in these boxes as wards of the province. When they were no longer wards, they should have entered other records. Tax rolls, marriage licences, death certificates. But we want to find boys between the ages of ten and seventeen who disappeared from these institutional records and whose names never appeared again."

"May I ask why you are interested?"

She looked over at Wingate, whose face was a blank. "We're working on a book."

"About?"

"The history of children's homes in Canada."

Cutter blinked at her a couple of times. "I was hoping you were police."

"We're writing a book," Wingate said.

"My mistake."

He left them to it, and Hazel and Wingate began to cull. She went on to the Ontario archives website again, and he began calling out names and birthdates. Dublin Home had been a train station for boys coming and going. For 1952, Wingate read out the names and birthdates of all the boys who left there and whose files contained a final entry. These final entries directed the reader to another branch of government if he or she wanted to read on, and they would be stamped FILE CLOSED on that last page. Adopted: see records at the Government of Ontario site. FILE CLOSED. Turned eighteen and left Charterhouse: check marriage and death certificates. FILE CLOSED. Died of scarlet fever at Charterhouse: see death records. FILE CLOSED. One after another, she could follow them. They bobbed up out of the chaos here and there, but they checked out. Boy leaves Dublin Home, boy eventually registers for Ontario Medical Services Insurance Plan, boy marries girl, boy's name appears on registration of live birth, and so on till death, should death already have come for him.

But the murdered boys, whoever they were, weren't going to have closed files. There would be no final entries for them. Hazel wondered if their files had been destroyed. "We need to find an admissions ledger of some kind," she said. "These personal files were kept individually, but there has to be something that was more basic. If our murderer was on the ball, he or she would probably have culled his victims' files."

"So you're thinking we need names that never made it through the records?"

"Something that is evidence they were taken in, but perhaps nothing else. Hints and shadows."

"What about medical records? Pharmacy records?"

"We have to find their names first, confirm they were actually at Dublin. Then maybe we can find them elsewhere while they're still alive."

Wingate leaned forward and cleared some folders from in front of him, and looked out into the middle distance. "What about a false paper trail?"

"It would have been hard to forge the right papers."

"Let's look for your ledger."

They called Cutter back in. "What about each institution's records, like admission books, ledgers, class lists? Is that stuff kept here?"

"Can you tell me what, specifically, you're trying to find?"

"Anything someone intent on erasing a person's records might have missed."

"Administrative records," Cutter said. "Something like that?"

"A loose end," Hazel said. "When could you have something for us?"

"Tomorrow," Cutter said. "I can call the number you left?"

"Don't," she replied. "One of us will come back in the morning."

That worked for him, and he led them back out to the foyer and exchanged handshakes. Hazel held the man's hand a moment too long. "If we were police," she asked him, "would you have shown us anything else?"

"No," Cutter said. "Down here, everything is a cold case. I figure who else would be interested?"

She was getting a tingle. "Where are you from, Mr. Cutter?" she asked.

"From? I've lived here my whole life."

"In the archives?" Wingate asked, and then laughed. Cutter laughed. Hazel didn't.

"We'll see you tomorrow, then."

Cutter held the door to the stairs open for them and they went through. "Listen," he called after them. "I sure didn't mean to question your credentials or anything. Whatever you're here for, you're members of the public and I'm here to make sure you get what you need."

Hazel led the way up the stairs, and they left the building without another word.

] 12 [

Wednesday, October 24, morning

Brendan Givens had failed to find satisfaction in his life. A career that paid decently (he didn't care to be rich, just comfortable) and allowed him to spend time with some nice people and also offered him the opportunity to get laid once in a while had been his sole ambition. But the modesty of his goals had not brought them within his reach. He hated the people he worked with, and not just the people who were on the corporate side at the Ascot Group, but also the upper management and employees of Tournament Acres itself, a wholly owned subsidiary. And also the residents of Tournament Acres, who were cheap, classless crybabies, with not a woman among them worth tapping. Except for Mrs. Freemey, but there was a police car in front of her house three times a week. So many single women – divorcees with settlements misled into buying "country homes" – but he'd not landed one of them. He'd not touched a woman in over fifteen years. It was over between him and women.

He sipped his whole-fat, extra-foam mocha in the window of a downtown café. He'd been in Toronto for more than twenty-four hours now, and he still had no idea what to do with himself. The bars opened at eleven and he'd walked from his dive hotel to a dive bar and devoted what remained of the morning to drinking. Now he was in a place called He Brews (*Where coffee and klezmer come together!*) applying caffeine to the problem and trying to come up with a plan.

Going back to Tournament Acres was out of the question. When fricasseed bodies start to turn up on a property you're managing, that's when your contract is over. No favours asked or owed.

And there'd been that text.

He shuddered and took his drink outside to the street. This was the rainbow part of town. Every city had one. All power to them, they never hurt anybody. He smiled at a couple of women coming toward him. When the sidewalk traffic thinned, he dosed his coffee from a flask. The cup, which had been about half-full for some time now, had changed from coffee with brandy to brandy with coffee.

He'd calmed down since booting it south on the 400 yesterday morning – in the Fremonts' car. It had been nothing to go into the house and find the keys to their Infiniti. If the person who had sent him the text was already on top of him, maybe he'd be watching for the wrong car. *That's good thinking, B.* He'd arrived in the city close to eight. He'd taken nothing with him but the cash in the safe, which amounted to eighty-five hundred or so. Beside one of the water traps, he'd burned all his IDs except his passport and driver's licence and then kicked the ashes in.

It was ten months since he'd last been in Toronto, but it felt like a safe haven now, a place to blend in. He'd left the Fremonts' car deep in the long-term parking at Pearson Airport and he was getting around in taxis. He'd get the car in a few days maybe, then go over the border in Quebec. He'd tell the customs guy he was going down to play poker in Connecticut. He'd leave the Infiniti on a side street in Chateaugay or Rouses Point. Then it occurred to him that there could be a problem if he went over the border in the Fremonts' car. Maybe it would be best to park it on the Canadian side and go over on foot.

He went back into the coffee house. It was starting to get busy. He didn't want to be around people now.

In his forty-nine years, he'd caught two people surreptitiously drawing him in one of those little pocket notebooks. In both sketches, his bulbous nose had looked even larger than it did in the mirror. God had given him this nose, and when he was younger his mother enthused to him that a big nose was character, a big nose attracted smart women. But a big nose had just made him look like a shorebird with good hair. Many times he'd considered a nose job, but he couldn't have done it while his mother was still alive, and now that she was dead, he still heard her saying, "God gave you that nose!" And there was also the problem with the surgery: the thought of being cut up terrified him. They would have to *cut his face.*

No one inside He Brews was drawing him, but the place was lousy with people typing on laptops. What if any of the people in this place were working for Ascot? Half of them had to be failed novelists, but who were the other half?

He looked over the shoulder of one of the typers as he drank some water. Gotta keep hydrated. She was an older woman wearing a couple of gaudy rings, her hands passing back and forth over the keys. She typed with only her two middle fingers and used her right index finger for the space bar.

Maybe everybody watches everybody else. *I watch people,* he thought. *I watch everything. That's how I knew when to blow town. I have a sense about things.*

Not all things. He was drunk and he could be honest with himself. After a certain amount of brandy, he knew the truth, but later he could never remember it.

The lady with the rings was typing line after line as if someone were dictating to her. He looked over her shoulder and read the line *The dead wear expressions of drunken stupor.* He shuddered again. She sensed him and turned around.

She had short hair with one thick streak of grey in it. "Can I help you?" she asked.

"How can you write something like that? Is that a diary?"

"Mister, do I know you?"

"I hope not," he said.

First thing Wednesday morning, James Wingate was back at the front door of the Westmuir County Archives and Licensing Centre. Cutter gave him a funny look as he unlocked the office. Then he took Wingate down and showed him the inventory of admin material from Dublin Home, some of it in steel boxes and dating back to the turn of the last century. Wingate dug through for the relevant years and pulled the logbooks from the home's registrar, as well as vaccination records. The vax records themselves were snapshots of boys passing through. They'd taken no chances: new boys got all new shots.

He kept notes on his laptop, although he would have preferred to put everything in pen in his notebook. He took down the names that they hadn't encountered in the personal files they'd pored through the day before. He used the summary cards from the wooden boxes in the cabinet drawers to look up names. If a name in the home's own vax records didn't appear among the individual records, then he looked for it in the name changes database. If it wasn't there, he checked the BDM. A kid who'd been vaccinated in 1955 – the form telling him so was signed in ink and stamped with a red sigil – who thereafter never once appeared in the public record, was an excellent candidate for murder, he thought.

Across platforms, the recordkeeping in various provincial offices and institutions was spotty, but it was possible to fill in the blanks. The spectres of dead boys began to fill the negative space between records, their names leaping out, singular in the welter of repetitions. He found a dozen names in the span of four years that fit his criteria. The period covered late 1955 to 1959. A big enough sample. It was a strange exercise to look for victims when he was usually tasked with finding perpetrators. From the dozen, he selected the six he liked most for further investigation.

Charles Shearing. Born June 9, 1945. Bounced around, ended up at Dublin Home in 1955, according to both the registrar log and vax records. Wingate logged into the archives' Wi-Fi and checked the federal databases: no passport, no SIN, never named in a criminal or civil suit. April 14, 1955, he arrived at Dublin Home and then vanished off the public record.

Valentijn Deasún. DOB November 30, 1944. Mother died at birth, no father. St. Patrick Home, 1944 to 1947. Transferred July 18, 1947, at the age of two-and-a-half to the Dublin Home for Boys. Fostered out to a family in Brigham; back in the system at Charterhouse in Renfrew County on January 15, 1958; transferred to Dublin Home for a second time later that same month. Record ends. No such name in the passport records, no social insurance number, no marriage certificate, no death certificate, no burial place on either Interment.net *or* the online Ontario Cemetery Finding Aid.

"The next two were at the Charterhouse orphanage in Renfrew County, though," said Wingate. "Both Charterhouse and Dublin Home were in the same catchment and there's a lot of back and forth between the homes." He turned two sheets of paper to face Hazel. She was sitting across from him in Uncle Pepper's, the burger joint on the highway between Mayfair and Port Dundas. The owners had converted a bunch of old train cars into dining rooms. "Brothers," said Wingate. "Claude and Eloy Miracle."

"Miracle?"

"That's what it says. Kahnawake Mohawks. DOBs unknown, but they had Indian Status cards when they arrived at Charterhouse in 1956. They put Claude as twelve and Eloy as nine. Then they were both transferred to Dublin Home. Claude was fostered out in 1960, but there's not another mention of Eloy in the provincial or federal records."

The fifth and six boys had come to Charterhouse without last names. In such cases, these children of nobody were given a local name or even took the name of the home. There had been quite a few St. Pierres in the records, after the name of a home in the town of Renfrew.

They asked for the check and split it. "We only need a single drop of blood to link one of these names to one of those bones," Hazel said.

"It's going to be hard to find the blood relations of dead orphans."

"That's why we should start with the brothers. The Miracles."

They arrived at the station house right at shift change. Wingate went quietly to his desk. By the time the afternoon staff came in, Hazel had found the couple that had adopted Claude Miracle in the records of the town of Gannon Lake: Thom and Georgia Wetherling. But she could find no record of Claude Wetherling himself. Nor of Claude Miracle. A name like *Miracle* would be hard to hide. Maybe he changed it, became someone new? There should have been a record of that.

There were plenty of Wetherlings. More than fifty, as it turned out, and by lunchtime, she'd spoken with fifteen of them — some kin and some not — trying to stay on an east–west tack from Renfrew County all the way to the Manitoba border. There had been a concentration of them around Dundas, Ontario. Cattlemen and sheepherders and corn farmers up behind the town and on both sides. There, the name went back to the early 1900s. She found a Wetherling outside of Dundas, in a gesture of a place called Copetown.

This Wetherling was named Hadley — she was her daughter Martha's age. She told Hazel that from the 1930s until the mid-1960s, orphan kids who'd come of age sometimes ended up working the fields near there and around Hamilton. Sometimes they'd ended up joining a family. Hadley Wetherling was the local family historian and she'd kept everything she'd found in relation to the family name, at least in Southwestern Ontario. Hazel highlighted the lady's number in her notebook and next to it wrote: *Has papers.*

She chased Wetherlings all the way to Fort Leonard, looking for relatives of the adoptive parents. Many of these Wetherlings thought they'd heard one thing or another about Claude Miracle/Wetherling, but none of the information she got connected together. Supposedly he had moved to Quebec, back to his band (the Mrs. Wetherling with this information did not know what the band name was); he may have, alternatively, died piloting a Cessna or a Twin Otter, although the date given for this Miracle's death was in the 1930s.

"Sir," she asked an elderly Wetherling, "have you personally ever adopted a boy?"

"No, sir, I don't believe as I have, though I don't have all my docaments nearby."

"My name is Hazel Micallef, Mr. Wetherling. I'm a woman."

"All right then."

"Can I ask you your date of birth?"

"You can. We were born Jan'ry ninth, ought nine."

"We?"

"Myself and Ewan. He's been dead these fifty-one years now."

"I'm sorry to hear that. May I ask you: have you ever heard of a person called Claude Wetherling, or Claude Miracle? Mohawk Indian; he was adopted."

"Claude. Black boy, right?"

"No. I don't think so. Could he have been Indian?"

"Maybe. I'm not so good with names anymore. Cousin Angie on my mother's side I'll say, could be wrong. Her parents had a boy when she went off to college. Got lonesome and adopted a boy."

"Up in the town of Lake Gannon?"

"Sir, it might have been, but I'm ninety-seven years old and on these blood-thinner pills and r'membrin' medicine, so I can't tell you about that."

"Is Cousin Angie still alive?"

"Oh gosh," he said.

"Could you give me her number if you have it?"

"Oh, she's moved a dozen times or more. Last I knew she was in the city."

"All right, thank you Mr. Wetherling."

"You're welcome, young man," he replied.

She replaced the phone gently. "Jesus," she muttered. She picked it up again and dialled Wingate. "Do I sound like a young man?"

"What?"

"Please tell me you are making the tiniest amount of progress."

"I have staff directories for some of the years at both places. It's pointless, though. People moved around. Half the staff of Dublin Home started there but did a stint at Charterhouse and versa vice. Both places had some lifers, like superintendents. Maybe one of them is alive."

"Don't bother with brass," she said. "See if you can find an administrator, maybe a nurse. Someone who served a while in both homes. I'd like to talk to one of those people." She hung up and looked at the clock: 1:30. She was going to have to eat lunch at her desk.

Brendan Givens left He Brews at 1:30 and started walking up to his hotel at the top of Church Street. Once he was out of Boystown, the neighbourhood turned drab. Construction hoardings advertised the condos that were going to appear in the hole behind them. *Life is easier – and cheaper – in Tournament Acres!* That had been the radio spot. It had sold a lot of bungalows. Here they built cubbyholes high in the air. When this all cleared up, he'd land on his feet with a more reputable company. He'd start again. He'd started again many times.

He strode past the billboard pitching *High-Class Living in the Heart of Downtown*, and he thought of the bottle he'd left behind in the suite. He still had the flask, though, and the flask wasn't empty. He was reaching for it in his hip pocket when he felt the ground jar beneath his feet. Then he was suddenly alert — a car mounted the sidewalk and blew past him a foot away from his body. He pressed himself against the hoardings, trying to catch his breath. "Why don't you learn how to drive?!" he shouted, but the car was long gone.

The hotel was an old apartment building converted to cheap suites, but they'd given it a highfalutin name: *Bristol Manor*. Givens said hello to the man behind the desk, a nice ruddy-faced man with a nametag that identified him as Tic.

He took the elevator to the third floor. In the room, he couldn't get a signal on his shitty Nokia. He went out onto the balcony and held the phone up. No texts. Just the one he'd gotten at 4:00 a.m. the day before. It had been pretty clear:

I know you have the files, Brendan. Why don't you bring them back? No questions asked.

As soon as he stepped back into the room, the phone in the suite rang. His heart was in his mouth, hammering. He felt his rib cage throb like a subwoofer. The phone rang and he stood paralyzed in the doorway. Then it stopped and a light on the handset flickered weakly, yellow and red, and in the sudden silence it felt like something had found him.

He checked the message, holding the phone not quite against his ear. "*Sir, Mr. Givens, the airline representative is here with your missing luggage. I send him up.*" Givens dialled the front desk. It was a woman's voice.

"Hello, Mr. Givens. How may I help you?"

"Uh, did your co-worker send someone up? Can I speak to him?"

"Who?"

"Uh . . . Tic."

"He's off now, Mr. Givens."

"But he just called me."

"He's off now, sir."

"Did you see the person he sent up?"

"Who?"

"The man from the airline!"

"I know no man from the airline."

He hung up and stared at the phone. It rang again, and he picked it up. "Yes?"

"Mr. Givens?" A man's voice now, but it wasn't Tic's. He couldn't place it. "Mr. Givens? Are you there?"

"Yes," he whispered.

"Can you hear me?"

"Yes."

"We have your luggage. Where would you like us to put it?"

"Who is this?"

"I can just leave it on your bed and you can sort it later."

He looked across the room, beyond the tiny, useless kitchen, into the hallway. He hadn't noticed the door to the bedroom was closed. His heart came back up his throat.

"Well, how would you like it?"

"You can leave it on the bed. That's fine."

"All right, then. It's on the bed."

"Thank you."

"You're most welcome, Brendan Givens." The man hung up.

There were no sounds from anywhere in the suite. Givens stood frozen to the spot, gripping the receiver. "Hello?" he called out. He walked as quietly as he could to the bedroom door and put his ear against it. The door handle was cold in his palm, and he held his breath to a count of three and then threw the door open.

There was no one in his room, but his suitcase was on his bed. He'd put it in the closet earlier in the day, but it was on the bed. He stood frozen in the doorway, his jaw set, breathing shallowly through his mouth. The phone rang again. "Oh Jesus . . . Jesus," he muttered. "Just get me out of this." It rang three times and then stopped.

Givens heard footsteps behind him. A man came into the hallway holding the phone receiver in one hand and a knife in the other. "I think it's for you," he said.

Givens leapt into the room and slammed the door shut. There was no lock. He backed up until he felt the mattress against his calves. The door opened.

"How did you find me?"

"Where are the files?"

"They're back in the office. I hid them. To keep 'em safe."

"And then you ran away?"

"I don't take my orders from you!" Givens spat.

"And I don't take mine from you," the man replied. "Do you know who gives me my orders?"

"Look, I don't know anything – *please* –"

"*Please*," said the man. "That's nice. When people scream, it makes it harder." He clasped Givens by the upper arm and pressed the tip of the knife into his ribs. Brendan Givens stood still.

"I'll do anything," he said.

The man clamped his hand over Givens's mouth and leaned against the knife. "The first inch isn't too hard," he said. "The second inch is where the trouble starts."

Givens doubled over, holding the man's wrist with both hands. "Stop . . . stop . . ."

"Stop what?" He leaned down to listen to the answer and the knife-edge turned, eliciting a groan of helpless agony. They both watched the pool of urine spreading out of his pant leg, and the man slid one of his shoes away. He pulled the knife out and Givens sank to the floor.

"No," Givens begged. "Don't." Blood poured out of his shirt.

"Have you protected *your* investment, Brendan?" the man asked, not without tenderness. He shoved the knife in again.

Givens said, "Oh," very quietly. His sinuses cleared and the light started changing. It smelled like coffee. He thought of his mother.

] 13 [

1957

By the end of November, it had already snowed twice. Northern New York State got six feet in one day and people lost track of their cars under it. Port Dundas was farther north than both Toronto and Buffalo, and far enough from the Great Lakes that the town rarely had any accumulation of snow.

Hazel was getting impatient for Christmas. Her father had been playing seasonal records since the first of December, trying to match his sweet tenor to Bing Crosby's. She tried for the second year in a row to explain how Christmas was "coming" to Alan, for whom abstract concepts were difficult. She showed him the calendar on the kitchen wall. "Each row is a week, and one page is a month, and the whole thing — the whole *calendar* — is one year. Got it? Mom can get you one and you can cross off the days as they go by."

"What if you cross off the days that haven't come yet?"

"Then your calendar will be a mess."

He shrank from the word. "A mess?"

"What're you getting upset for?"

"I'm not messy!"

"It's all right, Alan. We were only talking about the days of the week."

Sometimes she'd see her father looking distantly in Alan's direction. He'd be staring over the table, watching Alan eat. Or he'd sit in his club chair, but instead of watching the television, he'd be looking at Alan.

Alan said, "The Philco Miss America Television receiver has wrap-around sound from three speakers." This kind of stuff Alan knew. He had thin seams of genius. He could build a Meccano bull and make its tail move with a crank, and he knew the specifications of almost every television and radio receiver, as well as the makes of cars and the changes that had come in their subsequent generations. "It's better than ours."

"There's nothing wrong with *that* colour television, Alan."

"The Sylvania Andover only has a twenty-inch screen, and the speakers are rotten," he said. His voice had taken on a tinge of insistence or anger. "The Miss America has *three* speakers and pop-up tuning so you can see what channel you're watching from across the room!"

They'd had a scare with Alan a few weeks earlier. He'd claimed to have found a necklace in the backyard with a silver heart-shaped pendant. There was a rabbit engraved into its surface. Hazel listened to her mother and father interrogating him in the kitchen well past both their bedtimes. She crept out of her bedroom to the top of the stairs. She heard her mother's voice.

"This is serious, Alan. Daddy and I are not angry at you."

"For now."

"Evan," her mother said sharply. Then, softer: "Alan – you're not in trouble. But you do have to tell us where you found this pendant."

Their father raised his voice. "We know you're lying. And *you* know you're lying. So let's be done with the charade."

Alan was crying: a reedy, wet sound. "What does that mean?"

"It means it's time to tell the truth!" her father boomed.

"I found it in the backyard! Right by the fence! It was on the ground! It was in the grass! *And it's mine!*"

Hazel heard the crack of her father's hand on Alan's skin. It shocked her. He'd never struck either of them before. Alan sobbed. There were footsteps and voices and then, without warning, her father began to ascend the stairs. He saw her right away and stopped. "Hazel Micallef," he said. "Have you anything to add to this sad chapter in our family life? Seeing as you feel free to eavesdrop?"

"Why did you hit him?"

"Don't question my —"

"He's just a kid! He doesn't understand!"

His face heated up, cheeks mottling red. "Do *you*?"

"Do I what?"

"Do *you* understand why your brother is in possession of a missing girl's pendant?"

That stunned her to silence.

"Carol Lim's necklace. It had a rabbit on it exactly like this. We've shown it to Gord Drury, he showed it to the Lims. So where did Alan get it? How is he mixed up in this?"

"*This*? Is Carol *dead*?"

Her father looked away, chewing on the corner of his mouth. "No one knows where the girl is. But her parents haven't heard from her in more than a month. What would you be thinking?" She didn't have to answer that. "Go back to your bed immediately, Hazel."

Her mother's love for Alan had never and would never falter, but her father was unhappy around him, and Hazel worried he would send Alan away. It roused an instinct in her to protect her adopted brother, even though he was vexing and dirty and seemed always to be stuffing something into his mouth. Her mother had said it was a reaction to being in the boys' home for so much of his life. He'd never had enough to eat. It hurt Hazel like a punch in the stomach to think of him starving, and she couldn't begrudge him his ways. But it was getting to her father.

She closed her bedroom door and stood with her ear against it. Their voices were lower now and muffled. She could hear Alan's footsteps on the stairs and then he went past her bedroom, snuffling. She wanted to talk to him, but she didn't want to get him into any more trouble. His door clicked shut and she heard her parents' voices again, rising up from underneath her floor. "I will leave you to it then," her father said.

"He doesn't understand."

"All the worse then! If he doesn't understand —"

"I'll keep him with me. He can be at the office sometimes."

"Take him to see Gord Drury. Let Gord talk to him."

On the Tuesday night, her father did inventory and her mother stayed late at the town hall. It was Hazel's job, on nights when her parents weren't home, to watch her brother. At almost fifteen, Hazel already knew how to make ten different things, including devilled eggs, fried baloney, and a billot log cake made out of chocolate wafer cookies and whipped cream. To her friends, Hazel referred to Alan as *Spaceboy*, but it was not the truth about how she felt. She was mystified by the instinct that arose in her when he came to her for help or asked her a question that involved revealing some part of the world to him, such as how calendars worked, or how voices came out of the radio.

For dinner, he wanted dippy eggs and toast soldiers. Since she'd come home from school, Alan had already eaten an apple and an orange, two chicken legs, a serving of leftover scalloped potatoes, and there was a table-spoon-shaped divot in the butter. Although he ate con-stantly, Alan had the body of an Olympic wrestler: small and lithe, a tight bundle of energy. Nothing elegant about him.

He sat at the kitchen table fidgeting with his fork. She sat down across from him with her own plate, and silently they began to eat. Alan's focus stayed resolutely on what was on his plate, and he neither spoke nor seemed to hear anything when he was eating. Sometimes she imagined him as a rescued dog: frightened, but hungry for food and comfort. She said his name and he looked up at her quickly and then back down at his meal.

"Alan? Do you like it here?" He didn't answer. "Do you love Mom and Dad? Can you look at me and answer me? Sweetheart?"

The affectionate moniker made him smile in a mysteri-ous way. "Can I have another egg?"

"Yes. But are you going to answer any of my questions?"

"After my egg."

She got up and put the flame on again under the pan. The lard began to liquefy right away. Hazel cracked another egg and watched the whites spit fat. "What was it like at the Fort Leonard home, Alan?"

"They didn't have eggs for dinner."

"I bet. Were you scared there?" She flipped the egg.

"Don't break my yolk!"

Like a starving animal, he watched her slide the egg onto his spotless plate. He burst the yolk and watched it flow. "There was mean laughing and sad crying and scared shouting. And it was cold."

"It sounds awful."

"There was two dogs tied up outside the door and I could see them from the top of the stairs on the second floor. They trained them to bite kids." He paused to chew a flap of egg white. "I don't like dogs."

"So you must be happy here," she exclaimed. "To have a place where you're safe and people love you."

"People don't love me," Alan said. "They want to chain me up."

"Now, why would you say that?" She reached to put her hand on top of his, but he twitched it away before she could touch him.

"It doesn't matter," he muttered. "I know how to escape."

She gave him a bowl of butterscotch ice cream afterward and they sat down in front of the television to watch *The Phil Silvers Show*. Alan got the broad humour of Bilko and his hapless cohorts. Hazel preferred *I Love Lucy*. Her own mother was nothing like Lucy. She had none of Lucy's joy,

Lucy's tears, Lucy's crazy passions. And her father wouldn't have known what to say to a man like Desi Arnaz. But when they watched together, they laughed together. Alan was doubled over on the floor, laughing at the ludicrous exploits of the denizens of the army camp.

"You know real life is nothing like this," she whispered into his ear.

"It should be," he said.

Their parents came home earlier than expected, and Gord Drury was with them. The three adults patted a light rain off the fronts of their coats. "Bilko!" said Drury. "I love this show."

"Me too," said Alan. He'd met Drury before and the two liked each other.

"Come on," said her mother, gesturing at Hazel. "Let's put the kettle on and let Gord and Alan finish watching the show." Hazel followed her mother through to the kitchen, looking once over her shoulder to see if her father was staying with the commander and her brother, or if he was coming in for tea. He stayed put.

"Boil the kettle, Hazel." Her mother leaned against the stove and lit a cigarette. Hazel started the flame for the kettle. "How was he tonight?"

"Hungry."

Her mother laughed. "He's more expensive to feed than a team of horses."

"What's happening in there?"

"Don't worry about them. Gord knows how to talk to people."

"Does he know how to talk to *Alan*?" Hazel asked. "I don't think Alan understands what's going on."

"He will."

Her mother's voice sounded wrong. "Do *you* think he had something to do with Carol's disappearance?" Hazel asked.

"Stranger things have happened."

"You don't believe him," she said quietly. "You're his mother. How can you not believe him?"

"It doesn't matter if I do or not. He's still my child and I'll stand behind him just as I would stand behind you."

"What kind of thing is that to say?" Hazel cried. "If you don't believe him, why don't you just send him back? Maybe he'd be better off in Fort Leonard. At least there no one pretends to care about him!"

She stormed out of the kitchen before the kettle began to sing. The doors to the den were closed and hushed voices spoke beyond it. She wanted to go in and tell them what she thought of their suspicions. If anything, Alan finding the silver pendant was a sign that Carol *was* alive. Maybe Carol herself had planted it! She hadn't been particularly nice to Hazel that afternoon at the Pit – why put it past her to complicate life for her and her family?

Maybe the adults knew better; maybe both of her parents loved her new brother, their new son. It was going to take time to civilize him, but he was no monster. He was a sweet kid, only twelve; he knew nothing about the world.

She changed into her nightgown in the bathroom. She tried not to look at herself in the mirror whenever she was changing, but she stole a glance when she was down to her underwear. Two years ago, the body in the mirror hadn't existed. She lifted one arm and gazed upon the three black hairs that straggled out of the scoop of her armpit. There was more below now and she was growing the beginning of some curves. She remembered Andrew Pedersen dancing with her at the Christmas Dance at school. He had danced with the body in the mirror. There'd been only three or four layers of fabric between them, and she'd felt him against her. She knew he'd been aware of her as well. He'd go into grade thirteen next year and then who knew where? He'd told her he was thinking of law school.

The voices continued to filter up the stairs even after Hazel had closed her bedroom door and climbed into bed. She couldn't make out the words, but her mother was in there with them now; Hazel recognized the song of her voice. She closed her eyes and listened to the murmuring. It changed into something else, and then finally into a colour and a feeling, and long before her parents and Commander Drury were finished with Alan, she'd fallen into a featureless sleep.

———

Micallef's department store had been run by a Micallef for five generations and almost everyone in the county shopped there sooner or later. It was the Eaton's dealer north of Mayfair for central Ontario, which made it a hub for travellers. A steady stream of people stopped at Micallef's to pick up a shipment. The big red *Eaton's* name – printed right onto the kraft paper the packages came wrapped in – was one of the commonplace sights in her life. "We'll see about you being the first lady Micallef to run the place," her father sometimes said. But once, last summer, he'd put his hand on hers and said, "That's not going to be the life for you, is it, Hazel?"

The occasion for this comment was an early morning fishing trip. They'd gone out for walleye and bass and pickerel in Gannon Lake. By the age of twelve, Hazel was coming out in her father's banged-up rowboat a few times each summer to drop worms and bits of liver on hooks into the underwater reeds. She didn't like fishing with live frogs, but they'd compromised on how he treated them: he could only fish with them if he didn't hook them through the mouth. If her dad could scoop one up on the end of the emergency paddle, he'd hook it through the foot and throw it in. "If no one wants him, all he'll have is a hole in his foot."

He'd convinced her that it wasn't cruel in principle, since frogs got eaten by fish all the time. But she didn't like the part where they helped the fish get the frogs. Frogs had eyes. They saw what was coming. She was certain they felt fear.

Her father maintained that they, with their fishing rods, were just part of the life cycle. "Some frogs get eaten by fish that get eaten by *us*. How is that wrong when it's all about eating in the first place? There should be enough to go around, and if there isn't, then everything might go to you-know-where in a you-know-what."

On this morning in early June, he had been smoking a rare pipe against a pink sky, the colour of spring trout before they get their fill of insects. They could see the dark backs of the bass lurking in the glowing milfoil below them. The bass were logy, but the walleyes rose to the stinktaste of the bait as soon as they put their hooks into the water. She and her father began hauling them in. He stunned them with a small club and gutted them. There was something present in the thrashing silver muscle when he pulled them in over the gunwale that was no longer there after he'd drawn the knife through the tender white belly.

Out of one of the walleyes came a living spring peeper, blinking its eyes in the sudden light. "You remember the argument about frogs we had? You argued me in circles, saying we were *abetting* them. The fish." He laughed at the memory. "Isn't that what you said?"

"I said I didn't like you hooking them through their mouths."

"OK, so . . ." He held the frog out to her at arm's length by one of its feet. It flapped its other leg without convinction.

"Here's a free frog, pre-eaten, half-dead. Even you could fish with this one."

"No way," she said. He narrowed his eyes at her. "It's double jeopardy." (She hoped she'd remembered what that was – she hadn't been able to focus all that well when Andrew was explaining it to her.)

He narrowed his eyes at her. "What about survival of the fittest?" he asked.

She pointed at the water. "Let it go."

"What about getting two fish with one frog?"

She shot her father a menacing look. "So there's no mercy if it's just business?"

"Touché. And no, there isn't. Or there shouldn't be. There's only mercy in life. Sometimes."

"That's why you should let it go."

He did. He dropped it into the water, and it kicked gamely and then just floated above the weeds. What did it mean to rescue that frog from its fate only to send it to another, identical fate? Interrupting a cycle didn't change its outcome. What kind of lesson was that? Below the frog, a dark shape was beginning to form.

Her father leaned forward and put his hand on top of hers. "I used to hope you'd want to manage the store one day."

"I don't want to sell clothes, Dad."

"No, I know you don't. I was hoping, but that's not going to be the life for you, is it, Hazel? You're your mother's daughter," he said. "It's not mercy that either of you wants, though."

"What is it?" she asked, watching the column of fish coalesce. They became a single muscle surging upward.

"Beware a man seeking justice, my Uncle Manny used to say." He relit his pipe. "You didn't know Manny." The tossed match made a tiny sizzle in the lake. That was when she saw the frog was gone.

The morning after Gord Drury's visit, the house was gravely silent. Hazel found her mother standing at the kitchen sink, smoking and looking through the window. In the den, Alan was watching *Gerald McBoing-Boing*, the volume turned down all the way. His spoon traced a metronomic arc between a punchbowl full of Rice Krispies and his mouth.

She heard the sound of a newspaper being folded in the library. Normally her father would be at the store by this hour, but when she crept silently down the hall, there he was, dressed in his suit, all but his left shoulder and leg hidden by the high-backed chair. She wanted to ask him a question, but she couldn't think of how to put it. She moved away from the library door and stood paralyzed against the wall. It wasn't until she heard her mother utter a single, choking sob, that she knew for sure that Alan was a suspect in the disappearance of Carol Lim.

] 14 [

Wednesday afternoon

Hazel had not thought of her brother or her father except glancingly in many years. Her father had been dead for eighteen years; Alan, for twenty-three. That had been a hard time, managing her own and her mother's grief, while almost single-handedly looking after two young children. The question of justice for Alan would be forever left open. He'd never speak in his own defence again. He was twelve years old when Carol Lim disappeared, and he'd been big enough to hurt someone. Maybe without the protection of his adopted parents they'd have scooped him up for it. And then who knows what might have happened to him. The present case was a trap door to her past.

And they were really off it now. There was full radio silence from the RCMP and they'd all been warned that they were to carry on with cases that had been *assigned* to them, and nothing else. The Mayfair unit had been told the same thing: hands off, stand down. Macdonald was still on Renald's disappearance, but it felt like a formality now. Mel was gone.

She crumpled up the paper bag her lunch had come in – a meatpie and an apple: Cartwright's idea of a balanced meal. She was a tiny bit sleepy and beginning to feel mired in names. One of them – *Angela Wetherling* – had already come up three times. The twin Mr. Wetherling had called her Cousin Angie. Another Mr. Wetherling had called her Angela. And the family historian, Hadley Wetherling, had also mentioned an Angie. Hazel called Hadley again and asked if she had a number or an address. She did. Angie/Angela had been one of the Copetown Wetherlings, and she still lived there.

Hazel didn't speak to Wingate on the way out and she didn't take her cruiser. She was pretty sure Ray would hear about it if her squad car drove past the exit to Dublin. She took her own car and headed down to the 400.

To go by records as old as the ones she had at her disposal was a farce of sorts. Why presume that there was a connection between unknown bones and dead-end records? Out of hope? A maze suggested both entry and exit, but this case was more like a labyrinth, complete with a monster in the middle. She already sensed its form. In her mind, it was a shimmering outlined in tiny sparks.

The name *Wetherling* was on the mailbox at 52 Orkney
Road, so at least the intelligence had been good. Hazel
walked up past the black Dodge Ram in the driveway
and knocked on the door. There was a doorbell, but Hazel
always knocked.

A man answered. He stood behind the screen door in a
tracksuit and tan slippers. "What's she done now?"

"Oh, well, I may not be here for what you think I am.
I'm Detective Inspector Hazel Micallef. I've come down
from Port Dundas on an investigation. I'm wondering, does
Angela Wetherling live here?"

"Yeah?"

"May I come in?"

He didn't budge. Then he pushed the screen door open
with a meaty forearm. Two voices were coming from somewhere on the main floor, and then a woman emerged, looking flustered.

"Are you Angela Wetherling?"

"I'm not gonna answer that," the woman said. "I say
yes, you serve me papers!"

Hazel took out her badge and showed it. "I'm not a process server, I'm a police detective. I want to ask you some
questions about a man called Claude Miracle. You're not in
any trouble."

The woman examined Hazel's ID. She handed it back.
"Turn on some lights, Moe. You want a coffee, Detective . . .
Meek —"

"Mi-*cay*-liff," Hazel said. "And no, thank you. I take it you're Angela Wetherling?"

"I'm not. I'm Angie Wetherling, after my mother."

"Not Angela."

"No ma'am, not even on my birth certificate. My *mother*'s name was Angela."

Hazel frowned. "You just said you were called Angie after your mother, but your mother's name was Angela?"

"Everyone called her Angie."

Hazel made busy looking for her notebook so she could hide her exasperation from the woman she needed to be friendly with. "And what's your last name?" she asked, pencil ready.

"It's Wetherling," she said. "I married 'im but I didn't take his name. What's this about, Officer? Where did you say you were from?"

"Port Dundas. About an hour north of here. Past Barrie."

"Ah."

Moe had finished snapping switches and the front room glowed with lamp-flung light. Angie Wetherling led her in to sit. Hazel put the woman in her sixties, about her own age. She was dumpy with pasty skin. "I want to know if you've ever heard the names Claude or Eloy Miracle. Or Claude Wetherling."

"I don't think so. Not the Miracle names. But there's a cousin Claude."

"What were his parents' names?"

"Georgia and Thom."

Good, she thought. "Is Claude still alive?"

"Oh yeah. I would've heard."

"When's the last time you saw him?"

"Moe?" she asked her husband.

"You want me to go get the social registry outta the archives, Ange?"

"Come on. When was that? Twenty-five years ago at least? We went up for a family reunion. Last time we ever did *that.*"

"Jesus," said Moe. "You were married to your first husband then."

Angie's eyelashes fluttered. "You sure you don't want any coffee, Officer?"

"Detective. No."

"Well, it was a long time ago." She stretched and looked aslant at her husband. "Before my hysterectomy, for sure."

"Claude looked like his mother," Moe volunteered.

"Claude looked like Georgia?" Hazel asked.

"Both of them, high foreheads."

"Do you know if either of his parents is alive?"

"Oh no," said Angie Wetherling. "They're all gone. My mother, my aunt, Thom, and *his* brother Hugh. My dad. Claude's my only cousin."

"Great story," said Moe, without enthusiasm. He'd continued to hover in the opening between the living room and the dining room. "Are we done?"

"Of course," said Hazel, rising. *When fact-finding, be light of touch and go when asked. It keeps doors open.* But. "One more thing," she said, putting her cap back on. "Did you know that Claude had a brother? Name of Eloy. Did Claude ever talk about a brother?"

"He didn't *have* a brother," said Angie. "He was an only child."

"He wasn't. And he didn't look like Georgia Wetherling, either," Hazel said. "He was adopted."

She stopped in Mayfair to gas up. Was Miracle living under a different name? If so, why had there not been a legal name change? Would he have been born with the name *Miracle*? She called Melanie. "You busy?"

"For you? Never."

"Look something up for me. There's, uh, gotta be a website for the Mohawk Nation. Get the number off the site and call them, would you?"

She heard Melanie's pen scritching on paper. "What am I asking them?"

"Ask them if *Miracle* is a common name in Kahnawake."

"Quebec?"

"That's right. And get back to me as soon as you can."

"Skip's asking for you. Where are you?"

"Working a case. Hurry up." She hung up and tore into a cinnamon raisin bagel. Toasted, with butter.

She called Wingate next. His brother answered. "He's asleep."

"At —" she checked her watch " — five o'clock?"

"Yes. He's asleep. I appreciate all the support he's getting from the department, but you people are rushing him."

"He told me you thought he was ready."

"He's not. This week he went three days without sleep. Does that sound ready to you, Detective Inspector?"

"OK. So maybe there's some . . . over-exuberance about his recent improvements. I understand what you're saying."

"You're undoing my work you know. When it's his day off, leave him alone."

"We're on a big case, though, Michael. Dead children. Scattered bones."

"He's told me. He's also told me about the people he found steeping in their own blood. Do you think he was ready for something like that?"

"He wasn't supposed to go down there. He went on his own."

"If any harm comes to him, I won't forget it."

She was shocked and didn't know how to reply, but he'd hung up. She stared at the phone in her hand. It was good she hadn't mentioned that James was actually on the job. He was probably in his bedroom with the doors closed and his laptop open. She'd call him later and tell him about her meeting with Angie Wetherling.

Back at the station house, Melanie had got nothing from Kahnakwe, but two people had promised to call her back. Hazel told her to keep on it. She made a point of popping her head into Ray's office. "I hear you were looking for me?"

"I was. You were gone half the afternoon. Sleeping one off?" He tapped one key repeatedly on his keyboard.

"Something wrong?"

"Oh, you know. Missing officer, dead kids."

"Maybe someone other than Macdonald should be hunting for Renald."

"Why do you say that?"

"I just think maybe Sean's not up to it." She imagined he was knocking off early to see Freemey. She wasn't surprised he'd not made much progress.

"Do you want to take over?"

"No."

"I left you a treat."

"You did?"

"Noise complaint. From a music school, if you can believe it."

"Thanks. Any update from the mounted constabulary?"

"None, just as they promised. They are thorough as well as succinct." He squinted through his glasses at the screen. She remained in the doorway, her mind milling troubling connections between Ray Greene and Chip Willan. "Why are you staring at me?" he asked.

"Just admiring your calm under pressure. I'll go sound out the music school."

He grunted some kind of goodbye, and she went back to her office. Melanie was typing at her desk and didn't even look up when Hazel went past. She opened her desk drawer to get the tennis ball, but it was gone. There was an apple beside her blotter. She threw it at the Plexiglas window.

"Argh!" cried Cartwright. She came lightly stomping into the office with the tennis ball gripped in her hand. "I'm a jumpy person, Inspector."

"Mohawk names."

"One."

"Well, let's have it!"

"First, please agree to pick up the phone and dial my extension. It's as fast as throwing something at the window."

"Fine. Agreed."

"*Maracle* is a common Mohawk surname. That's what the lady said when she called back."

"Just now?"

"Yes."

"Goddamn it, why didn't you come and get me, Cartwright."

"You were talking to the skip."

"Spell it."

"*M-A-R-A-C-L-E.*" She put the tennis ball on Hazel's desk.

"Uh-uh," she said, passing it back. "I don't need the temptation."

———

Maracle. Was it possible? Her hands shook as she entered the variables into Canada 411. She came up with a number of Maracles, but no Claudes. No *C*s even. She sat zazen in front of the screen, willing it to do the work for her, her mind wandering. If only she knew where to look and what to look with. Was Eloy in there under *Maracle*? She typed it in. There was one hit – in Toronto – but it practically leaped off the screen. *Eloy Maracle.*

She dialled the number. A man picked up. "Claude Wetherling?" she said, and the man hung up. Her pulse whacked in her neck. She dialled again and there was no answer. A machine picked up. She heard *"This is the home of –"* then someone picked up the phone again.

"What do you want?"

"Are you Claude Wetherling? Born Maracle?"

"Who am I talking to?"

"Detective Inspector Hazel Micallef of the Port Dundas Police Department. Are you really Eloy Maracle?"

The man hesitated. "Eloy is dead."

"You're listed under his name in public records."

"Easier to stay hidden if you're a dead man."

"Where is he buried, Mr. Maracle?"

"I don't know. Eloy was taken with some kind of a flu is what they said. Why are you asking about him?"

"How long were you at Dublin Home?"

"Two years."

"Boys came and went I'm sure. But there must have been the occasional death as well, like your brother's. Were you there when any other boys died?"

"What are you investigating, Detective . . ."

"Micallef. Missing boys."

"Eloy died of the flu."

"Where is he buried? Was there a graveyard or a memorial garden? On the grounds?"

"No. A potter's field in Mayfair. The county puts the indigent dead into a communal hole. They're not too sentimental about dead orphans, homeless rubbies, people found dead in the street."

"Is that what happened to boys who died at the home?"

She heard the sound of ice cubes in a glass. "I don't like to think of that time in my life. I'm sure you understand."

"I do. There must be some very painful memories." She hesitated, unsure how to put the next part. "I have to tell you that we found bones in the fields behind Dublin Home. Scattered over acres of land."

"And you think Eloy . . . ?"

"He might be," she said. "We looked into the records from Dublin Home in the late fifties, when you were both there, and they show you were adopted by Thomas and Georgia Wetherling. But there's no such record for your brother. No death certificate, no transfer order, no release. In fact, you're the only one who still has a file in the archives. Your brother's has been destroyed."

"Well, he was dead enough that Indian Affairs stopped sending his cheques. I know, because my parents put up a fight to keep getting them, but IA told them he was dead. They had to be satisfied with the eleven dollars I brought in every month through my benefits. While I tilled their fields for my room and board."

"I understand they're deceased."

"So I hear. I had nothing to do with them after the age of twenty-one. Came to the city, took my brother's name and worked teaching grade-school math."

"Mr. Maracle – Claude – would you consent to giving some hair for the purposes of DNA analysis?"

"What bit of difference could it make? He's dead. He's never let me know otherwise, so who cares what they did with his bones? Why *not* in the fields outside of Dublin?"

"What if it was murder? What then? Wouldn't you want to know?"

He took a breath in slowly through his nose. "Ironic what they changed our names to. Life was no miracle for us. Eloy was bigger'n me, by almost five inches, although he was younger. He always said no one would take us together because he was too strong. He'd been trouble in all the other places we'd been."

"What kind of trouble?"

"There wasn't a person that could hold Eloy down when he got mad. He broke a bunch of chairs one day because there'd been no meat in our suppers for a whole week.

They put a shot of barbiturate into him and he kept going anyway. We were in four homes between when I was five and twelve. The Wetherlings didn't want us both. They wanted a good boy, not a gorilla. I didn't want to go. I was Eloy's only protection in that place. I kept a lid on him and calmed him down when it came off. But I had to leave. No one ever passes up an opportunity to leave a place like that. I went."

"Claude, let us do the test. I can have someone come out and take a single hair from your head; that'd be it. At the very least, if there's no match we can rule out Eloy's bones among the ones we found in those fields."

"Fine," he said. "But don't tell me nothing about it. I don't want to know."

"If that's how you feel."

"I'm sorry for whatever happened to my brother, but I'm too old to think differently about the past. I only know what I know, and that's all I want to know."

"I can accept that," she said. "Thank you."

He gave her his address. She called Jack Deacon and had him dispatch a technician to collect the man's hair.

Hazel heard her mother moving around in the den. She'd napped after supper and Hazel was prepared to leave her to sleep for the night, but she'd woken and come down-stairs asking for breakfast. There was no harm in it. Hazel heated a pot of oatmeal from the fridge and topped it with cream as well as maple syrup. Her mother's appetite was fugitive at the best of times, but even she could not resist the siren call of maple syrup. The kettle sang, and she poured out the water over decaf crystals. She saw her mother making for the stairs. "Where are you going?"

"I'm going to floss."

"You're coming back down, I hope. I'm making all this for you."

"Is it ready?"

"Not quite."

"So tie up your horses."

"I wasn't —" she started, but her mother had already begun her journey up the stairs. She was so thin now that she couldn't make the steps creak.

Someone rang the doorbell.

"Oh, for . . . Hold on!" she called to the stairs. She ran, wiping her hands on a tea towel, and opened the door on Kraut Fraser's nervously smiling face. "What's wrong?" There was no one behind him. "Are you here to warn me to keep away? Because I'm away."

"Remember the hanging file Brendan Givens gave to Wingate?"

"What? When did Wingate see Brendan fucking – ?"

"Never mind." He produced two sheets of folded paper from inside his jacket. "He gave them to me. I spent a couple of days on the Internet, tracing titles and boards of directors.

That kind of thing. What if I told you that some of these files might explain why the RCMP is on the case now?"

"Fine," she said. "Come in."

"Smells like coffee."

"You're going to make a hell of a detective, Kraut. Want one?"

"If it isn't a problem. I'm on a double."

No cop ever drank decaf. She made fresh for him, but instant. The kettle was still hot. "If you see my mother, keep it simple."

"How is she?"

"Her Honour has been a little gaga of late." He handed her the document. It was a printout with six-digit numbers down one side and a series of contact names on the other. "What am I looking at?"

He sipped on the hot coffee. "That's a list of Ontario numbered corporations that are shareholders in Tournament Acres."

"OK?"

"This one," he put his finger on one of the numbers, "is owned by a Paige Willan."

"*Paige?*"

"I'll spare you the exposition: she's the commissioner's paternal grandmother."

"Chip has a living grandmother?"

"No. She's not living. But she still has sharp taste in real estate."

"Holy shit." She clasped his upper arm and squeezed it. "Have you told anyone else about this?"

"Hello Dutch," said Emily Micallef. She'd been standing in the doorway.

Hazel stilled herself. "Dietrich and I are just going over some papers, Mom."

"What did I call you?" Emily asked Fraser.

"Dutch. That's OK, I go by a lot of names."

Emily poured the rest of the decaf Hazel had brewed into a mug. Hazel watched her as if she were armed and dangerous. "Indian cigarettes, I bet," her mother said.

"What?"

"You two are taking orders for cigarettes?"

"No, Mom. Dietrich and I are on an investigation."

"Oh yeah?" She took a seat at the kitchen table and arranged her housecoat around her legs. "What about?"

"I can tell you later."

Emily got up suddenly and clasped Fraser by the shoulder. "I called you Dutch, didn't I? Oh my god, I'm a crazy old woman." She laughed and it was her old laugh. A bit of birdsong. She came closer to him, to speak into his ear. "She's been hiding my cigarettes. Get me a carton of DKs."

She took her coffee into the den.

"There but for the grace of god," Hazel said. "She's OK when we sit down and eat together or we're in the car. Then she seems to lock in. But otherwise she drifts. At least she's sleeping." She gestured with her coffee mug that they should step back into the hallway. When she was sure she was out of her mother's earshot, she said, "Although she woke up last night hacking and coughing and telling someone to get away."

"I wish I knew what to tell you."

She put the list back into his hands. "Hold on to this. Don't make any copies."

"All right. Surely you don't like Willan for the Fremonts?"

"No. He's just one more thing in the hopper."

"What about for Renald?"

"You think Willan has whacked Melvin Renald? Maybe he had the RCMP whack him?"

"You don't think having the dead boys case stalled improves matters for the shareholders?"

"The RCMP taking over those fields isn't an improvement for any of the investors. Even if our commissioner is posing as his dead grandmother to buy property, I'm not sure it has anything to do with Renald, or the Fremonts, or the bones in the dirt."

"You think the Mounties would suppress evidence?"

"I don't know the lofty workings of the RCMP or who they really answer to. But I hope not."

"Hazel, you should go to Ray with this." He held up the pages he'd brought. "Willan might be a case we could work."

"We're going to do what Ray told us to do. One: don't go to Tournament Acres; and two: get to work. Children died in this county, Fraser, under the eyes of its citizens. That's our case."

"But if *Willan* is the case, maybe Gateway Plaza won't happen. So what if he didn't have anything to do with the Fremonts? *In the course of our investigation* blah blah blah *evidence of illegal investments* blah blah *serious conflict of interest*."

"Gateway Plaza is a done deal. The groundbreaking is in six days. Put that stuff away until we need it."

] 15 [

1957

Commander Drury had both families into his office, which easily fit the seven of them. Because of her mother's stature in town, or so Hazel believed, they had not been taken into one of the interview rooms.

Drury sat in his high-backed chair, a lit cigarette burning on the rim of a standing ashtray beside his desk. The three children sat on the couch under a map of the county, and the three adults were in chairs in front of his desk. He spoke first to Hazel's mother. "You understand, Emily, no one is being accused of anything. But if your son did in fact find the pendant in your yard, then how did it get there? And is it possible, despite his protestations, that he may have found it somewhere else? Somewhere he shouldn't have been, maybe? Alan —" Drury said, raising his voice a little.

"Yes, sir?"

"Let me ask you. If I told you, as a man of the law, that you had done nothing wrong by finding and keeping Carol's pendant, and that you would not be punished for anything you said in this room, even were you to admit to a lie, would anything about your story change?"

"Excuse me?"

"Are you afraid you'll be punished, Alan? If I told you that you will *not* be punished for telling the truth, even if it is different now than it was before, would you change your story?"

Alan's eyes darted around. Could he be lying? Hazel wondered. If he were lying, though, surely something would have given him away by now.

"I want to tell you everything," Alan said. "I am trying."

"What is the point of this?" asked Dale Whitman. "Master Micallef is a boy of twelve, and a very backward boy. You can't interrogate a child."

"I must question him, if he is able to answer," said Drury.

"And why are *we* here?"

"Dr. Whitman – your daughter was one of the last people to see Carol Lim five weeks ago. Memory is a strange thing." He returned his attention to the trio of children on the couch. "Sometimes we remember what happened, but not all of it. Like you did, Gloria, when you recalled the man you saw. And sometimes when we remember, what we're remembering didn't actually happen. But then you hit on it! A vital detail. Something someone said. The colour of a person's jacket. A little teaspoon of truth." He stood up, and when Gloria's father began to rise, Drury gestured him back down into his seat. He moved beside the desk to face Alan, Hazel, and Gloria. "That's why we're here, under your parents' supervision: to see if we can help you remember. You see, children, the finding of Carol's pendant is a very significant thing. It tells us that someone interacted with her in some way."

Alan put his hand up. "What if she threw it away?"

"Why would she have thrown it away?"

"She was angry," he offered.

"At whom?"

"I don't know," Alan said, meekly.

"And so why did the monkey run off with the seahorse?" said Dr. Whitman, rising from his seat. His face was red. "You obviously don't need us here."

"Sit," snapped Commander Drury. "You are not the authority here, Doctor. Gloria, did you see Hazel's brother at any point that day? Before or after your encounter with Carol? Gloria . . . ? I'm asking you a question."

"Apologize to my father." Her voice was cold.

"Answer his question, child," Dr. Whitman said.

"Did you see him?" Drury repeated.

"I probably did," said Gloria. "He's always around anyway, with his dopey face covered in chocolate, looking for sticks or frogs. But I don't know if I saw him that day or some other day. I don't know. And I've told you everything. I wasn't feeling well. Hazel can tell you. I was woozy."

"Do you recall Gloria being woozy, Hazel?"

"I guess . . . she was a little out of breath." Hazel felt like there was a train speeding toward her. "But I know she didn't see Alan after I saw her. I went right home and he was waiting for me. I took him out for a float. Dad gave us money."

"I did," her father said.

Drury turned his questioning to Dr. Whitman. "I haven't asked you what your memories of that day are."

"I wasn't there. I have none."

"I mean when your daughter came home. Did you notice anything untoward?"

"Her homework was done and dinner was ready. So no. Everything was as it should be." He beamed at Gloria. "If you think my daughter is involved in the –"

"No, goodness no," said Hazel's mother, and she reached out and touched the doctor's sleeve, smiling. "We're all very upset about the Lim girl. Commander?"

"Mrs. Micallef." They all noticed that he did not call her Emily or Madam Mayor, and the temperature in the room ticked up. "If you can hold your comm –"

"She must know a lot of people in Toronto," Emily said.

He wasn't going to answer her, but she stared at him. "What do you mean by 'a lot'?"

"In addition to her relations. Wasn't there something about a boyfriend?"

"Yes. We've already checked him out. Tom Landers. He's at the University of Toronto. But he hasn't heard from her since the day before she disappeared."

"He could be protecting her."

"We've looked into it." Drury's voice was hard. He looked at each child in turn and shook his head. He let a silence stretch out. "All right," he said, rising, and it was as if air had been pumped into the room. Dale Whitman stood and shook the commander's hand. Everyone but Alan did, in turn. "You don't shake, Master Micallef?"

"I don't want you to take my fingerprints."

Drury laughed. "That's not how it's done, young man."

Emily ushered Alan out with the rest of them, but she stayed behind in Drury's office. "Give us a minute," she said. She closed the door, and then Hazel could hear nothing from inside the office.

"Well, I suppose we should be going," Dr. Whitman said in the corridor, and he offered his hand to her father.

Evan Micallef shook it, but he spoke to Gloria: "We don't want you to feel scared to tell your father or Commander Drury if anything else comes to mind."

Whitman put a protective hand on his daughter's shoulder. "Do you believe your own daughter, Mr. Micallef?"

"I do."

"And I believe mine. I think she has told us everything she knows. This has been traumatic for everyone, and the best thing now is for us to carry on and hope and pray that

Miss Lim will make her whereabouts known. Then we can be sure we'll get the whole story, and any suspicions about your boy can be put to rest."

"Suspicions?"

"Why do you think we were asked here, sir? To question *my* daughter? Gloria and I are here as a courtesy."

"A *courtesy*?" said Evan Micallef. "My son is neither more or less capable of lying than anyone else here."

"Now now, Evan, I mean no offence. But you haven't known him your whole life. You don't know what he is capable of. *He* doesn't know!"

"I suggest you go back to your offices, Doctor. Where you are helpful and useful."

For the first time that afternoon, Hazel made eye contact with Gloria. The question of Carol Lim's fate had become so urgent that it seemed anything was possible now. *Does she think I know something?* she wondered. *Does Gloria know something?* What if Gloria was helping Carol? They hadn't acted like they were friends, but maybe that had been for Hazel's benefit. Gloria could have used the necklace as a diversion. It had been so easy to conclude that things were just as they'd seemed that day. But because she was in the story she'd been telling, Hazel had not considered till now that her role in it might have been unwitting.

"Come," Dr. Whitman said, holding his hand out. Gloria took it and they began down the hall to the lot at the rear of the building. Then Emily emerged from Gord Drury's office and kissed Alan on the crown and Hazel on the forehead.

"That's all, my darlings. It's still early enough for the breakfast special at Ladyman's. Why don't we go park ourselves and have a feast?"

"I'm hungry," said Alan.

"You're always hungry," Hazel said, eyeing her brother.

"I'm energetic."

"You're a human garbage can."

"Be nice to him," their mother said. "He's been through a lot today."

All through the breakfast, Alan applied himself to his plate like a miner hammering at a seam of coal. The food went everywhere, but by the end, as at most meals, Alan had thumbed up the crumbs and pinched the stray fleck of meat off the side of the salt shaker. "You do clean your plate . . . and the surrounding area," their mother sometimes joked, but to Hazel it seemed as if her mother admired his appetite. Hazel she warned about getting fat, but she couldn't feed Alan too much.

Over the pancakes and coffee, Hazel watched her parents communicating silently with each other through the occasional held gaze or a look askance. Once, they locked eyes and then simultaneously looked at Alan. They traded copious information with each other without so much as uttering a syllable.

The feelings of adults were difficult to decipher, and Hazel had long ago stopped trying to understand who her parents were together. One day, in the distant future it felt, a man would look at her and just like that she'd know everything he was thinking and feeling. But for now, she was lost in a sea of signals. She didn't know how she felt about Andrew Pedersen, really. Was it enough that someone was nice to you?

She was aware of her heart beating. She looked up and her father's head seemed very far away, as if she were looking down the wrong end of a telescope. It was a scary feeling. She could hear every sound in the place. The dirty dishes clattering in the sinks; laughter and voices; the cough of a car starting. Calls from the street, a horn in the distance. Then her heart felt like it stopped. A high-pitched whine sounded inside her head that reduced all the ambient noise to something distant, and she looked at her brother. He was sitting on the other side of the table, picked out in a column of light as if the angels were going to take him away.

] 16 [

Thursday, October 25, morning

At their appointment earlier that week, Dr. Pass had suggested a visit to a neurologist in Mayfair, a specialist in
aging and changes in the brain. After making a phone call,
he wrote a referral and marked it URGENT. "Most people
have to wait months for a visit with Dr. White – I can get
you in Thursday morning at eight."

However, after she'd made some scrambled eggs and toast,
Hazel found her mother unwilling to get out of bed. "This is
ridiculous," she told her. "Adults don't behave like this."

"I'm taking a stand," her mother protested.

"Would *you* accept this kind of behaviour from anyone?"

"I'm not *anyone*," Emily snarled. "I am your mother."

"That's correct. And, right now, my mother needs to
get her skeleton out of bed so I can take her to see the nice

doctor and then go to work."

"What's her field?" asked Emily. "This nice doctor."

"Gerontological neurology."

It took further cajoling, but eventually Hazel was able to get Emily dressed and feed her a couple forkfuls of egg before leaving the house. Emily took forever to lock the front door and then she turned around and saw Hazel had brought her cruiser. "Mother of Jesus," she snarled. "Are you taking me in *that* goddamned thing?"

"I'm on duty, Mom. But we can go fast."

"How fast?"

"I can punch it to one-fifty on a straightaway."

Emily got in and sat glowering in the passenger seat, and Hazel had to do her seat belt for her. Then they headed towards the 41, passing the turn-off to Port Dundas where the new headquarters was going to go. A banner hanging between two stanchions on the prow of land below the granite cliff read:

FUTURE HOME OF SOBEYS SUPERSTORE,

ROOTS, GALAXY CINEMAS AND MUCH MORE

ON THE MAIN THOROUGHFARE OF WESTMUIR COUNTY

and

THE NEW HEADQUARTERS OF THE

ONTARIO POLICE SERVICE, NORTH–CENTRAL DIVISION.

Deputy Commissioner Charles. S. Willan

GROUNDBREAKING OCTOBER 30, 2007

"An abomination," said Emily. "Main Street will be dead in two years."

"Just think: if you could drive straight north from Toronto and have all your needs met without ever having to pull off into some ratty little town, wouldn't that be wonderful? How much you want to bet there'll be a McDonald's here in six months?"

In the rear-view mirror, Hazel saw the outcrop of scrub with two roads joining in front of it. One led to the heart of Port Dundas, the other would soon be applied like a garrotte to the throat of the town.

"When you get to my age, try to stay out of doctors' offices," Emily said. "They are employed by government forces to make people shuffle off their mortal coils, thus saving the economy billions a year."

"It would be nice to put an end to that plot."

"There's no plot. When it's your time you don't have any say in it."

"You talk like I'm driving you to your execution."

"You could be," Emily said. "Too bad it isn't covered."

Hazel had read recently in a not-entirely disreputable women's magazine that sometimes when people expressed negative feelings they weren't looking for advice or a counterpoint, they just needed someone to hear them. Someone to listen. And listening was easier than responding to the carping. She would try harder to hear what her mother was saying.

———

The clinic was in a house at the end of a rural road outside Brigham. Aspens in full colour hung over the roof and there was a basketball hoop at the side of the house. It had a calming effect. By the time Emily was welcomed into the doctor's office, all the fight had gone out of her. Sooner or later in your life, you have to put yourself in someone else's hands. Just surrender. Hazel watched her mother being walked away. A small figure following a white coat down a hallway.

The magazines were atrocious. They were a contributing factor to the ongoing fall of civilization. The television suspended from the ceiling played a game show silently. The grand prize was plastic surgery. No one should be surprised by anything people may be capable of, including competing on television for a new face.

Her phone rang. Ray Greene. "Brendan Givens is dead."

"What?" She went out into the hallway.

"Stabbed to death in a hotel room. Yesterday. In Toronto."

Toronto? "And who caught *that* case?"

"Fifty-one Division."

"God. I feel like we're on the losing side of a game of keep-away."

"Did you look into the complaint I left for you?"

"The racket ruckus on Fraser Street? I put Eileen Bail on it. She won't punch anyone."

"Then what have you been doing?"

"I haven't been in Tournament Acres."

"But you *have* been . . . ?"

"Doing research."

"On?"

"These boys lived in our county, Ray. They weren't even given the courtesy of an unmarked grave, they were . . . murdered, incinerated, and their remains were scattered in the corn. They have a right to their names."

He moaned something unintelligible. "You're as reliable as tides, Hazel. You don't have a case, but someone says no to you and you see a red cape."

"You can't stop me from reading public files."

"Is that what you're doing?" Silence. "You've got Wingate on it, too?"

"Yes."

"You know, I got a pretty furious phone call –"

"From Michael Wingate? He tore me a new one, too. Don't change the subject. James has the names of six boys who vanished off the public record after doing a stint at Dublin Home. Six candidates for murder. There'll be more. All we have to do is attach a name to one victim and we have the foundation of a huge case."

"How do you propose to do that?"

"Find a relation. Do a DNA test. And, um, well . . ."

"Well what?"

"I've actually already found a relation. Deacon sent someone to get a hair sample. They can get markers in three days to compare to the results Deacon's lab got on the bones."

"Do you have an assignment for me?"

"What do you mean?" A nurse entered the hallway and gestured for Hazel to come through.

"I mean, since you're still obviously in charge, what do you want me to do? Should I go down the chimney at Fifty-one Division and steal the file on Givens?"

"I might have something for you later." It made him laugh, but she knew he was mad as hell. Before he could form another objection, she said, "Nothing on Renald?"

"Nada. How do I know he didn't disappear on your say-so, huh? Maybe you have him out there dressed up as a Mountie."

"I gotta go, Ray." She went back into the doctor's office. Emily emerged from the back with Dr. White in tow. Her mother wore a look of frank triumph.

"Not a thing wrong with me. Tell her."

"Hello Hazel. Nice to see you again."

"Nancy." Her eyes shuttled back and forth between her mother and the doctor. "So we're to carry on?"

"Come back here for a minute, and we'll talk about it in private."

Hazel followed Nancy White, but her mother stayed behind. "You don't want to be a part of this conversation?"

"I've seen all I need to see back there for now. I'll wait out here with the hopeless cases."

Dr. White's office was the standard-issue professional inner sanctum, with diplomas and wood accents and a steel lamp on the desk. "People weren't meant to live into their nineties," Dr. White said. "What's happening to your mother is normal. She forgets, she remembers, she's herself, she's not herself. She's been working with that brain since she was in her mother's tummy. Things get old."

"What about the myeloma?" Hazel said with half a smile.

"It could be contributing, but it doesn't really matter. There's no sense in pathologizing the aging process — not all of us are lucky enough to have one! But we do live in an era of options and one of those options is drugs. I could, for instance, put your mother on five milligrams of Aricept. Good drug. My father was on it. I think it kept him going, cognitive-wise, maybe an extra year or two."

"Do you have a drug that can make me *forget* stuff?"

"I know of one, but it's around three hundred dollars an ounce." They both laughed. "We don't know very much about the brain, I'm afraid. We go at it with the equivalent of boxing gloves on."

Hazel had begun to feel heavy. "Can we think about it?"

"Of course."

"What did she say?"

"Your mother? She asked me if I could euthanize her with Jim Beam." They both laughed again, but Hazel found herself snorting back tears.

A Mountie leaning against his cruiser at the corner of Sam Snead and Pebble Beach held up his hand to stop the approaching OPS cruiser. Hazel rolled down her window to report she had an appointment with the CO up in the command truck. She didn't, but the Mountie read her warrant card and let her through anyway.

Hazel drove up and parked her car. The RCMP remote command vehicle was an RV decked out in red, yellow, white, and blue. Stairs led up at one end and down at the other, like a haunted house at a county fair, but with Mounties in it.

She walked up to the door marked IN and knocked. The big, bearded man who answered smiled at her. "Ya?" He dried his hands on a white tea towel.

"Detective Inspector Hazel Micallef. OPS. I was wondering who the commanding officer here is?"

"That role falls to me. Superintendent Martin Scott. Come in. Which OPS?"

She stepped up into the vehicle. "Port Dundas."

"That nearby?"

"Not too far." It was a single room inside, complete with red carpeting. There were a few desks and a white eraser board on one wall. A kitchen and a curtained-off area took up the far end. It smelled of sock. "We were actually on the case here. You know about . . . the bones of the kids, and also the dead couple. The Fremonts. Do you know about them?"

"I do."

"Is that your case?"

"Sort of. Tea?"

"Sort of?"

"I can only make small talk, Detective Inspector. Tea?"

"Do some of you live in here?"

"There's always someone on the barge," said Scott. "And we've got one guest in the cell."

"You have a suspect?"

"No, I have Mr. Givens's secretary. Justine. She got apoplectic."

Hazel looked at the near end and noted a locked door flush with a particleboard wall. "And you locked her up?"

"She's tanked."

"Can I see her?"

Without hesitation, Scott tossed her his keys. "Green key fob thingy."

She went to the door and unlocked it. Behind it was another door, a steel one, with a large, barred window in it. A woman was sleeping under a Hudson's Bay blanket on a comfortable-looking cot. "Justine," she called. "Hazel Micallef. Everything OK in here?"

"I threw up."

"All right, sweetheart. You can probably leave now if you want."

"No," she said, and Hazel heard the sound of her throat working. "I think I'd better stay here a few more hours." The girl sat up partway and blew her nose. "I can't believe he's dead," she said. "He was gonna take me to see the horse circus."

"Get some rest."

She closed the outer door and locked it. She walked back and put the keys into the palm of Scott's outstretched hand. "I'll have tea." He was rugged-looking, about fifty-five, with a barrel chest, and his bushy beard was starting to streak grey under his mouth. "Superintendent Scott, are you aware that one of our officers has been abducted?"

"I am. I'm sorry. I understand there isn't much progress just yet."

"It's hard to carry on an investigation when the crime scene is locked down by another police force."

He was in the little galley, busy swirling hot water into teacups. The cups – Royal Doulton, she was sure – looked silly and small in his paws and he wore a look of engrossed concentration. He swirled water in the teapot, too. "It feels sometimes like the world is coming apart at the seams. A cup of tea helps."

"I'm not sure Sergeant Renald would agree with that sentiment," she said. "Are you doing *anything* in those fields?"

"There's not much in the way of shovelling going on right now," Scott said. "Our instructions are to keep the site secure. When they saw you lurking around, we were told to lock down every corner. Which we have carried out with ruthless efficiency." He smiled.

"You knew it was me?"

"I think it only took one phone call."

She wondered how good a policeman he was. He had a soothing manner that was also charming, in a practised way. She'd missed a few words; he was still talking: ". . . would have seen him by now. We've inspected every dwelling in the development. And we've checked every ID. Your sergeant is not on these grounds."

"How do you know he's not under them?"

"If he is, then I'm afraid the investigation into his death would be ancillary to our current command." He held both cups aloft in their saucers and splashed a bit of tea into them. Hazel reached out to take one.

"Which is what, specifically?" she asked.

"Which is to collect evidence."

"Well, we have similar aims."

"But at cross-purposes."

"Why is the RCMP taking over this investigation?"

"We have not taken anything over, Detective Inspector. We're on our own investigation." The door to the command centre opened and a young woman in uniform entered. She saw Micallef and Scott sitting there together and she apologized, and left.

"You're not investigating the unrecorded murders of children from fifty years ago? You're here for another reason?"

"I wish I could tell you more."

She put her teacup down on its saucer and pushed it away. "I wish you could, too," she said. "You're impeding *my* investigation. You're not even keeping it alive. I'd like to know what for."

"I would like to tell you. But I can't."

"God. I've always found you guys inscrutable, you know?"

"Us *guys*? We are also women and dogs and horses."

"Sometimes I wonder if you're just pretending in those shiny uniforms of yours."

He looked at her steadily for a long count. It made her feel she shouldn't blink. "I assure you," he said, "we are not pretending."

She rose and pushed her chair away. Its feet bumped awkwardly backward over the red, tight-pile carpet. She reached out, a little stiffly she thought, to shake his hand.

"It's true you have to watch out for the horses," he said

to her at the exit. "They are both inscrutable and mischievous. Come back if you like. Command is lonesome."

James Wingate spent his Thursday in the archives and he was home by six with copies of complete personnel lists for both boys' homes between 1951 and 1960. He faxed them to Hazel, and once they'd both had their suppers, they sat on the phone together and went over the data.

"Get this. One of the physical education teachers at Charterhouse was named Greer Knockknock," he said.

"Do you see any personnel who shuttled back and forth? Listed at both institutions at the same time maybe?"

"I haven't looked." They both heard papers being shuffled. "Tell me," said Wingate. "How much of this do you think went on? Crimes like this, ones we only discover by accident?"

"You shudder to think what's under the ground anywhere. I had an aunt who lived in Tunisia. She had six mummies in her garden."

"I have some contacts in Renfrew now . . . I'm dying to ask them to sniff around the local history. But if they've got anything in their fields like we do in ours, they'd be smart to keep a lid on it or maybe they'll get their case snatched too."

"I don't think our case has been snatched," Hazel said. "I met the guy in charge down there. Martin Scott. He was pretty straightforward about the situation. His position was to be very kind and polite and also immovable. But he did tell me their case is not the missing kids."

"The Fremonts then?"

"He wouldn't confirm it. But why would the RCMP be interested in people like the Fremonts?"

"What's that mean?"

"Bit players. Those homes went for under a quarter of a million, most of them. What kind of criminal enterprise was Oscar Fremont in that paid off this poorly, but the RCMP would investigate?" Wingate arched his eyebrows. "The Fremonts – and everyone else on that cursed bit of land – are sideshows to a sideshow, and the RCMP is doing something altogether unconnected. Or connected in a way that's not obvious. Scott acted as if the discovery of the bones created an opportunity for them."

"Let's keep going," he said.

She heard him turning pages but she had no idea where he was in the document when he started talking. "There's some commonality, besides oversight, between the two homes in the time frame we're looking at. A couple of administrators, a bookkeeper, some medical and nursing staff. I think there might have been a provincial circuit for the docs because these records show their salaries were paid separately by inhibition. Institution. Very small amounts, though. In 1958, this one – Harald Groet – was paid two hundred and seventy-five dollars by Charterhouse and three hundred by Dublin Home. That's not a lot for a doctor even in 1958, don't you think?" She heard him tapping on a keypad. "Three hundred bucks in 1958 is like two thousand now."

"Why does this matter?"

"I don't know."

"Does knowing doctors' salaries in 1958 move our case along?"

"None of them were on staff. That's what I mean."

"Fine. Janitorial staff. Did you find any?"

"Some."

"Any night guards or overnight staff?"

"I can't tell from just this."

"OK." She thought about it for a moment. Then she started flipping pages again. "How many doctors?"

"About a dozen."

"Why aren't they all together in here?"

"I can refax —"

"Never mind, I'm pulling them out. Donald Rosen. Frank Inman. Frances Kelly."

"Which Francis?"

"The female."

"Female doctor? Hold on, I found her," he said. "*Frances.* Not a doctor, a nurse. And there's a Peter Lynch. Back and forth in the region for twenty years. Frequently at both Dublin and Charterhouse. Dale Whitman —"

"Dale Whitman?" Hazel said. "I knew him. I grew up with his daughter, Gloria. We lived on the same street."

"Do you remember him?"

"Oh yeah. I remember him well. He was what people used to call a 'community leader.' I think I even remember that he volunteered his time at various homes in the county."

"He didn't volunteer. He was paid."

"Well, there's nothing wrong about it if he was. He raised Gloria alone. I liked him, but last time I saw him I'm sure it was fifty years ago. And I was a kid." She leaned back in her chair to flip the stapled mass of paper back onto her desk. "I guess it would have been pretty good cover, being a community leader. With all these hockey coaches and priests, how could you be surprised by anything?"

Hazel checked with her contact in Toronto about Claude Maracle's DNA. They'd put it on rush, but they still wouldn't know anything until Monday at the earliest. It could make one boy real and prove the effectiveness of their investigative methods, but it still wouldn't bring them any closer to who had put the bones there. Or to getting back to the crime scene. She began to realize that the cohort of boys who'd known Eloy Maracle was as important to find as the victims. Most of the former wards of Dublin Home would be in their sixties and seventies now; it wouldn't be difficult to locate a couple of them. She called the archives and put Leon Cutter on it.

Hazel got up from her desk and shut the door to her office. She turned off the light. A chair wedged between file cabinets served as her thinking spot, and right now the setting sun was picking it out in a column of light. She sat down in it and closed her eyes.

Bones are found in a field on which an expensive development has been partially built. The people who bring this to light are murdered. Why? To warn others to keep quiet? And Givens hands files over to the police that can identify who might have something to lose if the development were revealed to be a crime scene. And he's murdered. And who knows what will happen to anyone else who helps?

"Jesus," she said aloud. "Honey Eisen." She got out her notebook, looked up Eisen's number, and dialled it. The clock on her wall said 7:10 p.m. There was no answer. She burst from her office and crossed the pen to Ray's. "Now I have something for you." She tossed him his jacket. "Get mad at me later. We might have another body."

"Let me guess: we have to go to Tournament Acres."

"I figure if you're in the car with me, I'm not breaking the rules."

She told herself the look on his face had a hint of frank admiration in it.

The drive, at the speed Hazel was going, took thirty-four minutes. She had Ray call down twice on the way, but Eisen didn't answer either time. When they got to the corner of Sam Snead and Pebble Beach, she stopped for the Mountie and rolled her window down. "I spoke to Superintendent

Scott," she told him, not lying this time. "We're going to drive around a bit so I can show my CO what I was talking to the super about."

"Oh, do you want me to call him?"

"No, that's OK. We'll just pop in later. No need to bother him."

"No, ma'am."

Hazel drove north up Pebble Beach until she was out of view of the gate and parked the cruiser. She dialled Honey Eisen one more time.

"When did you talk to the superintendent?" Ray asked her.

"No answer," Hazel said. "Earlier today. I came down. Nice guy. Not very helpful."

"Hazel, I —"

"I didn't enter Tournament Acres, I just went into the RCMP command vehicle. I didn't break any rules. Let's go."

He glowered at her, but he got out of the car. They walked up to Eisen's house. It was dark inside behind drawn blinds. Hazel went up the front stoop and looked in one of the side windows: she saw nothing. She knocked on the door and then rang the doorbell.

Ray stood back. She tried the door and it opened. "Aw, shit." They both drew but kept their safeties on. She put her finger against her lips and held the door for him as they stepped into the darkened house. She clicked on her flashlight and led the way down the hall, where Mrs. Eisen took her when she'd come to visit. The kitchen and the dining room were both empty, chairs pushed in under tables, like storeroom displays. Hazel beckoned Ray toward the bottom of the stairs.

"I hear something," he said. He stood on the bottom step and listened with a strained look. "Can you hear that?"

"I don't know what you're hearing."

"It's a hissing sound."

He snapped on his flashlight and began to climb the stairs. She followed behind and at the landing she heard the sound as well. It was coming from a room at the end of the hallway, behind a closed door.

"Do you smell gas?" she asked.

"No."

"We should be careful, Ray, I don't like this."

"Look," he said, shining a hard circle of light onto the hallway runner. It picked out a crimson streak. "What's that?"

On her knees, she looked at it closely. "I don't think it's blood. It could be an old stain. It could be a flick of paint."

He picked out a couple more of these maroon-coloured streaks as they crept to the door at the end of the hallway. Hazel's chest tightened. It was definitely a hiss, as if someone was slowly letting the air out of a big balloon. Ray paused at the door and leaned in to listen. "Mrs. Eisen? Are you in there?" Hazel came up beside him and rapped the door lightly.

The hissing got louder. Was it a spraying sound? A white-noise machine? A voice choked with terror said, "Why are you here?" From within, a rough, low moan began to rise.

They both took their safeties off and stepped back from the door. "Honey? It's Hazel Micallef. Are you in there?" Now there was the sound of a struggle and items being banged around, and it resolved into a muffled voice shouting, "Hey! Get out! *Get out of here!*"

Ray shouldered the door open, and Hazel came in behind him with her gun drawn and her light slashing across the darkened space. The beam fell on a bed alive with movement, a human form thrashing in the grip of a pale white serpent. Under the human shrieks, the hissing was louder and Hazel struggled to keep her beam on the forms wriggling in the bed. Then Ray found the light switch.

Honey Eisen was half off the bed, screeching and hollering and kicking her legs in the sheets. The serpent was a medical hose attached at one end to a breathing machine and, at the other, to Honey Eisen's face. She righted herself and stood before them and Hazel was reminded of the monster in the Alien movies. Eisen tore the mask off. "GOOD fucking SWEET baby Jesus! What the hell are you doing in my house?"

] 18 [

Hazel goggled at the scene in front of her. Mrs. Eisen slept in only a nightshirt and as she shook her arms at the two of them, she flashed them her black and grey bush repeatedly. "Mrs. Eisen," Hazel pleaded. "We're really so sorry – it's just we didn't expect to find someone sleeping and there was this noise –"

"What business is it of *yours*, missy, when I go to bed?" She turned on Ray, her face rigid in anger. "This is a lady's personal bedroom, asshole. You want to see my tits too? Huh?"

"Oh," said Ray. "I'm so sorry. No. Um, Detective Inspector Mic –"

"*Get out!*" the woman screamed. "How did you *get* in here, anyway?"

"Your door was open," said Ray, paralyzed.

"And you just *walked* in! Into a private home. You know

what? You give me a heart attack, and you'll both be breaking rocks somewhere!"

"We're very sorry," Ray stammered, backing out of the bedroom. He took Hazel by her arm to pull her out as well, but she stood her ground.

"*Look*," she said. Her tone of voice silenced both her CO and the thin woman in the nightshirt. She pointed at the east-facing window in the bedroom. There was a second OPS cruiser parked behind her own now. Hazel strode back into the hall.

"Where are you going now?" shouted Honey Eisen. "Off to terrorize babies and kittens?"

Ray followed her into the hall. "Hazel?"

"I thought we were leaving. We've given our apologies — and again, Mrs. Eisen, our deepest apologies for disturbing you while we were in the process of ensuring you hadn't been murdered by the same person who killed the Fremonts and now Brendan Givens — and we should go."

Ray stammered his objections while Honey Eisen pursued them down the stained runner. "I thought I was about to be raped!"

"Again, very sorry!" said Hazel from the bottom of the stairs. Ray took the remaining steps two at a time and got to the front door before Hazel was through it. But then she came to a sudden stop in the doorway. Ray almost ran into her back.

"Oh, fucking hell," she said. He looked over her shoulder. On the other side of the road there was a man leaning against her cruiser. It was Chip Willan.

"I'm going to guess this isn't a coincidence," Willan said. He offered Ray his hand. The way Willan offered a hand, you weren't going to refuse it. He thrust it at you like a dagger. "You two playing around with radio frequencies?"

"We were actually down here on Superintendent Scott's recognizance," Ray lied. Hazel felt briefly proud of him.

"Is *that* how we meet here at Tournament Acres?" he said to Ray with a smile. "I thought you'd stood down." Willan bent away to look down the street. "Who's in trouble?"

Hazel watched the two men carefully. She'd rarely seen them together, and to judge by the tension, they were either at loggerheads or they were trying not to say something in front of her.

"How did you end up here?" Hazel asked.

Willan pretended to notice her for the first time. "Well, I'm liaising with the local commander. Making sure they have everything they need."

"They're the RCMP, sir. And the local commander is a superintendent. They already have everything, so I'm not sure why they need your assistance, sir."

He squared himself to her. "They asked for it. Who cleared *you*?"

"She's here on my recognizance," said Ray.

"And you are on Scott's?"

"Actually, your grandmother cleared us," said Hazel. Both men looked at her blankly. "Page, right? Grammy Page?"

"What the hell are you talking about?" Ray asked.

"He's an investor in Tournament Acres," she said. "He's got money in this place under the name of his dead granny."

Willan smiled beatifically.

"What are you talking about?" Ray's voice was choked with alarm.

"Isn't that right, Chip? It's no skin off your knuckles if the RCMP keep the lid on what's happening here. What a stroke of fortune!" Ray put his hand on her arm but Hazel shook him off. "They have Renald, and there are two freshly dead bodies on this property and one in Toronto. Is that OK with you, Chip?"

It seemed to her that he wasn't even working on a reply; he was already serene with some foregone conclusion. When a predator looks upon helpless prey, it can take its time. Play with it a while before dealing the death blow.

Ray pulled her away. "Come on, Hazel."

Hazel remained silent until they were well up the 41, heading back to Port Dundas, and then she said: "Choose."

"Sorry?"

"Prove to me that your interests lie with the department and not with collecting whatever prize Chip Willan
has offered you."

He looked shocked. "Is that what you think of me? That
I came out of retirement to collect a prize?"

"What has he promised you when the new detachment
opens? CO of the amalgamated OPS Central? A salary
bump?"

"It hasn't been discussed yet. It's more than a year
away."

"Groundbreaking is Tuesday afternoon, though. It's
been decided already, all of it. And you've been told what
you'll get if you go along."

"Was that true?" he asked. "What you just accused
Willan of?"

"He's got a vested interest in that place. I bet Tournament Acres was just a dry run for whatever the Ascot
Group might have in mind for other fields in our county.
Who knows what kinds of future contracts Willan might
be looking at?"

"You disagree with him," he said. "That's all this is. You
have to let go of your conspiracy theories if you're going to
think straight."

"I still want you to choose."

"Between what and what?"

"Being a cop or administrating for Chip Willan, whether
you think you'll be rewarded for it or not."

His expression clouded. "I don't have to pass your tests anymore, Hazel. You have to pass mine."

As a peace offering, Ray Greene gave Hazel permission to find three of the living wards of Dublin Home. They had to be in Westmuir County, though, north of Dublin. He forbade her to investigate Willan, promising he would look into it himself. She didn't believe him, but now at least the investigation into Dublin Home was resurrected.

She returned to Mayfair first thing Friday morning. Putchkey held the front door open for her. He was agitated but doing his best to hide it. "Can I ask you something? Is there some kind of maniac on the loose?"

"What do you know about maniacs, Mr. Putchkey?"

"I hear a buncha people were killed over by Dublin."

"Who told you that?"

"I know people. Do you think we're safe here? Members of the public use this office, this is a public place. Do you think we should close up until he's found?"

"Will you buzz me in so I can go see the person I have an appointment with?"

"Oh, he's late. Said he wouldn't be in until lunchtime."

"Cutter?"

"Yeah. He left you an envelope." He went through the *Employee's Only* door and into the back. "So we're fine here then? Killer's probably moved on, right?"

"Can I have my envelope?"

He gave it to her. Cutter had left some names for her. Three, just as she'd wanted: Rex Clemson, Rene Eppert, and Hibiki Yoshida.

Mr. Rex Clemson lived a brief drive from the archives, in a trailer park. It was the lunch hour when she got there, and her stomach growled. She checked the address again and walked down the site to knock on number 5. The man who opened the door looked hard at Hazel through cloudy eyes. "I'm from the Port Dundas PD, sir. Detective Inspector Hazel Micallef. I'm wondering if I can talk to you about the Dublin Home for Boys."

The man in front of her was in his sixties, but he looked older. She showed him her badge, but his eyes were locked on her face. "What about it?"

"You were there in the late fifties for about eighteen months. Is that right?"

"Why are you interested?"

"May I come in?"

He shook his head. "Ask your questions from there."

"Did you know Eloy Miracle?"

"No."

"How about Valentijn Deasún? Or Charles Shearing?"

His face changed. Now he looked at her with suspicion. "How did you find me?"

"I'm a police detective, Mr. Clemson. I can do that."

"But how did you know to look for me? Why did my name come up?"

"May I come in?"

"No." She saw he wanted to close the door on her, but his eyes glowed with fearful curiosity. "Who sent you?" he asked.

"I wasn't sent by anyone. I was looking for survivors of a certain period at Dublin Home."

"And someone told you to come and see me?"

"Mr. Clemson, I can't tell you –"

"Leon Cutter," the man said. "Son of a bitch. Come in." He held the door open and she entered, not without trepidation. The cramped trailer stank of marijuana. Clemson stood aside and she stepped forward to find herself standing beside the bed.

"Why is Leon's name the secret code?"

"Leon is a righteous man. He told you to come see me?"

"Yes." He offered her a seat beside his muted television. He was watching *Animal Rescue* and out of the corner of her eye she could see a woman pulling a koi from a pool with her bare hands. A plate with a half-eaten sausage and slices of apple sat on the table in front of the couch. He went back around to his seat, moving with difficulty. She recognized his pain – he walked with a tilted head, an arm out at an odd angle to brace himself for every step because every step hurt. He walked like he was drunk. She guessed it was his L5 vertebra. "Who is Cutter to you?" she asked him.

"He was one of my dorm mates at Dublin Home. So was Valentijn."

She blinked a few times, quickly rearranging things in her head. "Leon Cutter was at Dublin Home?"

"That wasn't his name. But yes."

"And Eloy Miracle?"

"Yes," said Clemson, looking away. "Charlie Shearing, too. He was a Blackfoot Indian. He wasn't even from Ontario. But they took him anyway."

"Took him?"

"The Dublin Home for Boys. Last stop on a tour of hell if no one ever thought you a grand addition to their household. May I?" He held up a joint. She told him to go ahead. He lit it. "Too ugly, too stupid, too strong. There were a lot of reasons a boy ended up at Dublin Home, and just as many for why he might never leave it. I wasn't there long when Charlie disappeared. They told us he'd gone home. But no one would pick up a new family member in the middle of the night."

"So what happened to him?"

Clemson lay the joint down on a metal jar lid and speared the sausage with the tip of a knife. He bit a chunk off. "I heard things. The older boys told stories. One of them told me Charlie had struck an orderly, and a nurse came and gave him an injection and they took him away. The boy told me Charlie came back with a sort of comical look in his eye, like he'd been somewhere fun.

"And he was a smart boy. Charlie knew how to draw and write his own comics. And he could do a handstand walk across the room. Sometimes he defended the smaller boys, but at other times he was just as bad as any of the monsters who were in there. He must've gone too far."

"Who took him in the night, Mr. Clemson?"

"I don't know. I didn't even know he was gone until the next day." His attention returned to the television and he winced at something. Hazel looked at the screen: a woman was holding a purple starfish with two of its legs missing.

"They grow back," she said. "Do you mind?" Clemson gave her his attention again. "What about Deasún? Or Ronald Morristown?"

"I didn't know a Morristown. I knew Valentijn. He and Lionel . . ."

"Lionel?"

"Leon. Valentijn and Lionel and me. A couple other boys. We stuck together. Valentijn was tall and strong, but he was an imbecile. If he got upset he would pound his own head with his fists and the orderlies would come running. They beat him to stop him. We took to protecting Valentijn because he was more helpless than even we were.

"Then one night, they came for him. I was in my bed with my eyes shut tight and I listened to footsteps come down the middle of the room between the beds. Normally, the dormitories at night were full of sounds – squeaking beds and coughs and sniffles. But that night, it was silent. I lay still, every boy in the room lay still. And then there was a little movement, something shuffling. Footsteps came back through the room. I opened one eye just a bit in time to see Valentijn's bare feet bobbing in the air as someone carried him past my bed." He put his fingertip on an apple slice and pinched it off the edge of his plate. "You shouldn't take my word for anything," he said. "It was a long time ago. A lot of water under the bridge. I can't even remember his face."

"Did Leon . . . Lionel see this as well?"

"After you'd been at Dublin Home long enough, you didn't have to see anything in order to know what was going on," he said. "More or less everyone knew. And knowing meant you could be next. Our survival depended upon our silence. I don't even know if it's safe to talk now."

"What is Leon up to?"

"He promised to find out who took our friends."

] 19 [

1957

Evan Micallef's Christmas buying trip was his most important of the year. It was when he purchased most of his stock for the following year, and he was charged with the sacred duty of buying the gifts Santa was bringing his children. Alan still believed in Santa. But Hazel had known by the age of eight that there was something fishy about the whole thing. Her dad had fallen through to the hip fixing the roof; there was no way reindeer could land on it.

He timed his annual trip carefully, scanning the advertisements in the *Toronto Telegram* every day starting the second week in December, waiting for the right moment. The moment came when the smaller department stores and specialty shops finally crumbled under the pressure of Eaton's and started advertising desperately deep discounts.

Prices were especially low in the stores of the Ward, where the prices were low to begin with. Everyone undercut. For Micallef's, it was the best opportunity all year to stock up on things that never went out of style: underwear and scarves at sixty per cent off, nightshirts in every colour for half a song, trenchcoats, and ladies' gloves. One Christmas he'd bought a huge lot of three-for-one, gold-plated cuff-links, which it took him seven years to sell out. For the family, he bought a year's worth of soap, sugar, and batteries at the same time.

Hazel had been asking to come on his Toronto trips since she was eleven, but last year was the first time her father had agreed to let her join him. She'd been to the city before, but all she could remember of it were the crowds of people going in every direction at Yonge and Bloor, the rattling of the streetcars, and traffic everywhere. Cars as big as boats lined up at stoplights. At night it had seemed like a dream or a colour movie. When she went down with him that first time, she was still struck by the number of people and the impression the city gave her of ceaseless industry. She made sure to be useful to her father, ferrying things to the car and watching for meter maids. She liked being alone with him and asking him questions: *What would happen if there was a flood in Port Dundas? What would they do? How did you meet Mom?*

She listened in on her father's deals. Because he was a soft-spoken man, people had to stand close to hear.

Occasionally he would have cause to touch them on the arm or shoulder. He made friends easily and he was likeable, unlike her mother who could get angry and was at times sarcastic. Her father was soft but he was direct. He'd say, "Ivan, I don't negotiate, I just buy if the price is right. I'll pay you a hundred and fifteen dollars for all the pants and last summer's blouses." They might protest that the merchandise was already at wholesale prices, but he dealt with his suppliers laughingly. "I must be crazy offering over a hundred! Everyone in Port Dundas gets the Eaton's catalogue. I can't charge a lot more than I'm paying. I'll make it a hundred and twenty-five." He'd take the money out and start counting. "Goodness knows I have half of what I bought last year *still* in inventory!" Ivan or Mr. Wing or Mrs. Ferguson would take the money. Later, Hazel asked him if anyone ever walked away from one of his offers.

"Sure," he said. "A good businessman knows when to turn down a deal. I respect someone who won't accept my offer."

"What do you think of the people who accept them?"

"I thank the lord that they exist. Or I might have to stock at Eaton's wholesale prices."

He put his purchases in overstock and brought them out as he needed them. Hazel's mother used to joke that he was the Roebuck of Port Dundas. If it made him mad, she'd pinch his face and coo, "No-oo darling, you're Sears. Everyone knows you're Sears."

This year, they didn't go to the city until the twenty-fourth, in part because the weather had turned nasty around the fifteenth and the roads were unsafe. It was dark when they left Port Dundas at 6:00 a.m. on Christmas Eve, and the sky was grey and flat when they got to the city at 9:00 a.m. It was as if the sun hadn't come up at all. It was so cold that the streetcars seemed to grind along on stone rails, screeching. Her father beat his hands together when they got out of the car. He gave her a nickel for the meter and it swallowed the coin with a rattle and a clunk.

They'd been warned to be back on the road by lunch-time so as not to be late for when their guests arrived. Three of the four grandparents were coming for Christmas dinner, and "How many more Christmases are we all going to be together?" her mother had asked him, rhetorically, at the door.

"Your mother will outlive us all," he'd replied.

Queen Street West radiated both opportunity and danger to Hazel. Kids a lot younger than she were selling newspapers and cigars on the street; others were just on their own doing who knew what. Some of them weren't properly dressed for the cold. Back home, when someone fell on hard times their neighbours helped them out.

They went into a store called Cardinal's, below Queen on Bay Street. Although Cardinal's was only three hundred metres south of the Ward, you could feel none of its bustle and noise. South of Queen Street, life was orderly and everyone spoke English, but north of it, you were in another world.

The man behind the counter greeted her father warmly. "I thought you weren't coming to rob me blind this year!"

"Mr. Cardinal, I still have thirty fedoras. No one wanted fedoras in 1957."

"They'll probably want them again in 1960," said Mr. Cardinal, still clasping her father's hand. "You'll make a killing."

"What can I take off your hands, Sam? Undershirts?"

"I have a double order of bootblack, you know. Mrs. Cardinal can't keep a thing straight. I can give you a case for under wholesale and I also have more of the good denim overalls you took last year. And one of my customers brought me a bottle of rye, so you might as well fortify yourself before you head out into the cold again."

"Sweetheart, Mr. Cardinal and I are going to chew the fat for a while. You must be hungry." He took a dollar out of his billfold.

"Bowles Lunch at the corner has a fine breakfast special: two eggs, peameal bacon and sausage, two flapjacks, a rack of toast, imported butter, preserves, and a pot of tea, all for sixty cents," said Cardinal. "You won't need to eat again until the ham is carved!"

She took the dollar.

"Maybe I'll fit in my visit to Mr. Yoon up Elizabeth Street

while you're gone, sweetheart. Will you meet me back at the car at noon?"

She agreed she would. Last year he hadn't allowed her to explore on her own.

"D'you hear?" asked Mr. Cardinal. "They're going to raze Chinatown. All the way to Dundas, they say. They're going to build a new city hall."

"You don't say. Well, it is a tip in there, isn't it?"

"But where will all the people go?" Hazel asked.

They appeared to have forgotten she was still in the store.

"Halfa them Chinese already moved west. To Spadina with the Hebrews," said Mr. Cardinal. "There's two Chinatowns now, but it can't get any worse for the ones who have to stay in this one while they tear it down around their ears. Even half empty, it's a pestilence. Don't you go on up there without your father, you hear?"

"I won't," she assured them. The doorbell dingled when she stepped back out into the cold weather. A species of arctic wind roared along the sidewalk, picking up speed, accelerating at times from gust to blast. She went up to Bowles and looked in. The room beyond the steamy window was crowded with businessmen finishing their breakfasts. A layer of pipe smoke hung under the ceiling and twisted in the fans. Since arriving in Toronto, she'd had one thing in mind and it wasn't eggs and flapjacks. She turned her back on Bowles Lunch and hesitated before crossing Bay

Street. Then she walked west along Queen, away from the restaurant. She stood at the corner of Queen and Chestnut. Her father had spoken of Toronto's Ward many times. He had friends in the Ward, other merchants, people who were "struggling to make it in a new place," her father said. It was a place of gathering, where people freshly arrived, speaking neither much English nor any of the other languages they would encounter in the Ward, found themselves a spot to sleep in ramshackle rooms behind crowded shops. Her mother talked of the Ward as a place where everyone was an orphan.

In her purse, Hazel carried a small pad of paper, a sharpened pencil, and two newspaper clippings. In the first one, from the *Westmuir Record*, Carol Lim's photograph was printed below the headline: LOCAL GIRL GOES MISSING. Dated Monday, October 28, 1957. The second one was a clipping from the *Toronto Telegram*, dated December 12, less than two weeks ago. It had picked up the Toronto angle, and featured two clear pictures of Carol. It asked its readers in "Greater Chinatown" to keep an eye out for the girl. This presumed the *Telegram* had readers in Greater Chinatown. The reporters from the *Telegram* had since been silent on the story. She wondered if they'd been kind and thoughtful in their approach. Or if maybe it was an assignment just like any other. Eight inches of type. They had all of Toronto to choose from, what did they care what happened to a girl from some other town? No one had yet treated Carol as anything more than a story. Somehow there were stories but there weren't any facts.

Hazel crossed Queen Street and walked up Chestnut, into the Ward.

Chestnut Street was not as crowded as Mr. Cardinal had said it would be. There were some closed shops, but the sidewalks in front of the boarded-up windows were alive with trade. A tarp, tied down tightly against the wind, protected one man's wares – as well as him – from falling icicles. The few things he had for sale were arranged on crates and wooden boxes. Onions, carrots whose leaves were so frozen that they had gone a deep, translucent green, and a few pieces of salt back pork. The man had a big yellowy face and blue eyes. Her instinct was not to talk to any men if possible.

She went up to Louisa Street and turned right. Some of the Chinese restaurants that looked like they had been there forever were open. Various cooked pig and duck parts hung in the windows. None of the signs were in English. She went into the most brightly lit one first. It was halfway between breakfast and lunch, and the booths were empty, but there were a number of old men sitting at the counter. "Excuse me," she said. "Hello." Silence. "Can I show you a photograph?" She approached the nearest man. He waited patiently for her to come closer. "This girl. Carol Lim," she said. "Do you know her?"

He looked at the picture and back at her. He said something and shrugged. None of the others, nor the man behind the counter, seemed eager to look at what she was showing around.

"My name is Hazel. Carol is someone I know. Her parents think she might have run away to Toronto. Her name is Carol Lim."

One of the men behind the counter waved the back of his hand at her. "You go please," he said.

The command to leave made her want to try harder. She put a photograph on the bar in front of the man who'd spoken. "I don't mean to be rude. This is important. She's been missing for two months, and someone I know has been falsely accused –"

"Wrong place."

She left the restaurant and crossed the street. There were a few more, mostly empty restaurants on that side and she was met with much the same response in them. The green lights running up the beacon on top of the Canada Life Building showed it was warming up, although two or three degrees would do little good in this cold.

She looked at her watch. It was not yet ten-thirty in the morning. The Ward was a ghost town of empty storefronts with signs in a dozen languages, the words in peeling paint. Behind her there was a huge field of rubble where the houses had already been torn down. She could go to the new Chinatown and show Carol's picture there and be back within the hour.

She wrote her father a note and ran back to Bay Street to stick it under his wiper. It read: *Went to find something special for Alan. Back before 12:00. H.*

] 20 [

Hazel walked back through the Ward on Elizabeth Street. The street itself still existed, but on either side, both the businesses and homes were in ruins. Here and there, like a remaining tooth in a mouth, there would be a house amidst the mess of broken stone and brick. All the trees had been cut down and their naked stumps levered out of the ground, rocks still clenched in their gnarled roots.

Farther up, she found the kiosk of an abandoned gas station. She went up to it and pushed its door open. Inside there was a banged-up cash register with an empty drawer hanging out. *The victim was found in the kiosk with his tongue hanging out.* A map of the city stapled to the wall confirmed that she was going the right direction to get to the new Chinatown at Dundas and Spadina.

When she came to Dundas Street, she saw people once more. She walked over to Spadina Avenue and went north in the bustle. On both sides of the avenue the signs were either in Hebrew or Chinese. There were barely any in English.

There was nothing to do but begin with the first place where there wouldn't be too many people. She didn't want to create a scene. She went into a Chinese bookstore. Coloured lanterns hanging from the awning spun in the wind. There were hundreds of books on the walls of the tiny shop. Everything was in Chinese. A young woman approached her. "I'm sorry, do you speak English?"

"I speak a little."

"Will you look at a picture?" she asked. She held out the clippings, as if to show her credentials. The young woman allowed her to spread the pages out on the glass counter-top. "Do you know this girl?"

"No," the woman said right away.

"Can you look at all the pictures? There are three of them. Maybe one of them looks more like her."

The woman took her time and looked closely at the images of Carol Lim. She adjusted her glasses once and looked closer, focusing. "No," she said once more. "Thank you."

"Is there a place where young people go to have fun? Maybe somewhere they could drink?"

"You want to have a drink?"

"No. I wonder if there's a place that would let *this* girl have a drink?" She tapped Carol's smiling face.

"I don't drink, so I don't know."

Hazel thanked her and left. There had been a pleasant if unidentifiable smell in the shop. Smoke and flowers.

She got nowhere in the next three stores. Some of the shopkeepers looked at her with frank distrust. There was a Jewish butcher next and then more restaurants. A store selling televisions, all its signs in Chinese. Was there anything in Chinese to watch on television?

She crossed Spadina and entered Kensington Market. It stretched away behind the storefronts on the west side of Spadina. She'd heard about the market from the grade thirteens – one of the classes had made a field trip. "Never seen so many fish and chickens and goats and pigs all in one place," Andrew had told her. He hadn't told her it stank like a barnyard.

She walked deeper into the market and the sounds of the city began to diminish. They were replaced with clucking and snorting, and voices calling out in different tongues. A small, fragile-looking truck on three wheels ambled by and turned into an alley. The market smelled of meat and smoke and rot and tobacco. She spied a tower of egg trays in a store window, a pile maybe three feet high, thirty eggs a layer.

The smell of roasting meat drew her to the kosher butcher. The Chinese displayed ducks, the Jews chickens. She could get a quarter roasted chicken in a paper bag for sixty-five cents. Next door was a used bookshop with English titles in a bin on the sidewalk and in the windows. She went inside. A man wearing a wool vest and smoking a short pipe greeted her. "Can I help you find something?" he asked.

"Actually, I'm looking for someone, but there aren't a lot of people around here who speak English."

"Why are you looking for someone to talk English with?"

She fumbled the clippings out of her coat pocket. The folds were starting to crease and fray. He took them from her and began reading. "Uh-huh. You looking for this girl?"

"I am, sir. Her name is Carol Lim."

"She's not from Toronto I'm guessing."

"She said she knew people here. Some people think she had a boyfriend."

"You got a name for that boyfriend?"

"Landers. That's his last name. But the police already spoke to him. He says he hasn't seen her."

"Did you go pay him a visit yourself?"

"No. I don't know where he lives."

The man scratched his beard with all five fingers of one hand. "Ha," he said, thoughtfully. His eyes were big behind his glasses. He walked away from her, puffing his pipe, and went down one of the rows of shelves. "You're smart," he called over his shoulder. "You shouldn't poke your nose in other people's private doings. That's how people get hurt. Ah, here it is."

"Listen, it's OK," she said, getting nervous. "You wouldn't know her and I have to get back to —"

"I ask myself: what would Marlowe do?" He emerged from the row with a small paperback in his fat hand and he laid the book down on the counter. Hazel was already folding up the newspaper clippings and putting them away. "What's your hurry, darling?" he said. "My name's Izzy."

"Hi. I'm . . . I'm Gloria."

"Hello *Gloria*. Do you read much?"

"I do. I like a lot of authors."

"Like who? Do you like Raymond Chandler?"

"I don't know him."

"Detective writer. What about Jim Thompson, ever heard of him?"

"I'm sorry, I haven't."

"What would Jim Thompson do?"

Behind her, Hazel heard a door opening. She looked over her shoulder. It was an old woman with a tray of coffee and biscuits. "Sorry Izzy, I can come back."

"That's good, Ma." She smiled and Hazel's palms went icy. His mother backed away and closed the door behind her. "I know what Jim Thompson would do," he said. "Someone would die and then someone *eltz* would die. Probably both sharp-looking chicks playing angles, had it coming. Sound like your scene?"

"No," she said quietly.

"Have a cookie." He pushed the plate toward her. "Then Chandler. More scenes during the daytime, won't make you as jumpy." He put his chin on his hand in a mockery of thinking. He squeezed his eyes shut. "Hmm," he said, and: "Let's see, let's see." She thought of making a run for it. "Marlowe knows from living near Chinatown that Chinese people don't call each other Carol and Joe. They got a different way of saying their names to each other."

She knew that was true. Carol had told Hazel her birth name. "Shen Yu," she said.

"Lim Shen Yu then. Marlowe'd go out with the real name, see if anyone twitches, you know what I mean? You tried grass yet, sweetheart?"

"No. But if I wanted to get a drink? Could someone my age get a drink in this neighbourhood?"

"I got a jugga homemade vodka upstairs. You want a schnapps?"

"No, thank you . . . Izzy. I appreciate your help."

"Not enough to have a drink with me, I see."

"Sir, I'm only fourteen."

"Once you come a woman, you're a woman, sweetheart. I like you, have a schnapps with me." He leaned against the counter, his fingers laced over his belly. "I'm not so old. How old do you think I am?"

She began to calculate what she might have to do. Her mother had never minced words: if any "boy" tried to touch her, she was to shriek, and if that didn't work, she was to slam her knee into his man parts. That always worked.

The door jingled and a customer came in. Immediately, Izzy resumed a professional affectation and smiled at his customer. "Hello," he said, and to Hazel he whispered, "Stick around."

She didn't. She ran out the door clutching her papers. If that was what the English-speakers were like, then she wanted no more of their assistance. She walked deeper into the market, looking for a girl her age or younger. Carol's English had been perfect, and her parents knew more than they let on. But no one here wanted to talk. After her fourth rebuff, she turned up Augusta Street and walked along the middle of the sidewalk holding the clearest photo out for people to look at.

"Do you recognize this girl? Carol Lim, from Port Dundas, Ontario. Shen Yu Lim. Have you seen her, ma'am? She disappeared on October twenty-sixth." In a store, she held the picture up before a startled crowd of spice-shoppers. "You may know her as Shen Yu Lim." Hazel wasn't sure if the silence she faced was friendly or menacing. She wasn't sure if anyone in the room was breathing, and then she realized she wasn't either. She exhaled. They exhaled. "I'm sorry if you don't understand me."

"I know her," came a voice near the back of the room, and instantly the other women in the shop moved toward the walls, like line dancers, and a girl came forward between them. She was eating something with pits in it and spitting into her hand. "How do you know her?"

"She ran away from home."

"Ah-ha. Is she your father's whore?"

Hazel was struck dumb a moment. "Carol — Shen Yu — lives in my town, in Port Dundas. She's missing. Have you really seen her?"

Hazel saw the girl — she was about her age — wasn't eating a piece of fruit. It was a fish head with gelatin stuck to it. She was spitting bones into her hand. "Why should I tell you anything? Who are you, anyway?"

"My name is Hazel. I'm visiting . . . I came here to find Carol."

"Lim Shen Yu."

"Is that how you say it?"

"Yes. Hazel. Do you think Shen Yu wants to be found if she is so hard to find? She must have her reasons."

"But she's safe?"

"Are you Carol's chum or her enemy? How do I know?"

"Why would her enemy be concerned about her?"

"Maybe you are pretending."

"I'm not."

The girl shrugged. "The person who cannot be trusted will never say so. What happens if you ask a liar if he is a liar?"

"He'll say no."

"And if you ask a truthful person? He will also say no."

"And they will both answer yes if asked if they're telling the truth." There was some snickering in the room. Apparently the girl was not the only one who understood what she was saying. "Look. Could you pass a message on to her?"

The girl considered for a long moment. "Maybe. What do you want to say?"

"That her parents are frightened for her and hope that she'll come home."

"That is a nice message. But still, I don't know who you are."

Hazel didn't really think about it. She just knew she had to do something to make this girl see her in a different light. She took the fish head out of her hand. One side was mostly eaten, but when she turned it over there was still a lot of meat. A stupid fish wasn't going to intimidate her. She plucked the shrivelled, cloudy eye out of its socket and put it into her mouth. She swallowed it, keeping eye contact with the girl the whole time. She handed the head back.

The girl smiled, and Hazel felt like she'd guessed something correctly. "The most delicate part is always for the welcome stranger. Why don't you come back in two hours? Then I might have something for you."

"Really?" She looked at her watch. "I don't have two hours. Could you make it one hour? I could come back in one hour."

"Is this important to you or not?"

"It is, but I'm here with my father and he says we have to get on the road by noon. It's Christmas Eve."

"I know it's Christmas Eve." The girl studied her. Hazel burped softly into her hand. "OK," the girl said. "Come back in one hour."

———

Hazel followed her nose north. She was going to have to wash down the fishy hors d'oeuvre somehow and there was a very appealing smell borne on the wind. She took out the dollar bill her father had given her and checked her watch. It was 11:00. She could kill an hour eating lunch somewhere. At the top of Augusta, close to College Street, she picked up the scent again. She wasn't sure what it was, but it made her think of someone's home. The food your granny makes. It turned out to be a delicatessen called Litwin's. She rode her nose into its steamy interior and sat down at the white countertop. The lunch rush hadn't begun yet, and she was the only kid in the place as well as the only girl. Behind the counter, a bunch of men stared at her. One came forward. "Kinna help you?"

"Are you serving lunch yet?"

He stepped out of her line of vision so she could see a man lifting a huge, wobbling hunk of meat out of a steam compartment. The meat was almost black on the outside. About six more hunks lay on a wooden chopping block, vapour wafting off them. "That appeal to you? Pastrami, corned beef, baby beef? I got smoke meat too, sliced turkey, kishka —"

"What is kishka?"

The man, whose nametag identified him as Max, flipped a steel lid and filled a ladle to show her. It looked like a pale-yellow sausage with cut-off ends. "You know what derma is, kid?"

"No," she said.

"Then you don't want kishka. Siddown. I'll make you your first corned beef sandwich, from the looks of it. You want it regular?"

"Regular?"

"Mustard. Yella mustard."

"How much is it?"

"Fitty cents a quarter pounda meat, seventy you want a halfa pound."

She put her dollar on the counter. "Half a pound, please. And a Coke."

Less than a minute later Max put down two towering halves of a sandwich on a chipped, white plate, each half held together by a single toothpick. She could see the scent of the sandwich curling up from the brilliant red meat. A bulging pickle cut into four spears lay beside it and there was a small paper cup of creamy potato salad.

"You gonna ask it to marry?" Max asked.

She dug in. The first couple of bites, her eyes rolled up. Slowly, Litwin's lunch crowd showed up. Workmen sat at the counter on either side of her, and the tables filled with men and women out from their offices for an early lunch. She ate slowly, keeping her eye on the Coca-Cola clock behind the slicers. When she was done, Max dropped a little plate with a piece of cheesecake drizzled with cherry sauce in front of her. "On the house," he said, "seeing you don't know your elbow from a pickle."

She couldn't imagine how she was going to eat a hunk of cheesecake after that sandwich, but it turned out to be easy.

At the end, she left the whole dollar on the change tray. A twenty-cent tip. Extravagant, her mother would have called it.

Out in the street, she checked her watch again. It was 11:48. She was in good time to see the girl, but she was going to be late for her father. She hightailed it back down Augusta to the spice shop. When she went in, she didn't see the girl she'd spoken to. Different women were going about their varied business, oblivious to her, and she felt too shy to talk again and draw attention to herself. She walked down one of the aisles, pretending to shop for something. There were dried items in bins that she'd never seen before. Withered, speckled, black, dusty: none of them looked like something you'd eat, but the customers were filling paper bags with them.

She wandered aimlessly in the shop for five minutes and began to lose faith that the girl would show. Then she felt a hand on her shoulder and almost left her shoes. "Hello. You are late."

"I was on time!"

"Where? Where were you on time?"

"It doesn't matter," Hazel said. "I'm sorry. Did you find her, though? Is she here?"

The girl produced a small paper scroll tied with string. "She sends a note to her beloved parents, to calm their souls."

"Oh, that is wonderful!" Hazel cried. "And she's well? You saw her?"

The girl slid the string off and unrolled the paper. There were Chinese characters in columns on the page. "Lim Shen Yu writes: *Beloved Mother and Father. Forgive me for leaving so suddenly. I am a woman now and must seek my own fortune. When I am married, I will bring my husband to you and you will see that I have become a wife and mother, just as you have wished for me. Forgive me my strong-headedness, and do not upset yourselves over my absence. We shall meet again.*"

She tied the note up with the string and gave it to Hazel.

"Thank you very much. Honestly, thank you. Please tell her I'm looking forward to seeing her again."

The girl suddenly clamped her fingers around Hazel's wrist. Her skin prickled just as it had in the bookshop and she tried to wrest her arm free.

"Excuse me?" the girl said with a snarl. "You think everything is cheap or free in Chinatown? Maybe I just like doing favours for white ghosts like you?"

"I didn't know . . . I don't have any money. But I can send you some."

The girl bent Hazel's hand back and she stumbled and cried out. "Hey, let go of me!"

Now everyone in the shop was looking at her again. "Longines," the girl said. "Nice watch."

"It was a gift from my grandmother," Hazel said. But she stopped resisting. She would have to explain it later, or use her own money to replace it before anyone noticed it was missing. She let the girl unstrap the watch from her wrist and drop it into a pocket.

She released Hazel from her grip. "Have a nice day. OK?"

Hazel backed out of the store, enraged and frightened to about the same degree. The girl just stared at her.

Hazel ran as fast as she could out of the market and back to Spadina Avenue. The last time she'd looked, her watch had shown 12:03. She ran toward Queen Street, her head down and her lungs aching. When she got to the corner, there was still at least a kilometre to go, but there was an eastbound streetcar waiting at the light with all its doors open. She snuck up the back steps and hid herself among the other riders. Four minutes later, the conductor called Chestnut Street. She didn't want her father to see her coming from the west, so she waited until the streetcar got to Yonge. She got off and waited a moment on the sidewalk. Then she strode quickly, but calmly, back to Bay and turned left. She saw her father approaching the car from the south. "Ah," he said when they arrived at the 1955 Packard at the same time. "Reliable as Old Faithful, I see." He was lugging a number of parcels with him, all of them tied with jute string.

"Let me help you." She took them from him one by one and put them down on the sidewalk. He unlocked the trunk, and she helped him load everything in.

"You had a good lunch I trust. Any change?"

"Actually, no," she said. "I used it all."

He clasped her on the shoulder. "It was your dollar to spend anyway. Come on, or we'll be late for Mother."

She got into the car and they pulled out into traffic. She felt in her pocket for her own little string-wrapped parcel, the one with Carol Lim's voice rolled up in it, and when her fingers brushed over it, she closed them and held it tightly in her palm.

] 21 [

Friday, October 26, afternoon

Clearly, Leon – Lionel – Cutter had worked his last day at
the Westmuir County Archives and Licensing Centre.

Mayfair OPS could not find him or his car at the archives
or at his home address. Instead, they found someone else at
that address, someone with no connection at all to Cutter
or the case. They went back to the archives and discovered
that entire card catalogues and their corresponding files
had been removed. DC Torrance called Hazel on her cell
and reported what they knew. "Want an APB?" she asked.

"Do you think there's any point? He's planned this out
pretty meticulously. I mean, I doubt he's driving anything
he actually owns."

"We have two licence plates registered to him," Torrance
said. "We might as well cover all our bases." Hazel agreed

and thanked Torrance for her help. Mayfair had already sent a picture of him out to every PD in Ontario.

Hazel hoped Claude Maracle's test result would come in today – she needed the link and it would be good to have it before the weekend began. It felt like the case was beginning to consolidate. They had uncovered only six names in the archives, but the DNA test results she'd glanced at yesterday afternoon had proved the existence of sixteen victims. All twelve to eighteen years of age. Most of the evidence had been scoured by fire – it was impossible to know how the boys had died. But some fragments of their scorched bones had survived, despite the attempt to obliterate all proof that they'd ever walked the earth.

There had to be more witnesses. The people Cutter was sending her to were three men out of many who must have heard the whispers or had even seen something. These three were perhaps the ones he knew best. Clemson had given her the impression they were friends; that Cutter had promised him something. But maybe the remaining witnesses were dead or had left the province. Or changed their names, like Claude Maracle had.

Caplin was the last town on the northern shore of Lake Gannon, thirty kilometres from Port Dundas. It was a twenty-minute drive along the scenic end of Highway 117, where the speed limit was, ridiculously, thirty kilometres an hour. A woman answered the door – the wife, Hazel presumed. She presented her credentials. Looking them over, the woman said, "Oh, he doesn't like to talk about those years. He doesn't have much good to say about Dublin Home when he does."

"It wouldn't take very long."

"He's in a wheelchair, Detective."

Hazel tried to see around Mrs. Eppert, but she reacted by moving her hips to block her view. "What if you tell him Leon Cutter sent me? Maybe he'll talk to me then."

"Wait right there," she said, indicating a tile on the floor. She disappeared into the house and then there was silence. After a minute, she returned. "He's got five minutes, OK?"

She led Hazel into a spacious front hall. An empty chair lift was at the bottom of the stairs, ready to take someone up its track to the second floor. "He had an accident down on Beech Road five years ago," she said *sotto voce*. "Collided with a Canada Post van. He's not the same person. Rene? Sweetheart?" she called. "Can you meet me in the den?"

She beckoned Hazel down a hall. A man in a wheelchair navigated toward them using a little stick shift on the arm. His head was thrown back, as if he were about to catch a peanut in his mouth. "This is Detective Inspector Micallef, from the OPS."

"How do you do," said Rene Eppert. She'd expected him to speak with difficulty, but his voice was clear. She wasn't sure where to look. "Will this take long?"

"I don't think so."

"Coffee?" Mrs. Eppert offered, and they both said they'd have a cup. Her husband gestured to an open doorway, and Hazel went into the den and found a seat that wouldn't cause her to sink too much into the cushions. He parked across from her.

"How do you know Leon Cutter?" she asked him. "And what's his birth name, if you know it."

"Lionel Couture." He tried to lower his head a bit, but the best he could do was to lay it on his shoulder. "His bed was in the same dormitory as mine."

"And you were friends."

"I suppose."

"Why did he send me to talk to you?"

Eppert looked uncomfortable. "To let me know he's keeping his promise."

"To you?"

"Yes."

"And to Rex Clemson and Hibiki Yoshida?"

"I don't know either of those names."

"What about Claude Miracle?" His eyes jumped away. "You knew him. And Eloy?"

"Claude is alive?"

"You know Eloy is not?" He didn't answer. "You were a ward of the province of Ontario at the Dublin Home for Boys from 1951 to 1958."

"Yes."

"Where did you go after 1958?"

"I was eighteen. I was on my own." The coffee arrived. His mug had a lid and a bendy straw sticking out of it. "I got a job in Uxbridge. I met Helen." His wife put a warm, proprietary hand on his shoulder and fitted the coffee cup into a harness. He turned to suck.

"Did you stay in touch with any of the boys you knew there? Did you keep in contact with Cutter or anyone else?"

"I haven't spoken to Couture in almost fifty years. And no. Why would I want to know anyone from that time? If you've been looking into the history of that place, then you know what it was."

"What was it, Rene? In your own words."

"An abattoir."

Helen Eppert's left eye started to twitch. "Inspector, I don't want Rene to –"

"Do you remember the names of any other boys from back then?" Hazel asked.

"I remember a lot of them. Orman Vadum, Jimmy Tirana – Italian – a bunch of black kids and Indians, the Miracles, Sammy Rideout. Ronnie Morristown –"

"Charles Shearing?"

"Yes."

Hazel took a sip from the mug. The coffee was merely warm. She imagined this was the hottest it could be for him. "Do you know how Eloy died?"

"No. One morning he was gone."

"Did you hear or see anyone in the night?"

"No. I heard the bell and I closed my eyes and pretended to sleep."

"The night bell."

"At the back of the home. The front entrance had a buzzer, but the back door had a small brass bell over it. The door struck it when it was opened. It was a little jingle, very distinctive."

"But if you heard it, you knew that someone had come into the building. And you would be scared?"

"Yes."

"Who was it?"

"You didn't dare look. Maybe that was the reason he took someone. Because they looked at him."

She'd taken out her notebook, hoping he'd continue to talk freely. "Was there anyone at Dublin Home who frightened you? Among the staff?"

"All of the adults. You were never shown a moment's compassion in that place."

"How did Eloy die?"

Eppert took a deep breath, as if he was going to hiccup, and he moved his upper body to get upright. It threw his head back farther. "You had to keep your group small in that place. At one point in the . . . in the fifties, there were almost two hundred of us in Dublin Home."

"Do you know how any of the missing boys died, Rene?"

"He's told me some of the things that happened there,"

his wife offered, to speed things along. She was watching him with a worried, tender expression. "I've told him that a lot of people write their memoirs and get them published. It lets the public know the truth about something that's important."

"M-may-m-maybe I will some day," he assured her.

"Did you know any of the medical or nursing staff? Did you ever go see the nurse, or get sick? Kids must have gotten hurt from time to time." Hazel read from the papers in her hands. "What about Dr. Donald Rosen?" Eppert made a cancelling sound in his throat. "Frank Inman? Harald Groet? Frances Kelly? Nothing?"

Rene Eppert was making an effort to bring his eyes down. He pulled his skull forward, but his eyes stayed rolled up as if they were locked to some point in space. "I don't . . . I don't. Know." He swallowed hard. "Those names."

"Inman was at Dublin Home for over twenty years, Rene. You must've seen him at least once. What about Peter Lynch?"

"Idaknow."

"Dale Whitman?"

"No," he said, in a strangled voice.

His wife leapt up. "Oh my god!"

Eppert's left hand sprang open and he said "*Oh oh oh!*" like he was having a panic attack.

"He's seizing," Helen Eppert said, trying to hold his arms down.

"Oh, I have a nurse!" Eppert crooned. His irises swelled from pinpricks to nail heads.

"Is it Whitman?" Hazel asked him urgently.

His hand jammed on the joystick and the chair rumbled toward a wall. Helen pulled his hand off the stick and righted him. "I'm sorry Detective, but that's all for now I think."

"He's scared. Rene? They're all dead. No one can hurt you now." Eppert shook his head spastically. "Did you know Dale Whitman? Did you know Peter Lynch?"

Mrs. Eppert pushed her husband out of the room. "Please see yourself out —"

"He knows something! What do you know, Rene? Who was killing children at Dublin Home?"

Eppert's head ticced violently over his shoulder, a physical stammer that denied knowledge of what had brought on his terror and shut him down.

At the station house, Ray brought both Hazel and Fraser in for a debriefing. Wingate was overstaying his hours again, but he was not in uniform, and Hazel had him looking through name change records on a provincial database. If Cutter had been Couture, were the trio of names he'd given them authentic? Clemson, Eppert, Yoshida? Wingate confirmed that all three of them appeared in the Dublin Home records under the same names. Wingate asked her if he could sit in on her and Fraser's debriefing with the skip. She told him he couldn't.

Ray Greene agreed with both of their assessments of the case: Cutter wouldn't reappear until they'd gone through all the hoops, and that meant locating and interviewing Yoshida. Hazel had already tried the number for him she'd found, via Motor Vehicles. He wasn't home or he wasn't answering. If he was where he was supposed to be, someone was going to have to make the two-hour drive to Dunneview. They agreed Hazel would continue to call.

She briefed both of them on her interviews with Clemson and Eppert. "I'm going to look more closely at the medical and nursing staff. Someone who knew what was happening, but has never told. There's got to be somebody who can tell us about the other people who worked there."

"Are you concluding it was someone on staff at the home?" Ray asked.

"No. Not concluding. But my interview with Eppert ended with him literally seizing up at the mention of some of the doctors' names."

"Which ones?"

"Peter Lynch and Dale Whitman." They both wrote the names down. "I knew Dale Whitman. He was a GP in town, and his daughter and I were the same age. We went to school together."

"Do you think it could be him?" Fraser asked.

"He was a nice man. He was well respected in town, and he was a presence in the community. But I always did get a strange feeling in their house. It had cold, stone floors downstairs that I didn't like, and there was gas lighting all through the house. They lived there together, just the two of them. Gloria's mother died when she was nine. But could Whitman have killed children?"

"Well?" said Ray.

"Anyone is capable of murder," she said after a pause. "We know that better than most."

"Is he still alive? Or his daughter?"

"I don't know about either of them. I'll check. Gloria and I kept in touch by letter for a year or two after high school, then she went to Toronto for work. I think she tried modelling for a while. I don't know when we stopped talking, but I think it was mainly my idea."

"Would you rather someone else locate her?"

"No. I'll look her up," she said. "Her father is probably dead, though. He was in his forties when I last knew him."

"Maybe you could just call Cutter for the information," Fraser said.

"Haha," she replied, flatly. "I don't know if he's *that* far ahead of us. He might have gotten to this point – to thinking about medical staff. But I think Cutter wants proof."

Fraser scoffed. "Maybe he's forcing Renald to work the case inside a locked closet."

"Renald isn't a detective. Cutter left us all our detectives. He took Renald to force us to solve the crime."

"And then what?"

"Then justice?' She shrugged. "Listen to me. Cutter's known the shape of this case for decades. He needed us to start pulling on the threads. So now we're his puppets because one of our own is at risk. He calculated well."

"Oh shit," said Ray Greene, slapping the tabletop. "Maybe Cutter *has* been reading our minds. Renald's radio was found destroyed. But what if he got Renald to . . . ? Goddamn it." Greene picked up his phone. "Melanie? Ask MacTier if Melvin Renald has logged onto any of our servers since his disappearance. I want to hear back from you in sixty seconds." He hung up. "Fuck."

Silence fell on them and Hazel found herself staring at Ray's phone. Her eyes fixed and it began to blur and throb.

"Cutter could be in Quebec City by now," Fraser whispered.

"No. He's nearby," she said.

"How do you know that?"

She narrowed her eyes at him like he was some species of idiot. "Stop whispering," she whispered. "He's nearby because he wants to be ready when we find our man."

"Or woman," said Ray. "Maybe there was a crazy nurse in that place. Why does it have to be a man?"

"Sensitivity training has worked wonders for you," Hazel said as Ray's phone rang.

Greene spoke. "Yeah . . . Uh-huh . . . OK, thanks. I'll come out and talk to you in a couple of minutes." He hung up. "He's been logged on remotely since the night of his disappearance."

Fraser began to offer excuses right away for why no one had thought of it. "It couldn't have occurred to any of us that they were *using* Renald –"

"MacTier is going to log him off and change his password."

"You don't think that could put him in danger?" Hazel asked. "You don't want to make Mel unnecessary."

They all thought about that for a minute.

"We can get MacTier to redirect his logon to a dummy site and falsify its updates," Ray said. "And, just to be safe, we should all switch to another secure channel when we're discussing our movements. MacTier will find us a frequency. Do everything else on the regular channels."

"Should we feed some false information down those channels?" Fraser asked. "Maybe match it up to the bogus updates?"

Ray held up his hand: STOP. "MacTier will call you with the new channel. And Hazel?"

"Yes?"

"Send Wingate home."

ChemLab Forensic in Toronto had two more unnamed bodies for them based on their DNA testing of the bones.

This brought the total to eighteen victims. The Maracle DNA was still being run. By three in the afternoon, all the weekly reports were done. Eileen Bail had gone down to the cacophonous dispute involving the music school and explained to both parties the importance of getting along. Maybe so-and-so could do this, and so-and-so could do that, and everyone would be happy. She reported that both took her advice, but not without one more verbal lashing from each of them trying to get the last word. "Men," she said.

Yoshida didn't answer his phone.

Wingate got ready to leave, finally, at four – four hours after his shift ended, and two hours after Ray had told Hazel to get rid of him. He insisted on an update before he went home. "So I can keep thinking about auctions at home this weekend. *Actions*," he spat, trying to correct himself and failing. "*Options*."

"Those are fairly limited right now," she told him. "Dale Whitman died in 1965. I've ordered the certificate, but I have the listing. I can't find Peter Lynch. Whitman had a daughter and she's still alive. She's a hairdresser."

"Why are we not actively looking for Leon Cutter? Every hour that passes keeps Sergeant Renald in danger."

"We've talked about this," she said. "We're assuming a wait-and-see attitude over the weekend. It'll give me time to talk to this Hibiki Yoshida first, I think."

"When are you going?"

"As soon as buddy answers his phone!"

"*Hibiki* is a strange name," he said. "How does he spell it?"

She laughed. "I imagine he spells it the way all the Hibikis spell *Hibiki*." She spun her computer screen around so he could see. "But he goes by Hiro."

] 22 [

Saturday, October 27

Hazel did her normal Saturday shift, but the case was quiescent, as if lying in wait, saving its strength for the next wave. Cutter was silent now and Yoshida unreachable. She had an urge to go up to Dunneview anyway. Yoshida didn't know what she'd discussed with Eppert and Clemson; that information was only in her notebook. Unless Cutter had wired their houses. Unless they were all in on it. How many people might it take to stay ready for fifty years, to see justice done? His or their methods suggested justice wasn't enough. They had raised the bones to the status of holy relics: sacred objects that could not be touched except by a priest. Or the police. The murders of innocent homeowners were ritualistic in this way, cleansing and vengeful.

It was becoming increasingly clear why and how the boys' killer had chosen his victims. He was practising the ultimate form of birth control: removing genes from the gene pool. What did the three identified dead boys have in common? The younger Maracle was an Indian possessed of uncommon strength; perhaps he had been an easy choice. Deasún was a simple boy, of Slavic or Irish origin, based on her searches. Big as well. Shearing was dark enough to look black and maybe that was enough to get you crossed off this person's list. It was pure eugenics. Their release into society would likely have meant the continuation of their line.

She felt some relief that Dale Whitman was dead. Lynch was probably dead, too. Or he would be in his nineties.

If any of the other doctors were living and findable, she hadn't turned them up. However, on Thursday Wingate had tracked down one of the nurses who'd worked at both Charterhouse and Dublin Home. Frances Kelly was living in Toronto. James had had no trouble getting her on the phone, but she'd declined to discuss Dublin Home right then, saying she had her hands full with her sister, who was dying of MS. She offered to call after her sister was asleep. But she had not called Thursday night, nor Friday, and James had turned her name and number over to Hazel.

Wingate wouldn't be in again until Monday. Recently, he'd been protesting how infrequent his shifts seemed; this case had made him hungry to get back and he was raring to go. Hazel promised she'd talk to Ray about it, but this was just to put him off for a while. She knew he wasn't ready. It wasn't just his cognition (as evidenced in his malapropisms) or his physical deterioration. She recognized a drug addiction when she saw one. She'd had her own battle with painkillers, and she knew he was living on pills. It showed in his eyes, which were sometimes merely tired, but at other times glassy. (Michael may have had him on organic vegetable juices, and who knows what other supplements. Whatever it was, was it any worse than the pills — *plural* — she saw him popping into his mouth almost every day?) She knew Ray was aware of the changes in his detective sergeant. He wasn't going to clear James for normal duty until he was cleaner than he was now.

Cleaner. That was an achievable goal. She'd stopped taking painkillers because, eventually, they're something you have to give up completely. But she still drank. Not a lot, but she drank. So did Ray, and so did Geraldine Costamides and Dietrich Fraser. First you saw things, then you drank. She was still of a mind to give James the greatest amount of slack possible — to let him do whatever he needed to do — and to trust Michael to keep an eye on him. She wanted to spend more time worrying about James, but her mind was trained on dead children.

Sunday, she stayed at home. Emily watched *Thelma and Louise*. For supper, Hazel made a chicken casserole with toasted Ritz crackers on top. Emily had a few hearty mouthfuls before running out of appetite. Hazel piloted her back in front of the television and turned on Discovery for her to watch *MythBusters*. After a while, Emily's head drooped. Hazel turned the volume down and listened for her mother's breath. She was still breathing.

She took out Frances Kelly's number and went into the dining room. They hadn't used it in more than two years. It had been a long while since she'd heard the voices of her mother's friends cackling over cards in here. She dialled, and after a few rings a woman's voice answered.

"Miss Kelly?" Hazel said.

"This is she."

"I believe you spoke to a colleague of mine, Detective Sergeant James Wingate. My name is Detective Inspector Hazel Micallef. Do you have a few minutes to talk about the Dublin Boys Home and Charterhouse? You worked at both facilities in the fifties and sixties, correct?"

"That's correct. I'm sorry I didn't call back, but my sister has taken a turn for the worse and we were busy with her all weekend."

"I hope she'll be OK."

"She won't," said Miss Kelly with calm finality. "She's dying now. In and out of hospital. You'd put a dog down that was as sick as she is." She sighed and sniffed back tears. "We are a cruel species."

"I wish you and your family well," Hazel said. "Is now a good time?"

"Yes."

"Can you tell me: what were your tasks at the two homes, and were you employed by any others?"

"I worked a tick at the Fort Leonard Home, but most of my time I was at Dublin Home and Charterhouse."

The name of Fort Leonard sent Hazel into a moment of dark reverie. That had been Alan's home before he came to Port Dundas and became a Micallef. A good name, a trusted name in a small place, in a time when that was everything.

"How would you describe Dublin Home? When you were there in the late fifties?"

"Things were different then, as you probably can imagine . . ."

"I've lived in Port Dundas my whole life. I know things were different then. How were they different at Dublin Home?"

"I don't want to give you the impression we were completely unenlightened. I worked in the infirmary, and I did my overnight shifts, as we all did. I can't say everyone who lived there was happy — a lot of our boys came to us from real trouble, and there wasn't enough money in the system back then, same as now. Society's least gets least of its bounty. They squirrelled them away — the old folks, the unwanted kids, the natives and the mentally ill.

"From birth to age ten, it wasn't unusual for some children to see the insides of five institutions. And some of them were born broken and some of them were special cases. Every child, if you want to know the truth, was a special case. I wanted to put each and every one of them in a warm house with a mother and father and maybe a sibling or two."

"What happened if one of the boys died?" Hazel asked. "It must have happened."

"Of course it happened. Boys weak to begin with sometimes succumbed, for instance if there was a flu or meningitis outbreak. We suffered our share of epidemics. If whooping cough came through it might take one or two with it. There were polio scares. And earlier on, before I did my RN, I heard they'd dealt with TB a number of times. Those old government homes incubated germs."

"Were there ever any unusual deaths or suspicions of foul play?"

"Not that I was aware of."

"Did you ever hear rumours that sometimes children disappeared in the night?"

Miss Kelly took a moment. "I don't pay attention to rumour. It is almost always wrong."

"That doesn't answer my question."

Suddenly Miss Kelly's voice was raised. "I'll be there in a minute, dear! Yes, this is my house, dear. You are sleeping in my house." Hazel heard the phone being muffled. She imagined Miss Kelly had pressed the receiver against her clothing. Then she was back. "There was a boy one time who made it onto the roof and slipped on the stone slate and tumbled to his death. That's the only time something like that happened, if you are looking for something unusual."

"Do you recall when that was?"

"New Year's of '58 or '59."

"Do you remember his name?"

"Not his last name. He was called Valentijn. A simple boy, big and playful. Covered in hair by the age of thirteen. The other boys liked him, but he was trouble."

"You saw this Valentijn? You saw his body?"

"No, I wasn't on shift, but I came in the next morning and all the children were upset, talking among themselves."

"What did the children think had happened to him?"

"They were worked up about it," Miss Kelly said. "Especially the younger boys. They were sure Old Father Crumb had come in the night."

"Old Father Crumb?"

"It was a ghost story," she said. "Something the older boys terrorized the little ones with. If you heard the night bell, it meant Old Father Crumb had come in the night. It was a sort of campfire story, you see? I never met a person named Crumb though, but that day they were buzzing with it."

"Where was Valentijn buried?"

"Back then, I'm afraid, if you had no next of kin to take your body, you were just buried in a potter's field. I think there was one in Mayfair. No names, no markers. Poor boy he was, and now no one knows he walked the earth."

"You know," said Hazel. "And I do, too."

The new week began with an email message from Cutter that came in the form of a jpeg. It was a photo of Renald beaten black and blue. He was holding a piece of card on which was written: THIS IS NOT MY HALLOWEEN COSTUME.

Hazel looked away. "Jesus, Ray. Don't spread that."

"What do you want to do?"

"What's the email address?"

"Tell me what you want to say."

Something about the tone of his voice. "Why? Show me." She went around his desk and looked. The sender was named *gonnakillhim@yahoo.ca*. She grabbed the keyboard away.

She clicked reply and wrote: *If you harm him any further, I'll make sure you never go to trial.*

"Hazel!"

She pressed send.

"Is there anything that pops into your head you ignore?"

"I mean it, too," she said.

Cartwright appeared at the office door. "Sorry to interrupt, but you just got a call from ChemLab Forensic in Toronto. It's a match."

"Is he still on the line?"

"Nope. He just said there was a 98.9 per cent chance that Mr. Maracle is related by blood to the sample you provided. That was it. He said it was a yes or no proposition, and I was to tell you yes, although if you want more certainty than that, it'll take another week. But –" she looked down at the note she was holding " – he also said that there was only one chance in forty-six billion that it was a false positive."

Hazel and Greene looked at each other. "That closes the circle, then," she said. "Eloy Maracle. We know one of our victims now." She got up.

"Where are you going?"

"I'm going to deliver the news to his brother in person. And I think I'll have a couple of new questions for him."

"In the meantime?" he asked.

"Keep Wingate working the records. Let him stay as long as he wants."

Hazel was in Toronto by 9:30. Claude Maracle's address was in Mimico, down by the lake, the southeast corner of Etobicoke. An old enclave of the city. There was no answer at his door. She went over to Lakeshore Boulevard and had a coffee.

ChemLab had faxed their report. She went over it again. Its stark math was certain: Claude and the bones shared the same parents. Fate had divided them, but science had made them brothers again.

The second time she rang, a tall, dark-skinned man answered the door. His eyes were blue and tired. "Help you?"

"We spoke by phone last week, Mr. Maracle. I'm Detective Inspector Hazel —"

"Yeah," he said, and he stood aside. "They came and took hair *and* blood."

She waved the folder with the report in it as if it could do the talking for her. "I've got the results from the lab."

He led her into a room where a chair, upholstered in a worn beige fabric, faced the television. There was a couch and a coffee table to one side, but it was clear no one had sat on the couch for some time. He gestured to it, but she felt she couldn't sit yet.

"I'm afraid I have bad news."

"What other is there?"

"Some of the bones we found behind Dublin Home belong to your brother. It's all in this report," she said, leaning sideways to put the folder down on the coffee table.

"I believe you." He was resigned in his manner. "I don't need that. It doesn't change anything. So now you think he was murdered. That's what you've come to tell me?"

"It's my duty to tell you."

"Sit down now, would you? I'm not going to offer you anything because you're not staying long." She sat. "You know who killed him?"

"We're not sure yet. We have some ideas, but most of our suspects are dead. This happened so long ago now. We've found some men who were once in Dublin Home as boys, but you're the only one who can put a name to a victim. Tell me, did you know a boy called Valentijn Deasún?"

"Valentijn. Yes, I knew him. He was Eloy's friend."

"He died in 1959. But how?"

"He fell to his death. From a window or a roof."

"That's what you heard?"

"It was a sunny morning on a winter's day, then they drew all the curtains. That's all I remember. After that, we had to spend the day in our dorms."

"Did anyone see him fall?"

"I don't think anyone saw him fall."

"Do you think he killed himself?"

Maracle leaned forward in his chair, his elbows on his knees. "Most of us were just trying to survive. I don't know if he killed himself."

"Eloy was his friend?"

"You wanted my brother on your side. Or he might do the opposite of protect you. He was good to the weaker kids and the young ones. Everyone was nice to the babies. So he kept an eye on Valentijn, because he was big and clumsy and feeble-minded. I never saw him do too much violence to his fellow inmates. He saved his worst rages for the staff."

"Who did Eloy dislike in particular? Was there anyone he had a lot of run-ins with, or conflict?"

"He would get mad and do something about it. He broke the arm of an orderly fifty pounds heavier than himself.

But not taller. Eloy got tall genes. I got my grandfather's blue eyes and my mother's ability to suffer."

Hazel wondered when the last time was that this man thought he still had a chance. Maybe his brother had been the lucky one, his life arrested before he learned where it was headed. If he could see his surviving brother's fate, Eloy might think his own painless.

"What happened after he broke the orderly's arm?"

"They transferred him out. Juvie, I don't know. I didn't hear from him and then I got a letter saying he'd died of influenza. I'd been with the Wetherlings for six months by then."

"Tell me about the night bell. Or Old Father Crumb."

He looked away quickly.

"Are they just stories?"

"Who told you?"

"A couple of people. One of them named Frances Kelly."

"Nurse Kelly. She's still alive, is she?"

"I spoke to her by phone. Obviously she's much older now."

"Nurse Kelly lives, but my brother is chopped to pieces and forgotten on the tenth green."

"Along with others. Was there a night bell?"

"I don't know."

"Did you ever hear something you weren't expecting to hear in the night?"

"No."

"But boys were found dead. Or they disappeared."

"Boys came and went. It was not our place to ask why." He rubbed the base of his throat with his hand. "How many boys?" he asked without looking up.

"We're up to eighteen different DNA profiles. There may be more."

"What a piece of work is a man." He looked up. "What is going to happen to my brother's bones?"

"When we close the case, we can give them to you for a proper burial."

His eyes were far away. "I don't want to be part of your case, Detective Inspector. I won't testify, and I don't want to make a statement or whatever it is you call it. If it's possible for me to have Eloy's remains, someone can communicate that to me, but otherwise, I don't want to hear from you again and I don't want you to use my name. Do I have your word on it?"

] 23 [

The Ladyman Café was packed as usual for lunch, and Monday lunches, in particular, were desperate affairs with people escaping their kitchens for the first time in two days. Hazel had made it back to Port Dundas in record time. She and Ray sat at the counter.

"So the idea was to get rid of anyone who shouldn't be allowed to leave the home and enter society," Hazel said.

"Three boys is not a strong foundation for a theory," he replied.

"Valentijn Deasún – described as strong but simple by two people. Eloy Maracle – native, strong and out of control. Violent. Charles Shearing, a dark-skinned adolescent." She swirled the ice in her glass and watched the light bounce around it. "You'd have to do it differently every time. Cover it up differently. Valentijn's record ends at Dublin Home. He's shown as deceased in their records, but there's no death certificate."

"It's lost, someone screwed up – there're a hundred explanations."

"Eloy's record showed he was transferred to another institution. James checked every angle. The place he was sent to never registered him as a ward of the province. He never arrived. And we know he's in that field."

Ray turned his wedding ring on his finger, thinking. "Who could have gotten away with that?"

"Anyone, I suppose. But if you were efficiently killing and then getting rid of the bodies, nursing or medical training would be a good thing to have."

He shook his head and then moved his arms off the counter to make room for the two plates that had just arrived.

"Toasted western with mayo, fries."

"Me," said Hazel.

"Toasted western, fries, mayo on the side."

"You've been serving us the same lunch for twenty years," Ray said to the man behind the counter.

"I like saying it. How come you never sit where your dads sat? You move all over – booth, table, counter – but never where they sat."

"I don't know." Greene squinted at him in mock challenge. "I guess I want to establish my own legend."

"You know why your father sat at the end of the bar, Ray? Because the second time he forgot to pay, *my* father told him he had to eat in the corner where he could keep an eye on him." He patted the counter in front of them, laughing. "Eat up."

Hazel looked at Ray's plate. "Why do you ask for cold mayo on the side?"

"If they put the mayo on in the kitchen, it's practically leaking out of the sandwich when he brings it."

She took a bite and made a *yum* face at him. "We need a witness, Ray. Somebody who saw it with their own eyes. Maybe that person is Yoshida."

"No answer still?"

"I'm going to go up there."

"When?"

"If he doesn't pick up this afternoon, I'll go up and poke around. You ever been to Dunneview?"

"Sure. Half of the main drag's been shuttered since I was a kid."

"It's almost all shuttered now. Last time I knew what its population was, it was under six hundred."

"You better hope Mr. Yoshida is one of the people who stayed."

"Well, that's where his phone supposedly rings."

———

Hazel got back to her desk and looked at the time: 2:20 p.m. She could get to Dunneview and back in five hours. But in five hours at the station, she could start planning for the last phase of the case: naming the victims. That was going to be a whole other database: finding kin, collecting blood, matching genetic signatures, entering it into a database. She imagined the dead rising from the fields for roll call.

She was proud of herself – and of James even more so – for summiting the mountains of data that had revealed the missing boys they'd found so far. For how many years had someone been permitted to carry out the scheme?

"Hazel." Wingate was standing in her doorway. He was in jeans and a white T-shirt.

She laughed. "Finally."

"What?"

"You look gay." He laughed. She hadn't seen a smile on his face in quite a while.

"Only you and Kraut are confident enough to joke with me."

"Kraut jokes about it?"

"Oh yeah."

"And you don't mind."

"In the coffee lounge Forbes was talking about finding a new apartment –"

"He and Olivia break up again?"

"Yeah. He's poring over the rentals online and he says 'How big is a bachelor?' And Kraut says, 'Ask Wingate.'"

"Oh my god," she said, covering her mouth. "What did you say?"

"I said I counted on him to have my back."

Hazel laughed into her palm. "Please tell me that's what you really said."

"I did."

He was looking at her strangely, she thought. "Are you here to say goodbye?"

"Oh, yeah, I'm off. Any luck with Yoshida?"

"No answer. I was going to go today but I've got too much paper on my desk. I'll go tomorrow. Get some rest."

"I will."

Wingate pulled out onto Main Street. He took the bridge over the Kilmartin River and drove along the 117 below the Lion's Paw. When the town was behind him, he pulled off onto a patch of gravel, got out, and removed his uniform from the trunk. He got into the back seat of his cruiser to put it on. It was difficult enough to walk or sit down or stand up, but getting his long form twisted around in the seat to put on pants was black-belt stuff for his banged-up body. He hit his head on the roof when he shrugged his shirt over his shoulders. The motor and the lights were off, but someone would notice an empty police car. He struggled the jacket on and reached for his black shoes.

After a pause, he emerged dressed in uniform and got

back behind the wheel. He pulled onto the road and followed it away from town onto Highway 41. A few minutes
later, a sign went by that gave the distance to Dunneview
as 231 kilometres.

According to what he'd been able to find out on the
weekend, Hibiki Yoshida was a Japanese boy found on a ship
in 1950, a stowaway alone on a tanker that had last been in
port in the Philippines. He'd found a story in the *Toronto
Star*'s online archive. He was seven and he was sent to live
at Dublin Home, and he wasn't adopted for ten years. The
adoptive family was a childless Jewish couple who took
Hibiki back to Toronto. But when he retired, he returned
to Westmuir County and settled in Dunneview. He hadn't
married, and he was on the tax rolls at a Dunneview address.

Wingate got to the town just after 5:00 p.m. All its main
street was missing were the tumbleweeds. The side streets,
however, reminded him of North Toronto, where he and
Michael had grown up. Low-slung bungalows among old
brick homes. For a moment he thought he could smell the
particular combination of drying maple and willow leaves
that had once been proof of autumn there.

He pulled up outside Yoshida's house and parked. The
blinds were drawn and the house appeared empty from
the outside. It was one of the red brick houses, with yellow
brick trim around its windows and doors. An old house.
The driveway was wide enough for two cars, but nothing
was parked there.

He unfolded his body from the cruiser and walked up to the door, aware that if anyone saw a policeman they would be concerned and perhaps the neighbours would come to see. It took the entire walk to Yoshida's front door for him to straighten his body out. He rang the bell once. Hazel liked to knock, but he preferred a single musical tone to announce his presence. It suggested that something serious required the homeowner's attention.

There was no sign that anyone was at home. He waited. His mind flickered one way and the other, between the 1980s in Willowdale and here, more than four hundred kilometres and two decades away. For a moment, the door he stood before had his family behind it: his brother, their parents.

A man opened the door. He was Japanese, with deep-set, intelligent eyes. He wore drawstring pants and a light-blue T-shirt that hung over his narrow frame. "Yes?"

"Hibiki Yoshida?"

"Yes?"

"I'm Sergeant Detective James Wingate, from the Port Dundas OPS. I'm wondering if I might talk to you."

Yoshida looked to the street. "On all the shows, the police work in twos."

"Budget cuts. And this isn't a call. I mean, I'm not responding to a call. I just have a couple of questions concerning a case I'm working."

"Come in."

The house was small and very tidy, with blond-wood

floors and cabinetry. From floor to ceiling along one wall in the living room, built-in shelves of dark pine held books in a number of languages. There was a single potted ficus, and above a black fireplace one thing on the wall: a curved sword in its scabbard, mounted on wooden supports.

"That come in handy much?"

"It may one day."

"You should come to the door with it."

Yoshida guffawed. "*That* would keep the brush-sellers away! It's an antique sword," he said. "It belonged to my great-grandfather. I am an only son, so I inherited it."

"Have you always had it?" Wingate asked.

"No. I tracked it down. It's the only thing that connects me to my family. I had it sharpened."

"Why?"

"Maybe one day I'll need to defend myself. Or cut a tomato into paper-thin slices." He laughed again. He gestured for Wingate to sit in a chair before a large, potbellied stove. On one of the two burner plates, a cast-iron teapot was keeping warm. "That fireplace is two hundred years old. I don't trust it since it set the roof on fire, so I put this stove in. I can make eggs and bacon on top of it, and tea. Sometimes I sit here all day and read and drink tea. Would you like a cup?"

"OK," Wingate said. Michael had turned him on to the power of different teas. "What is it?"

"*Gyokuro*. A green tea."

Wingate accepted a small ceramic cup. His mind was still partly in a memory and it made the present unreal. "Why do you not answer your phone?"

Yoshida turned his head and pointed to his ear. There was a tiny pink hearing aid in it. "I don't wear this if I'm home alone. I like the way being hard of hearing is sometimes like being in a cloud, far away from everything."

"How did you hear the doorbell?"

"I have a light there – see it? – and one upstairs. They flash. Is this a test?"

"No sir."

"Then how can I help you?"

"The Ontario Police Services are looking into allegations of a . . . an . . . abuse at the Dublin Home for Boys. You were there between 1950 and 1960. You were adopted by Joe and Zelda Rubins of Toronto. You went back to your birth name?"

"Yes," he said. "My adoptive parents are dead. I have always thought of myself as Yoshida."

"I suppose it might have been a little strange in the sixties living with a Jewish family."

"I think that some tradition instead of none at all was good for me. And I make a mean brisket. I marinate it in soy sauce and mirin wine. Tell me what you mean by *abuse*."

"Do you remember a boy who fell from the roof?"

"Yes. I do. He was in the snow in the morning, on his back, and there was frost on his blue face."

"You saw him?"

"I was the one who found him."

Wingate took his notebook out. "Do you remember his name?"

"Desoon."

"Like this?" Wingate wrote *Deasún* on a page.

"I don't think I ever saw it written."

"Valentijn."

"Yes. Valentijn Deasún. They said he fell from the roof."

"Do you think it was an accident?"

"No. I don't, not anymore. I've spent my life reading about these places. Anything I can get my hands on."

"You mean anything Leon Cutter has sent you."

"We've kept each other up to date with our discoveries. His interests are more local than mine. I could show you many things you can't find at the archives."

"How many of you have been working on this case? Cutter's been in the archives, what – twenty-six years? He must have *got* that position to gain access to provincial records. What do you do?"

Yoshida smiled. He was a ridiculously calm and sunny man. "I was at the Ministry of Child and Youth Services. I worked as a placement officer for the public adoptions department. I'm retired now. But I had access to government records Leon could never get."

"Like what?"

"Well, the public knows now what the priests and hockey coaches were doing. But you don't know half of what went on in this country's asylums and nursing homes and foster care homes and even hospitals. I have evidence of forced sterilizations, abortion without the patient's consent, even euthanasia. And eugenics."

"Eugenics?"

"Selective breeding. Well, retroactive selective breeding."

"Murdering people before they can reproduce."

"There's also this." Yoshida rose from his chair and disappeared into another room. He returned with a small stack of stapled papers and put them down on a side table. "These are internal bulletins put out by a foundation called the Ontario Parents' Information Centre. It operated out of Kitchener and it had an office in Mayfair as well."

"What was it?"

"They advocated for contraception. There were a couple of court cases in the sixties when one of the centre's nurses was arrested for handing out condoms to women."

"Sounds like a pretty modern approach."

"On the surface. But the president of the foundation – his name was A.R. Merchant – established it in order to bring contraception only to *certain* communities. Places where English was not the first language, neighbourhoods where the skin colour was not white – that's where they went. In their internal literature," Yoshida said, pointing to the stack of bulletins, "the foundation called these groups 'welfare risks and underearners.' Merchant targeted women, hiding behind his foundation and spreading a gospel of 'choice' before the idea really caught on. Except he wanted to prevent them from passing on their genes . . ."

"What does this have to do with Dublin Home?"

"I saw Merchant there. He was a regular visitor. I didn't know who he was until I got older and undertook my research, but when I saw his face, I knew he was the same man." He took a bulletin and opened it to the third page, where a photo of Merchant was printed at the top of his monthly address to his readers. He had a warm, horsey face marked with laugh lines. "That's him. As he looked."

"Why would he visit the home?"

"I believe he went from orphanage to asylum to hospital, offering information and perhaps supplies at times. There are no clear records of the role he might have played, but it's not unreasonable to think that he consulted on sterilization at some of these institutions, and maybe even performed some of them himself."

"Was he a doctor?"

"No."

Wingate shuddered involuntarily. "Did someone perform those kinds of procedures at Dublin Home?"

"I don't know. In the ten years I lived there, doctors and nurses came and went."

"You believe that Deasún's death was not an accident. Were there other suspicious deaths? Disappearances?"

"Boys came and went. You never knew why."

"I heard some of them disappeared in the night."

Yoshida looked at him squarely, as if to gauge what he could trust Wingate with. "If a boy was going to another home or getting a family, we'd say goodbye to him at lunch and they'd leave in the afternoon. Some kids they took at night. No one ever heard from them, and no one ever talked about it. It was like they'd never been born."

Wingate put the bulletins into an evidence bag and tore the backing off the adhesive. "Would you testify?"

"Merchant is dead. The rest of them are elderly or dead themselves. Who is there to testify against?"

"I'm only asking if you would be willing."

Yoshida thought about it. "I suppose I would, except I don't know how admissible my memories would be."

"Was there such a thing as the night bell?"

"Yes." Yoshida's eyes were no longer laughing. "I know because I heard it. Twice."

"Will you tell me?"

He'd stayed longer than he'd intended – it was past 6:00 p.m. Michael was making kale soup and a raw-food chili. Michael's way of eating had no doubt helped his body recover in the last year, but kale soup was a cure worse than the disease. Still, he didn't want to hurt his brother's feelings. He sent a text: *Held up at work, home at 9:30.* He put the evidence bag of bulletins on the passenger seat and pulled away from the curb.

He drove through the dying town and out to the access road that led back to Highway 41 without seeing a living soul. At the last light before getting on the road back to Port Dundas, he felt the cold muzzle of a gun at the base of his skull.

"Don't turn around, buddy." A man's voice. "I won't hurt you if you co-operate." Wingate felt the cold steel rise into his hair and come to rest directly behind his eyes. He glimpsed at his rear-view mirror.

Leon Cutter said, "Now drive north." Wingate started driving. "Send your radio, your phone, and your gun back here. Careful now."

"I don't have a gun," Wingate said. He passed the phone and radio back.

"Oh right, you're on admin duty, aren't you? Do you even have your badge?"

"No."

Cutter laughed softly. "I like your style. I think I can lower *my* gun."

"I was hoping you would." Wingate's shoulders came down as he felt the muzzle pull away from his scalp.

"One false move —"

"Would kill us both," said Wingate. "Assuming you want to live."

"Don't assume anything about me."

Wingate watched Cutter in the mirror lean back in the seat. He made no eye contact with Wingate, choosing to watch the countryside go by. In daylight, he looked younger than he had at the archives, where the overheads had given him a dead-white cast.

"Is Renald alive?" Wingate asked.

"For now."

"Why did you take him? You killed the others."

Now Cutter flicked him a look. "The others?"

"The Fremonts. Brendan Givens."

"I don't know who those people are."

"You're kidding me. You didn't kill the Fremonts? Slice up Brendan Givens in a hotel room in Toronto?"

"No," said Cutter, amused. "I think I would remember that." He ran his tongue around inside his cheek. "Look, your colleague's alive. No one's killed anyone. And offing a cop is bad news. Although it makes you a hero in prison."

"If you ever get to prison."

Dead trees slashed past on either side. Wingate realized with a start that this was going to get him kicked off the force. He wasn't cleared for duty and he was hostage in a cruiser without his badge or gun.

He'd visited Yoshida knowing he was pushing it. But all he'd wanted to do was prove he was ready. If he did a good interview, moved the case forward, maybe they'd see he could work. Michael had been insisting it was going to take another year, but he could see in Hazel's eyes that she wanted him back. In *her* eyes he was ready, and she was his only champion right now. And would continue to be, he hoped, realizing he needed at least one.

He continued north on the 41 until Port Dundas was almost three hundred kilometres behind him. They'd crossed the border between Westmuir and Parry Sound. The autumnal changes were more advanced at this latitude. Many of the trees were bare already and the nostalgia of fall-in-progress had given way to the foreboding of the coming winter. Ice clung to the blasted granite sides of the highway, and the few fields carved out of the forest were denuded, empty. He considered the possibility that he was about to be murdered.

After almost an hour of silence, Cutter spoke: "You know that thrill of horror you get when you realize the chicken you just ate was undercooked?"

"I'm sorry?"

"That feeling that you might have just caught your own death the way you catch a cold. Once, I had a kebab that was cool in the middle and I could taste the bleach."

"What do you want, Leon?"

"I want to catch our man."

Cutter hadn't put on a seat belt, as far as Wingate could tell. A sudden stop might give him control of the situation. But it might also get them both killed. He'd had his dance with death and gotten away. He wasn't going to risk it a second time.

"Did you give the order to someone to kill the Fremonts or to kill Givens?"

"What case are you on, little detective?"

"I'm not so sure now."

"Ascot knew what was in those fields. Ascot knew, but they didn't report it. I waited fifty years to learn what happened to my friends, but instead of reporting their bones to the police, Ascot built a golf course on top of them."

"Am I driving you north at gunpoint for a reason?"

Cutter leaned forward suddenly, his head springing out to Wingate's right, between the seats. "I want their bones! I want them to receive a proper burial. And I want the person who killed them identified."

"Whoever did it is dead."

"I know that."

"And the remains are evidence in an ongoing investigation."

"Pull over," Cutter said sharply.

"Where?"

"Here! Pull over!"

Wingate crossed a lane and got onto the shoulder. Cutter stepped out of the car, training the gun on him the whole time. The muzzle felt like a human eye. His neck prickled. Cutter leaned down to the window and gestured him out. Wingate struggled out of the driver's seat and stood beside the car.

"I've done almost all of your work for you," Cutter said. "Now you have to carry it over the finish line."

"Why haven't you reported what you know?"

"We're not the law. We've had half a century to work on what happened to our friends, but if I reported what I'd found? The police were an accessory! So were the morgues. Even some local politicians. No one would listen to me. I want *you* and your partner to make it stick. And if you don't do it by Friday, I'm going to kill Melvin. Now give me the keys."

"The keys?"

"I'm going back for my car. I left it in Dunneview. I just need you far away for a couple of hours. You can hitch back in your uniform." He jiggled the end of the gun. Wingate handed over the keys. Cars had been going by in both directions for more than a minute now, but their drivers had been oblivious to what was happening on the shoulder as they zipped by faster than the speed limit. No OPS officer had passed in either direction. Never a cop when you need one.

Cutter got into the cruiser and rolled down the window. "Good luck, buddy. See you soon." He pulled out onto the road.

A few minutes later, Wingate saw him on the other side of the median, driving south.

] 24 [

1957

On Christmas Day, still stuffed like a turkey *with* turkey, Hazel reluctantly set the table for lunch. She had tried to press-gang Alan into doing it, but he was enjoying his new Meccano set and she was happy to let him be. He'd never know what his true Christmas gift had been, the one she found in Toronto's Chinatown. She could tell no one what she'd done; it had to be between herself and Carol's parents. She felt certain that the Lims would not report her secret foray. Perhaps now she would become the sole conduit to their daughter – they would go through her until Hazel finally figured out a way to get Carol home. They would need her.

Not every family ate Christmas dinner on Christmas Eve, but hers did. The huge meal provided fuel for the long but happy process of opening presents the next morning. The sluggishness induced by the previous night's meal invariably peaked around lunchtime on Christmas Day. On Christmas Day, only Alan attacked his food with his usual enthusiasm.

Her parents had done everything they could for the new member of their family. But they had chosen to. She hadn't. Watching him play with his new things – things he could never have dreamed of – made her at last feel love for him. She made herself a promise that as long as she was alive, he'd never go hungry again.

One way to get Alan's co-operation was to withhold dessert until he had helped clear the table. Their parents went upstairs to nap after lunch and told Hazel to encourage him to go outside and burn off some of his energy. Alan hobbled back and forth between the dining room and the kitchen, stiff with a full belly. "I want some trifle and custard as well," he said.

"You'll get dessert when the lunch things are put away. But be quiet, Mom and Dad are sleeping."

He walked as slowly as possible to the kitchen and back. "You know Mr. Bannerman?"

"Who is Mr. Bannerman?"

"Dad says he's rag-picker."

"I don't know what that is, Alan."

"He has a dirty store on Main Street." He kept talking as he walked away from her.

"I can't hear you anymore," she called. "You know sound doesn't jump up over your head and come back to me, right?"

"I'm not dumb," he said, red-faced, from the doorway. "His store is across the road from Herbert Lim's. Dad says they think he did it."

"Did what?"

"They think he hurt Carol Lim."

"Come here." He approached her. "I'm going to tell you a secret, but you have to keep it to yourself for a while. Carol is fine. I met someone who knows her in Toronto. She gave me a note Carol wrote to her parents."

"Really?"

"Yes."

"She'll have her necklace when she comes back."

"I guess –"

Without warning, Alan threw his arms around her and began to sob. "I lied!" he said in a tight, small voice between gasps of air. "I lied!"

Their parents were still upstairs. It seemed a long nap, but Hazel was grateful they were not seeing Alan in such a state. "Let me show you," he begged her. "Get Daddy's keys."

"He'll notice they're gone," she said.

"We'll be back before he notices. Please!"

His anxiety was so acute, she felt she had no choice. She

went into the closet by the door and felt up the wall inside until she came to the hook where her father's keys were. She took them down, afraid that they would jingle and attract attention, and clasped them tightly in her hands. She whispered to Alan, "Put on a coat and gloves," and she looked backward nervously as they left. The house was dark and silent behind them and the streets were almost empty. The occasional car passed them with a muffled sound – rubber tires on new snow.

She led her brother down Candlestick Alley and they stood for a moment at the mouth of it, looking out at Main Street for anyone who might recognize them. "OK, go," she said when she was sure the coast was clear.

They walked up the street to the heart of town, where the family store was. It was dark behind the glass and the mannequins in the window stood in shadow. They ran up to the door in fast, light steps. Hazel knew which key opened the main lock and she turned it until she felt it give under her hand. She took one more look at the street and then pushed the door open and held it for her brother.

Inside, it felt like an empty museum. Round racks of shirts repeated in hunched silhouette down the middle of the store. Usually when they were there, it was abuzz with light and talk, and fragrant with the smell of perfumes and colognes and *people*, their father presiding with a smile over it all. He had the knack for sales and didn't even have to try: he'd told her many times it is easy to sell when you love your own wares. He was being honest when he told a customer how fitting a certain colour was, how handsome you were in a worsted vest, how those shoes completed your look. He took pleasure. It mattered to him how people felt about themselves when they left his store.

The silence was particularly imposing in the dark. She felt Alan slip his hand into hers. "What is it you want to show me? I don't think we should be here long."

"We have to go in the back."

She was reluctant to go any deeper but Alan pulled her onward. At the back of the store were the changerooms, and behind them the stockroom where extra wares were kept. She was worried that he wanted to show her what was in one of the fitting rooms, and the idea that he might draw a curtain away and reveal something she wasn't ready to see kept her moving very slowly.

He wasn't taking her to the fitting rooms, though. He went to the door that led to the stockroom. "It's locked," he said. "The key is on the same chain."

She fumbled with the ring, trying different keys until she found the one that went in smoothly. "Why don't you just tell me what's back there? I'll believe you."

"You have to see with your own eyes. I have to show you."

"How did you get back here in the first place? The door is kept locked. Did Father let you in?"

"No," Alan said, blinking manically. "He leaves the keys

in the cash register until the end of the day. I took them when he was having lunch!"

"Why?"

"I wanted to see?" he said, hoping it was the right answer.

"Wanting to see where you're not allowed to go can get you into trouble. Don't you know that?"

"I know it now."

She felt for his arm to hold. The only light was the little coming from the high windows. There was grit on the floor and their footsteps threw dull reports against the shelving. Boxes ranged up on either side of them; she imagined their lids lifting up all by themselves.

She came to a sudden stop.

"What are you doing?" he asked her.

"What are *you* doing?"

"I want to tell the truth."

"So tell me."

Her eyes had adjusted to the stockroom's gloom, but she couldn't make out his expression. Surely he wouldn't hurt her. Surely the love she was beginning to feel for him would be in *him* too. For her.

He told her to wait, and he walked into the dark.

Hazel considered going back to the stockroom door and locking him in. But if she showed she didn't trust him now, who would he ever trust? It had taken the better part of two years for him to open up this much. All would be lost if she showed him he didn't belong.

She would continue to believe him. Even if it cost her.

After a moment, he returned with a small cardboard inventory box in his hands. He held it carefully, top and bottom, like it was a stack of something. "I found it when I came back here. I didn't think anyone would care. I didn't know."

"It's OK, Alan. What's in the box?"

"I'll hold it. You take off the lid."

She put a hand on either side of the lid and slid it up. There were many small objects in the box, filling it about halfway. She thought at first the objects were carved Indian arrowheads or flints, like the ones they found from time to time walking through nearby fields, or at the edge of the Kilmartin River.

She reached in and touched the small, cold objects. They jingled against each other. She took one out. It was a silver pendant in the shape of a heart. She ran her thumb over the face of it and felt the rabbit engraved in it. "Oh my god," she said. "Alan."

"I stole one!" he cried. "Please don't tell!"

She dug her hand into the box and scooped out a fistful of silver hearts. She almost laughed but her breath caught. She let them slide out of her hand, jingling, into the others. Her father must have bought them on one of his shopping trips years and years ago. Perhaps he'd sold a few of them — one to Carol Lim — and then forgotten the rest in the inventory. "Alan," she said. "You should have told them!"

"I stole it," he said, gasping and beginning to weep. "I stole from Daddy!"

She grasped him by the shoulders. "Isn't it better that he think you a thief than a murderer?"

"A murderer!" He shrank away from her, retreating into shadow.

"Don't you understand that *that* is what all the fuss was about, Alan? Why you had to talk to Commander Drury so many times."

"I didn't kill anyone!"

"No, obviously," she said, shaking a fistful of graven hearts in front of him. "But now you have to tell them the truth!"

"Why, if you know she's alive?"

"Before she comes home, it would be best if Mom and Dad knew where your necklace came from. Do you want to have to live with another secret?"

"No," he admitted, cowed by her logic. "But you're sure she's alive?"

"Yes. And soon everyone will know. We're going to take these home and you're going to tell them, and then it will all be over."

"No. You tell them if you have to."

"Alan, you're only twelve, and taking responsibility is hard to do, but it's a sign of maturity. They will notice that. It'll be OK."

"No," he said, jerking away from the hand she'd offered. He was suddenly terrified. "Don't ever tell them. Promise me."

"Why are you shaking?" Even his teeth were chattering. She put her hand out again and this time, he allowed her to touch him. "OK, OK," she said. "I promise."

He pushed the box away when she tried to give it back to him. "No. They're yours now. *You* keep them!"

After supper, when the only light was from candles and reflections in glass, Hazel said that she was going to walk down the street to give Gloria Whitman her Christmas card. It was a lie.

She also wanted to be out of the house: Alan needed to be alone with their parents in case he had a change of heart. She hoped he would.

She'd been allowed to go out alone during the day since the age of nine – walking unaccompanied to school, going on small errands, visiting her father in his store. It was only last year, after she'd turned thirteen, that they began to let her go out on her own at night. That had truly felt like independence.

The Whitmans were at the "high" end of the street. The closer to the river the house, the older and finer it was. She walked all the way to Gloria's, but then she continued on to River Street and turned left. It had snowed again after a short period of mild weather, and the ice in the Kilmartin had thinned. The new cold front gave the ice a thick coat of snow, and now the sound of the river ran muffled below it like a voice heard through a wall.

The walk to Herbert Lim Grocery took her all of three minutes. She felt nervous going up to the closed gate beside the shop that led to their apartment door. There was a little white button fixed to the gatepost. Beyond it, metal stairs went up.

She felt in her pocket for the little bit of fraying string that held the scroll with Carol's message on it. She rang the doorbell.

Footsteps came quickly. The door at the top of the stairs opened and Mr. Lim stepped out and shielded his eyes from the street lights. "Who is it?" he called.

Hazel stepped out to where he could see her. "I'm a friend of Carol's."

"You are the mayor's daughter."

"Yes."

"We are closed, even for the mayor." He sounded a little drunk.

"I need to talk to you," she said.

"It's Christmas don't you know!"

"It's about Carol."

He went back into the apartment. Then he came down the stairs. He wore a housecoat cinched tight around his waist with the ends of the sash hanging down over his bare shins. He was in socks and flip-flops. "You are not a friend of Carol's," he stated flatly. He stood facing her on the other side of the gate.

"I know her a little," Hazel said. He smelled like sweet wine and she felt a bit afraid of him now. "We were in grade school together. But I was a few years behind her. We didn't really talk that much."

"What do you want to tell me about my daughter?"

"I have a message from her," she said.

He'd been looking at her with his mouth fixed in a line, but now his lips parted. "Where is she? Where did you see her?"

Hazel held her hands up. "I didn't see her *myself.*"

"How did she give you a message?"

"I . . . I . . . met somebody when I was in Toronto yesterday with my father. Somebody who had spoken to Carol. I learned how to say her name in Chinese. Someone recognized it."

"Who?"

"I don't think I should say," she said, and she began to feel a little sick to her stomach. "I have Carol's message with me."

He opened the gate. "Come up. You talk to her mother." Mrs. Lim was now standing in the doorway, tying her housecoat up.

"Hello," Carol's mother said. "Merry Christmas."

"Merry Christmas," Hazel said. "I'm so sorry to bother you." They went into the kitchen and both Lims sat down in chairs facing her. "Like I said, I wouldn't have . . . but I . . . I brought something to you from Carol. She sent a message."

Mr. Lim said something to his wife in Chinese. "You did not see her?"

"No, but I met someone who knew her. Carol's name is Shen Yu, right?"

"Yes," said Mrs. Lim. "Let me see the message."

Hazel took the little scroll out of her pocket and laid it in Mrs. Lim's papery-white palm. Carol's mother slipped the frayed ribbon off and unrolled the message with her thumbs. Her eyes scanned it quickly twice. She pressed her lips together to hide her emotion, but when she blinked, a tear rolled down beside her nose. She looked at her husband and handed him the note. She held her hands out to Hazel. "Come here please," she said.

Hazel went to her. She took Mrs. Lim's hands. They were as cold as the silver hearts had been in their box.

"This is a very nice thing you have done," said Mrs. Lim. "Mr. Lim and I are very grateful that Carol has such a good friend."

"I wish I could have done more," Hazel said.

"No, this is more than enough," Mrs. Lim said. She spoke to her husband and he got up and left the room momentarily. When he returned, he was clutching a green bill with a black border. Twenty dollars.

"Please," he said, "take this."

"I can't," said Hazel. "I wouldn't feel right. I really just wanted to help."

Mrs. Lim took the money from her husband, and folded

it twice. She pushed the money into Hazel's front pocket. "That is more reason you should be rewarded. Now leave. It is Christmas Day. Go be with your family."

They saw her out, and Mr. Lim held open the screen door for her. "Thank you," he said, smiling at her in a pained way. "You are a good girl. Your parents are lucky."

That night, she sat on the edge of Alan's bed and dried his hair with a towel. "Tomorrow is no school either," he said.

"Nope, you are free to wreak havoc all day long." He smelled good after a bath, one of the only times he had a pleasing scent. "Did you tell Mom and Dad? About the pendant?"

"Yes," he said. "I did."

"You showed them."

"Yes. I took them out of your closet and went downstairs and I told them. They were angry."

"That's understandable."

"Mommy was very angry."

"Well, now you know how bad it is to lie. And Mommy was upset because she was disappointed. But she loves you. Everyone loves you."

"Not everyone," he said.

"Who doesn't love you?"

"Me," he said. "I don't love me."

She was speechless for a moment. "Well, then it's a good

thing that there are all these other people to love you. Lie down, Alan." He did and she pulled the covers up under his chin and smoothed them down along his arms. "*I love you*," she said. "That's a pretty good start."

He turned on his side and curled up like a bug. His big brown eyes looked up at her. "I got the heart from Daddy's store."

"We all know that now. It's over. Close your eyes."

He did. She watched him for a while. After a few minutes, one of his legs kicked a little and he was asleep.

Downstairs, she found her mother leaning against the wall in the kitchen, talking on the phone and smoking. Her father was in his library where she knew he would be until he went to bed. "I need to talk to you," Hazel whispered.

Her mother nodded at her, but it was a *come back in ten minutes* nod.

"No, now," Hazel insisted.

"Just a moment," her mother said into the phone. She covered it with her hand. "Isn't it pretty close to your bedtime?"

"Did Alan tell you?"

"Yes. For goodness sake, what a song and dance!"

"It's good for him that he told the truth."

"Yes. I'm talking to Grandma. Go brush your teeth."

"You never doubted him for a minute, though, right?" Her mother put the phone receiver against her chest. "You knew he was innocent the whole time. Right?"

"Yes, sweetheart, I didn't believe it was him. He's a good boy. Now go to bed." She put the phone to her ear again. "Your granddaughter. As mulish as your daughter . . . Yes, Ma, it does."

Hazel had seen in her mother's eyes that she'd lied. His own mother had needed proof, and Hazel would never forget this. She was the only one who believed in Alan. She was the only friend he had in the world.

] 25 [

Monday evening

An hour after being abandoned by Cutter at the roadside, Wingate was picked up by a pair of his colleagues from Fort Leonard.

It was humiliating to ride in the back of an OPS vehicle, although he noted the seats were pretty comfortable. He asked the constables to contact Hazel Micallef and she'd explain and get them to take him down to Port Dundas. But they weren't having it. No badge, no radio, empty holster. In addition to this, they weren't too keen on helping a Port Dundas gumshoe – if that, in fact, was what he was – since his job was a lot safer than theirs. Half of Fort Leonard's cops were being redeployed to Port Dundas; the fate of the rest remained up in the air.

They took him to their station house, where a man with

an air of dreamy distraction took his statement. Wingate told the truth. There was no point now in finessing it: he was done.

Maybe it was for the best. He had not yet passed a day since he'd woken up from his coma when he felt safe. He felt a constant shadow on him and he called it dread. He had wanted to die when they'd killed his lover, David, and he'd wanted to murder as well, but he had never feared *being* dead until that long night that followed being buried alive. Not the night itself, but the featureless sleep of coma, when he was dead to himself, unaware. A *not-thing*. Waking from that, his mind was changed, even more so than his body had been. Sometimes the dread was like awe. He'd been thinking that he was in an early stage of madness and perhaps everyone would know that now.

Hazel told them to hold on to him until morning then put him on the train. She did not want to speak to him. The station house had a quiet room with a cot. They gave him a cold can of Coke, a bag of ketchup chips, and a microwave pizza. Afterward, he had indigestion.

The groundbreaking for Gateway Plaza was set for next afternoon. Fittingly, it was the day before Hallowe'en, and it was even money that Chip Willan would come dressed as a pirate. It was an occupational hazard, seeing Willan in costume the week of Hallowe'en. Those on active duty, and those with ranks above constable, were expected to attend. All others were *encouraged*. "The union's line," Kraut Fraser said, "is that on-duty officers *should* attend the ribbon cutting except if it would interfere with their duties, and off-duty personnel are invited and encouraged to attend." He held his hands up for silence. "If you don't wanna go, find something necessary to do, but –" and here he reached out to stop Hazel from rushing past " – all ranked officers above constable *will* show their support."

"I'm going to pick up Wingate at the train station."

"He's not on today."

"I know that."

"You'll be at the groundbreaking, though. Two p.m."

"Yes," she said, exasperated with him. She pushed the door to the rear lot open a little too hard and it banged. She drove to the train station feeling so livid she imagined slapping Wingate's face. He was finished if she told Greene.

He came out of the tiny brick train station with his uniform in a cloth Loblaws shopping bag. He hadn't slept. She felt a pang for him that doused her rage and she leaned over to open the passenger door.

"Thank you," he said.

"There's something very wrong with you, James."

"I know."

She put the radio on quietly and drove up to Main Street. "What am I supposed to do with you?"

"Don't get into trouble for my sake."

"But *why* did you go up there?"

He couldn't make words for a moment. "I wanted to do my job."

"Your job is recovering. You know that."

"No," he said. "My job is police detective."

She stopped a couple of streets away from his apartment and turned to face him. "What did you find out?"

"Cutter didn't kill the Fremonts."

"He told you that."

"Yes."

"You believe him?"

"He was pretty proud of himself for what he *had* done. So, yes. He denied Givens, too. He wants us to solve the case before he lets Renald go. But Yoshida told me something."

"What?"

"Your theory, about someone practising eugenics? It might be right."

"Go on."

He told her about Merchant and his organization. She'd heard of Merchant because he'd endowed a wing of the college in Mayfair. "Yoshida gave me some bulletins that they published there. I have them in the bag in my cruiser. You recovered my cruiser?"

"Yes. Lucky for you."

"Merchant was a public figure. Yoshida says he saw him at Dublin Home. He says he looked like the man pictured in the bulletin."

"I'll take those and Fraser can go through them."

"Hazel," he said. "Please. Let me finish. I won't leave the apartment."

"How can I possibly — ?"

"It doesn't help the case for me to hand over my work when I'm just putting things together."

"But *you're* coming apart!"

The motor was still running. Hazel turned it off.

"I'm almost finished tracing the names of the survivors," Wingate pleaded. "There are already another dozen from Dublin Home, and some of them will be witnesses, too. Let me finish and I'll go back to Toronto with Michael. That's what he's been asking me to do. I'll do it when the case is done. Please, Hazel."

The day started grey and threatening, but by the time two o'clock came around, the sky had cleared. Under a large tent hastily erected in case of rain, Charles Willan was sitting in a throne-like chair on a raised platform, together with a half-dozen dignitaries. Instead of a costume, he was wearing his serious, metallic grey suit that Hazel thought made him look appropriately robotic. In front of the platform, a polite crowd was listening to the mayor extol the many benefits that the new plaza would bring not just to the town but to the province as a whole. Beside Willan, the local MPP — a round, gleaming Tory who was a fixture at such events – was nodding along, a grin glued in place.

After the mayor spoke, the developer expounded not briefly enough on what an exciting step forward in design the plaza would be. That made Hazel peer more closely at the billboard-sized rendering of the development that had been erected where the entrance would go. It looked the same to her as any other plaza: a sprawl of stuccoed boxes hemming a parking lot. The one in the drawing had boxes with green roofs, but Hazel couldn't tell if the green was supposed to be grass or metal shingles. She twisted around to see who else from the station had shown up to do their duty here until Fraser nudged her. Willan was standing up to speak. He glanced at some notes he then tucked into his pocket, clutched the edges of the lectern, and switched on a smile. "Thank you, thank you," he said to the silent gathering. "What a proud day it is for all us witnessing it, eh?"

A partial smattering of applause.

"This is a moment in history. We are sharing a historical moment together. This afternoon we will mark the beginning of a new *future* as a community, a county, and a police force!"

They had been lectured about pride, and so this time the police in the crowd led the clapping. Charles S. Willan beamed. He explained how the officers of OPS Central were like spies who hadn't been let in out of the cold yet. He was here to change that, to bring policing into the twenty-first century. The new North–Central police division symbolized that, by being at the heart of the innovative Gateway Plaza. "Come in from out of the cold, OPS Central Division. Come to the heart of Westmuir. Come to Gateway Plaza and be at the hub, where everything happens."

"Is it a heart or a hub?" said Fraser in Hazel's car. "An ass or a teacup?"

"Shh. I'm listening to the pontiff."

A voice shouted: "When you fire half of Fort Leonard, will we get driving allowances so we can work at the new Walmart in Port Dundas?" Willan registered the interruption with a flash of teeth and then he stepped away from the lectern.

After final remarks by the mayor, the five dignitaries descended the platform and were ushered over to a patch of dirt where each was handed a small ceremonial shovel by one of three little girls lost in their frills and two boys uncomfortable in boxy suits. The crowd *oooh*ed, then the men jabbed their shovels into ground that had already been loosened. Almost in unison, they turned dirt, grinning for the cameras gathered around them.

There was muted applause and someone shouted "YEAH!" but that was all the celebration that took place. The gathering immediately began to lose its coherence. Willan bent to say something to the MPP, then stepped into the crowd with his hand extended.

Behind Hazel in the tent, a man in a pair of filthy overalls and a yellow helmet came up to the microphone. "The,
uh, mayor was supposta say our permit is live as of the
hour of noon and we're gonna do some *blastin'*, folks. Stick
around if you want to see sompin' cool!" Willan intercepted
the man as he stepped away, and snarled a couple of words
into his ear before pushing him back toward the microphone. "Sorry, folks," he said, "I meant the deputy commissioner. Of police, I was supposta say."

Fans of loud noises seemed to be changing their minds
about going home. The average age in this group was thirty.
The others – mostly in uniform – left in a cloud of murmurs.
Willan came to where Hazel was standing with Fraser and
she touched her cap. He hardly acknowledged her, brush-
ing past and looking for hands to shake. The crowd had
been made up of anyone who cared to witness the historic
moment, including prominent businesspeople (those who
had to make nice at such events to ensure themselves a slice
of the pie), a couple of local sports celebrities, and Mayfair's
obnoxious morning show duo, Sally and Gonzo Pete. These
two were recording something for the radio's Web page.
Sally, the pretty half of the duo, on the mic: "Whaddya say
we spin some tunes to blast by? Or are we blasted already?"
There was a big cry of approval. Now Hazel understood
what this was: the crowd that remained was here because
of a radio contest. "Who's gonna be 107 the Thunder's
Plunger Pusher?"

Another huge cry. Ray drifted over to where she was. "You can watch this live on the Internet," he said. "I heard about it on television. One of those plungers will set off the ceremonial first blast."

She crossed her arms over her chest and looked on with nauseated horror. "The people who listen to this radio station will do anything for fun."

"The winning plunger gets three thousand bucks and a year's worth of cinnamon buns from the bakery," he told her.

"What is defined as a year's worth?"

"Exactly."

Sally called: "Who are our three lucky plungers, girls and boys?"

The other half of the duo, Gonzo Pete, stood with the contestants. He looked nothing like his radio voice. For one thing, he was white. "Imma got me a trio of plunger-pushing plenitude and pulchritude!"

"Haw haw," said Sally. The three contestants were given hard hats.

"Jesus," said Hazel, "this is *fucked*." She strode forward, toward the woman who was speaking into the camera.

"These three lucky plungers are about to see – oh . . . yes?" Hazel barged into the shot. "Oh, excuse me!" She laughed. "I think I'm being arrested! Officer, are you going to arrest me live on air?"

"No," Hazel said. "Can I have that microphone for just thirty seconds?"

"Of course! People, everyone, this is a policewoman! She wants to talk to you all for thirty seconds, OK? I think one of you left your lights on!"

Gales of laughter. Hazel took the mic. Instead of facing the crowd, she spoke into the camera. "For all you people out there watching a hill get blown up on the Internet, I want to ask if any of you even know what it's called?" A few answers lifted out of the crowd, some of them correct. She turned to acknowledge them. "That's right," she said. "We still call it the Lion's Paw. My mother, who grew up in this town, says her own mother called it that. People have been walking its bluffs since long before there were any towns or cities in this country.

"When I was a kid, you could see Highway 41 rolling away from the toe of the paw. And you could walk around, away from town, and look over the marshes, or you could come back where you started and look down into Port Dundas, founded 1841. And now someone's going to blow it up. I hope you're pleased with yourselves."

The crowd roared with delight. Hazel passed the microphone back.

"Awesome!" Sally shouted. Gonzo Pete primed the dynamite plungers like a race official with a gun, and set the first contestant to her plunger. People put their fingers in their ears.

Hazel retreated to stand with Ray. "Do you know Gonzo Pete got his explosives licence *just* so he could prime those plungers?" Ray said in her ear. "What do you think they'll call it now?"

"The Lion's Stump."

Sally wished the contestant luck and counted her down from three. The girl plunged and there was an enormous, ear-splitting explosion.

Hazel gasped. A cloud of dust rose before the crowd and chunks of stone began to rain down.

It took a couple of moments before she heard the screaming, and then people started stampeding for the road. The debris smacked into the dirt and asphalt and some people fell to the ground. A rock the size of a dinner bun smashed down in front of them, and Ray grabbed Hazel's elbow and pulled her back.

She tasted dirt and heard people shouting and calling out for each other. Ray's weight pushed down on her. "Not so hard!"

"Geddown, geddown!" he said, out of breath. She allowed him to put her on the ground.

"How deep were those fucking charges?"

"I don't . . ." he said. "I don't." He was becoming heavier.

"Ray?" She pushed him off and he fell onto his back. Blood trickled from his hairline. "Ray! *Oh my god!*" She scrambled to her feet. "I need help!" she shouted. "Somebody call an ambulance!"

People ran past her in both directions to escape or to help, and she saw bodies lying on the ground on the grassy verge below the hill. Sally staggered up to standing from where she'd been blown flat, and shook off the dirt and pebbles that matted her blonde locks. She wanted to keep going. She rolled her index finger forward in the air and her cameraman mounted his camera to his shoulder. More people were running toward the blast site now than were running away. Hazel followed the eye of the crowd. At the base of the blasted paw, people scrambled over fallen rock and climbed upward. "You!" she called to a paramedic. "Come here!" Ray coughed and lurched halfway up. "Stay where you are!" she said. "Do you hear me?"

"I hear you," he croaked.

She left him and broke into a jog to get to the front of the gawkers. Above the scattered, broken rock, Hazel saw the cameraman balancing on a stone ledge, his lens flaring with sun. Above him, Sally had a serious look on her face as she talked into the mic, her other hand gesturing over and over to something Hazel still could not see.

She clambered up to where the girl stood.

"You again?"

Hazel paid her no attention. She stood with her back to the camera, her heart pounding in her throat, and gazed upon the upper half of a skeleton: an unmistakable ruffle of human ribs arrayed in gentle arcs with shabby tufts of cloth still clinging to bone. Through the ribs, she saw a shamble of vertebrae and she traced those up with her eyes until they fell on the empty, grimacing skull.

] 26 [

Tuesday, October 30, afternoon

Hazel closed her front door on the world and stared down the empty hallway. She stripped to her blouse and underwear and left her dirt-covered clothing on the mat. She had already shaken her hair out in the driveway and she ran her fingers through the gritty strands.

She tiptoed down the hall to the bathroom and looked at herself in the mirror. Her eyes seemed bright, shining out of the grime. This must be what the survivors of Vesuvius looked like, she thought. She turned on the hot and began to wash her face. Black water rushed down the drain.

Ray was OK. He'd been struck by something large enough to produce a wobbly lump the size of a golf ball on his head. She'd last seen him in the back of an ambulance.

Others were hurt, too. Luckily, no one had been killed. The injured had lain scattered around, some of them badly banged up, the paramedics in their yellow jackets moving among them like bumblebees.

She opened the mirrored cabinet door and looked for some ibuprofen. She'd made a point of keeping any pain-killers – OTC or not – upstairs. She'd been thorough; there was nothing there. When she closed the mirror, her mother was standing in it. "Oh! Jesus Christ."

"You're a sight," Emily said. "Don't you dare use one of those hand towels. Those are for guests. What on earth have you been doing?"

"I was at the groundbreaking. And then they had this . . . contest to see who would start the blasting."

"What nonsense are you talking?"

Hazel smelled cigarette smoke. "Mom, are you smoking?"

"No. Paula Spencer is smoking."

"Who?"

Emily shook her head like she was giving up. "You've met Paula a thousand times. I couldn't find my cigs, so she came over. *She* still smokes."

Paula Spencer had been one of her mother's old friends. They'd played cards together until just a few years ago. But Paula Spencer was dead.

Emily said, "So where are they? My cigarettes?"

Hazel folded the hand towel over its rail. Without looking at her mother, she said, "I think I saw them in the kitchen."

In the mirror, she saw her mother leave the bathroom. Hazel followed her, mind racing.

"I don't see them in here," Emily called from the kitchen.

"No? Oh, right! I think I saw them upstairs," Hazel said. "Why don't I go get them."

"Don't you go upstairs still covered in muck. I'll find them. They must be with the ashtray." Emily spoke in a clear voice, at odds with the way she walked, which was like an old woman full of pains.

Hazel waited at the bottom of the stairs, still in shock. They'd blasted clear to the base of the bluff, tearing away fifteen metres of broken crag and boulder that had obscured it for half a century. The SOCOs had gotten to the skeleton before she could examine it any closer.

But it had to be Carol Lim.

And she *was* smelling cigarette smoke. Had her mother walked all the way to the convenience store to buy herself a pack?

She checked her cell. Nothing. The remains would be arriving at Mayfair any time now.

Emily came back down the stairs, flustered. Hazel cut her off at the pass. "Mom? Look at me. Do I look like I'm fifteen years old?"

"No."

"I'm not. And you're not in your forties anymore. You don't *smoke* anymore. You're confused, Mom. Don't you know that?"

"Ha!" she cawed. "Paula, do you hear that?"

Hazel took her mother's arm and brought her into the living room to show her it was empty. Except it wasn't. There was an elderly woman sitting on the couch smoking a thin white cigarette.

"Hazel," the woman said, looking her up and down. Hazel realized she was standing there in her bra and underwear. "You haven't changed a bit."

"Mrs. Spencer!" She began to back out of the room, all the while making white-hot eye contact with her mother. "I really . . . I had no idea . . ."

"It's a surprise to find some people are still alive. Henry Kissinger is still alive. So is Bob Hope."

Hazel stood outside the room with her back to the wall. "Bob Hope died four years ago."

"Oh shit, did he really?"

She went to the front hall and took a black raincoat out of the closet. She cinched it around her waist and went back into the living room. "You can't smoke in the house, Paula."

"I forgot," she said, looking not in the least contrite. "The rules have changed."

Her mother waggled the remote control at the television. "That thing is not worth the money your father paid for it," she said. "Alan was right."

"Was he, Mom?"

"He's got a good head for *things*, your brother. But I worry about him." She took Hazel's hands in hers. "It's up to you to look after him when we're gone, dear."

Tuesday was her normal day off, but she was just waiting for Deacon to call her so she could go down to the
morgue. Her stomach had turned sour with worry: would
the pendant be there? Would it have rusted away? Maybe it
hadn't been silver after all.

Wingate had texted her asking permission to go back to
the archives. It was highly unlikely that Cutter would be
there, and he knew he could talk his way past Putchkey. She
gave her assent. He wanted to look deeper into Merchant's
relationship with Dublin Home.

Paula Spencer left.

"You thought she was dead."

"It's hard to keep track these days, Mom. Don't you
find?"

"A human life is like a bead of water on a hot griddle. I
want to watch a movie."

Hazel found an old Natalie Wood drama and her mother
became engrossed. She joined her for a while, and then went
to the kitchen to make them both toast and peanut butter.
She cut thick slices of banana on top and drizzled a tiny bit
of maple syrup on it. Her father had come home one day
with a hankering for it and it had become a family favourite.
Later, it was implicated in the revelation of her father's
affair with Delia Chandler. It had been her recipe. Everyone
in that story was dead now except for her and Emily.

They sat together on the couch, eating toast. She left
her mother asleep before the movie ended and crept away

to clean up. In the kitchen, the light from the television flickered, a silent party in another room.

At four o'clock, her phone buzzed. It was Deacon, inviting her down to the morgue. She drove to Mayfair with her lights going but no siren and made it there in less than an hour. Ray, his head wrapped in white gauze, had got there first.

Deacon repeated the cause of death, but Hazel was barely listening.

"It's hard not to conclude it was a fall," he said. "Lots of blunt-force trauma. But I don't think that tells us much about what happened."

"Where are the personal effects?"

He pointed her to a table near the morgue door. In a deep plastic bin, she found the remnants of clothing and shoes and a coat, panels of which were still intact. Hazel put on a pair of latex gloves and dug under the rotted fibres: a desiccated pink elastic band, a couple of rusted rings, a pocket Bible, a rusted belt buckle, a metal container, and two small stamped gilt earrings, each in the shape of a leaf and eaten away as if they were real leaves.

At the bottom, leaning vertically against the side of the bin, she found the graven heart. It was tarnished black and smoothed like a river stone by its fifty winters, but the rabbit was still in mid-stride, running for its life.

"It *is* her," she said.

Ray lifted his head. "Who's her?"

She came over to the steel table on which the bones lay in an approximate human shape. She imagined that skeleton inside Carol's living body, and all the years it had lain undiscovered among the rocks in the ankle of the Lion's Paw. "This is a girl who went missing almost fifty years ago. Her name was Carol Lim."

"I remember her," Ray said.

"I do as well," echoed Jack Deacon. "How do you know?"

"She wore this around her neck." She put the heart into Ray's gloved hand. "I saw it on her the day she vanished."

"Where?"

"It was by chance. In the fall of 1957, when I was fourteen. I was out for a walk with a friend." She couldn't help pausing, watching his eyes. "Gloria Whitman."

"*Really*," said Ray in a tone of wonder.

"You remember her. They lived alone in the big stone house at the end of my street, overlooking the river. Just the two of them. Her mother died when she was a young girl."

"How did her mother die?" Ray asked.

"I was told cancer."

"What happened on your walk?"

"We'd gone to the Pit, so Gloria could smoke and drink some of her father's brandy. Fifteen minutes earlier, she'd stolen the cigarettes she was smoking from guess who?"

"Herbert Lim."

"And so, along comes Carol eventually. It wasn't ever clear to me if she'd seen Gloria stealing from her father, or if she was just out for a walk like us. She was seventeen. Long hair, black as crow feathers. She must have heard us or smelled the smoke and she came down into the Pit. I remember her talking about sex. She was sort of provoking us. Carol took one of the smokes – I think she took the whole pack, actually – and she wanted a drink from Gloria's flask. I remember what she said to us when she left us alone. She said, 'See ya later, lovers.' She walked away and as far as I know, we were the last people to see her alive."

Deacon inspected the pendant. "Do they still own that corner store?"

"Until about ten years ago," Hazel said. She suddenly felt dizzy, as if she were going to fall down. "Her father died. Her mother . . . her mother . . ."

Ray reached out and took her elbow. "Hazel?"

She returned to the box of Carol's effects, her stomach churning, and ran her hands through them again until she came upon the metal container. "No," she whispered.

"What's going on?" Ray asked.

"This is the flask. Gloria's flask."

"Carol took the smokes and the flask?"

"No," Hazel said. "I remember distinctly that Gloria offered me a drink from it after we had seen Carol. I declined. I didn't want to smell like brandy. Gloria finished it off . . . she put the flask away . . ." She put her face in her hands, and Ray came over and touched her shoulder. "Some people thought she was still alive . . ."

"After all this time? Who?"

She could barely speak. "Me." She shrugged off Ray's touch. "I have to go," she said.

"But what's going on?" he asked her, and she broke down, weeping, and left the room. "Hey!" he called, but he knew he had to let her go.

After a few minutes, he went up to the main entrance of the hospital. Kids in Hallowe'en costumes were walking through the lobby, and he saw a couple of them go up in an elevator. He found her standing in the dead grass by the entrance to the parking garage. There wasn't a cloud in the sky, but to him she looked like a black-and-white photograph. There was a look of pure despair on her face. "Hazel!" he called.

"I'm sorry," she said, trying to wave him off.

He stopped ten feet from her. "It's OK. I can go away and come back."

She muttered something under her breath.

"I'll go," he said.

"No . . . stay."

He went to her and she let him put his arms around her and she wept into his coat. He rubbed her back and said whatever soothing words came to his mind. When she was calmer, she patted his shoulder and he let go of her. She told him what she remembered about the days after Carol's disappearance: things she hadn't thought of in decades. She told him about their meetings with Commander Drury. "I'm sure I must've wondered about her even then," she said. "It was just too horrible to consider, but years afterward it would come into my mind: what if Carol's not in Toronto? What if Gloria killed her?" She looked at him through red, swollen eyes. "That's the first time I've ever said that to anyone."

He gave her a moment to finish collecting herself. All around them in the quickly dwindling afternoon light, people were streaming in and out of the hospital, including the early Hallowe'en celebrants. "Greater proportion of costumed patients than normal."

"Must be a full moon." She took a couple of deliberate deep breaths. "In my heart, I knew Carol was dead. Even though I found evidence she was alive."

"What do you mean, *evidence*?"

She got her keys out. "My first investigation. I'll tell you another time." He walked with her back to where they'd left their cruisers.

They held the press conference at 7:00 p.m. Ray Greene — wearing an OPS cap over the gauze wrapped around his head — and Willan flanked her on either side of the wooden podium at the front of the station's conference room. Behind them hung the OPS insignia on a white background. Willan's face looked painted white.

Cartwright had told her that eleven newspapers and TV stations had RSVPed, including CTV, the *Westmuir Record*, the *Toronto Star*, the *Hamilton Spectator*, and the *Mayfair Packet and Telegram*. There were a number of people at the back with video cameras on their shoulders: TV cameramen, news bloggers. On the rolling bulletin board to her right was a picture of Carol Lim taken in 1956 and, beside it, an image of her bones as they'd been found in the crater of the Lion's Paw. The reporters packed in close with their notebooks out, like policemen.

"Thank you for coming on such short notice," Hazel said. "Please keep your questions until the end, there's quite a bit to get through." She pointed at the board. "This is Carol Lim. She was born here in Port Dundas, on November 14, 1939. In October 1957, she disappeared, and despite concerted efforts to find or contact her she was never seen again. Earlier today, her bones were uncovered at the new Gateway Plaza site, during a groundbreaking ceremony —" here she gestured to her right, at Willan, and he raised his hand, half waving. "We don't have final confirmation of identity yet," she continued.

"Urbina Kellog, *Hamilton Spectator*," said a woman at the front. "I understand, and I can see from that other picture there, that the skeleton was discovered during blasting, not during the groundbreaking."

"You're correct," Hazel said. "I was getting to that."

"You said during the groundbreaking."

"It wasn't. You're quite right. In fact, it was a ground-breaking, and afterwards a blast." The skill of restraint came with practice. "There was a . . . an *inaugural* blast *after* the groundbreaking, and it was then that these remains were unearthed. We have every reason to believe, from personal items found at the site, that this is Carol Lim." A small hubbub erupted. She held her hands up. "This has been a very upsetting discovery, but it is the end of a fifty-year mystery. We send our condolences out today to the whole Lim family. We ask you to respect their privacy at this time."

"Was she murdered?" asked the reporter in the front row.

"Um, thank you. If you'll hold your questions till the end."

"Do you have any suspects?" came a voice from deep within the room.

"This is a startling development, and we don't have any theories yet about whether it was an accident or if foul play was involved."

"Is the discovery of her death linked to the discoveries in Tournament Acres?"

"Which paper are you from, sir?"

The reporter stepped forward so she could see him. He was dressed in a suit and tie, holding a notebook and pen in front of himself. There was no way of disguising his beard. "*Royal Canadian News*," said Superintendent Martin Scott.

"Sir, would you hold your questions until the end?"

"Actually, I had a question for the deputy commissioner."

"It can't wait?"

Scott stared at her fixedly. His gaze was about ten per cent mischievous. "I don't think it should wait," he said.

Hazel looked over at Willan, but if he knew Martin Scott, it didn't show on his washed-out features. He tried to smile as he stepped up to the podium. "Yes? Mr. . . . ?"

"Scott. Can I just offer my condolences on this sad day. It must be very difficult for you all."

"Thank you, yes, uh, thank you, Mr. . . . Scott."

"I mean, your new HQ and the whole plaza up there will certainly be delayed and perhaps even revisited, don't you think? I bet some people are going to lose a lot of money."

Hazel began to smile.

"Yes, that's a . . . something that we, as a unit –" Willan fumbled.

"Deputy Commissioner," Scott continued, "do you sit on any professional boards as a paid director?"

"Do I what? What has that to do with what happened to this poor girl?"

"Do you have a financial interest in the golf development called Tournament Acres?"

"I'll just turn this back over to –" Willan looked to Hazel for help, but there was none forthcoming.

"Where were you, sir, the night of October eighteenth?"

"What is this?"

A low hum began to spread through the room. Scott said, "How close were you to the murder victim Oscar Fremont?"

Willan decided to take the high road. "Sir, whoever you are, this a press conference about a missing girl –"

"I'm sorry for interrupting. It's just, seeing as I needed to arrest you for commercial crimes and major fraud, I thought it would be a good place to come find you. Was I wrong?"

The place erupted. Willan shouted, "Now hold on! Hold on a second!" but Scott was striding toward him and Willan elected to get out of the room fast. Hazel locked eyes with Martin Scott and mouthed *What the fuck are you doing?* The press was already streaming out after the deputy. Ray said, "Do you want me to stop him?"

"I'm guessing the superintendent," she said, pointing to Scott, "will have a small posse outside waiting for Charles." She saw Scott coming over. "Thanks for hijacking my press conference."

"You can have your fields back now. Isn't that what you wanted?"

"Are you telling me that *that* man killed the Fremonts?"

"Oh no," Scott replied. "Unless I'm very mistaken, he had someone else do the killing." He turned to join in what – from the commotion they heard – was certainly Willan's arrest outside the station house, but Hazel grabbed his arm.

"What has he done?"

"Let's just say he's found novel ways of benefitting from his position."

"You still can't tell me."

"No." He turned sharply to Ray Greene. "Commander."

"Superintendent," he said.

"Detective Inspector," Scott said.

"Yeah, yeah. I'll be in touch," she said.

They watched him walk through the pen, where he was looked upon as a sorcerer of some kind. "Is he allowed to do that?" Ray asked.

"Do what? Sashay? Have you never seen a big man sashay?"

"Make an arrest in the middle of a press conference?"

She pushed the front doors to the station house open and they walked out into the night. Up at the corner of Porter and Main Street, three RCMP cruisers were blocking traffic in all directions, and in the middle of the T-shaped intersection illuminated by street lights, Superintendent Martin Scott was putting cuffs on Chip Willan.

] 27 [

Tuesday evening

The moment she walked back into her office (still shaking her head in wonder), Melanie Cartwright was standing at her door. "What just happened?"

"The RCMP arrested Superintendent Willan."

"No way! For what?"

"Maybe just for being an asshole. And also other things. Apparently, we have to wait for the movie."

"Not a good week to be Chip Willan, then."

"No." Melanie stood in the doorway, a distant look on her face. "Is there anything else?" Hazel asked.

"Oh, yeah, this." She handed Hazel a printout. "DS Wingate sent this."

She took it from Cartwright's hand. Wingate had written across the top: *A link? Found it among the bulletins.*

A.R. MERCHANT
Merchant Rubber Company
130 Juniper Street
Mayfair, ON

September 19, 1952

Dear Doctor Whitman,

I am replying to you from our corporate address. Please do not write me at OPIC, which is for newspapermen and fundraising. It's an office where anyone might open a letter. In any case, it came to me and I destroyed it as per our arrangement. I hope you are not becoming forgetful.

On to your request. It is hard enough to get the courts to acknowledge our right to distribute information about contraception, let alone distribute our stock of it, so you can be sure Ontario is not ready for more novel methods of prevention. Our Foundation is engaged in activities throughout the country disseminating information about birth control and providing contraceptives to women who request it. A court challenge against one of our nurses was struck down and failed on appeal as well. But we are still on thin ice.

The prevention of the reproduction of less fortunate members of society is a boon to them and to society as well. I am in favour of sterilization for wards such as yours; indeed, they should be sterilized just as we spay our cats, and as I have said in past correspondence, I would be most happy to move forward with you as an expert witness in the pursuit of this goal. I would be happy to lend my not-inconsiderable Rolodex to you for the purposes of fund-raising and finding like-minded men.

What I cannot do is supply you with the substance you have requested because I am not a doctor. I'm certain my medically-trained colleagues here in Waterloo would feel the same way. So you are left to your methods for now, however work-intensive they may be. I hope there is a time when we can stand together as champions of our own species, but for now I can do nothing but wish you luck. Be careful.

Yours,

A.R. Merchant

Hazel read it again and then walked the letter down to Ray's office.

"Are you sure this is authentic?"

"Wingate is sure."

"Wingate is *off* today," Ray said. "Or is he?"

"He's still plowing through data. He's set up at home on two laptops, and he's also taking notes, I understand.

Everything is OK," she said, to stifle his rising displeasure.

"Whose laptops?"

"Company's. And he's doing all of it through our server, neat as a pin."

"When is this going to end? He's off duty as well as on leave, but he's sitting at home with two of our laptops?"

She'd come ready to fight. She'd foreseen she was going to need a heated conversation with Ray to keep his attention off James. "How come you don't get that there is some urgency to this?" she asked him. "One of *your* officers is being held by these people and so we are working for *them* now. What else is there?"

"What has that got to do with *Wingate* working from *home*?"

"It's all hands on deck now. He's got focus enough and it's good for him."

"Oh, fuck what's good for him now!" Ray shouted. "When this case is done, someone much higher than Willan is going to shit down our necks."

"Because they're going to shut down Gateway? Good."

"Who knows what they'll do? The skeleton of a young woman tends to change the meaning of 'shopping destination.'"

"Whatever form salvation takes, let's accept it."

He shook his head with disdain. "You think this will be enough to save this town? You're dreaming. I bet whatever comes next will make you long for Chip Willan."

"What comes next is death, right?"

He read the letter again, a small snarl forming on his upper lip. She hadn't seen Ray this angry in a long time and it made her faith in him suddenly deepen.

"What do you think Whitman wanted?" he asked.

"Something hard to get, maybe arsenic. Easy to weaken them slowly and then do whatever he wanted to them." She plucked the page back. "This is what Cutter wants. In exchange for Renald. That's job one right now."

"Then how do we get in touch with him?"

"He'd said he'd be in touch with *us*, but it would be nice to get the jump, get in front of him. In the meantime, I better find Gloria Whitman, and I'm thinking you might want to find a death certificate and a burial place for Mother Whitman. Maybe even an exhumation."

"What are you thinking?"

"Just covering the bases."

The following morning, a bright autumn Wednesday under a cloudless sky, Hazel made two phone calls from the road. The first was to Clipper Falls, where, according to her last tax return, Gloria Whitman now lived.

"Betty French Hair Emporium, how may I help you?"

"Hi!" She put the call on speakerphone. "I want to make an appointment to get my highlights done. I hear Gloria is the best for that."

"Gloria is booked solid through to the end of the week, ma'am. Our stylists are all fully –"

"Can she see me today?"

"She's not even in today, ma'am."

"Ah. OK then. I'll call back."

She dialled Wingate. He answered after one ring.

"Bingo," she said.

"She works there?"

"Yes. But she's not in today. I'm going to go to the house. How's the data crunching going? How many more names of survivors do you have?"

"Over a hundred now."

"Wow. Living?"

"More than half of them. A lot of these names we've come across before, but they weren't dead ends, so we put them aside. There are a lot of men still living in Ontario who were boys at Dublin Home when Whitman was employed there. I'm only just realizing now how deep it goes. How many people are affected."

"I think the government should cough up a lot of money to the men who lived through such terror. And people should know what happened. Any dead ends turn out to be name changes?"

"A couple. And then I caught a few more. I'll keep going."

"Thank you, James. This is my exit."

"Be careful, Hazel."

She hung up and drove along Concession Road 33 to Clipper Falls. Another half hour to the east.

"Was that her?" Michael asked his brother.

"It's almost over," James replied. "It's going faster now."

"If the union or the OPS learns what you've been doing and what they've been doing, they might shut the whole detachment down. And do you think they'll be willing to keep you on payroll if this comes out?" He set down a mug of hot marijuana tea.

"I don't want any more tea, Michael. It makes me drowsy."

"It's slightly sleepy or pain, you choose."

"Pain."

James had converted the kitchen table into a workspace. Both laptops were open on the table in front of him, and there were arcs of paper piles of varying heights on either side of him.

"Can you even focus anymore?"

"The pain focuses me. You see this?" He spread his arms and regally presented the investigating layout. "To my right, copies of personnel records from Dublin Home and Charterhouse, as well as copies of signed contracts for nurses, doctors, and staff. These over here are copies of some of the original intake and discharge records from the homes; there are over a thousand names in those piles there. Both computers are logged onto the secure server at the station house, the one on the right is —"

"Why the fuck are you —"

"The one on the right is connected to an archive of public records in Ontario, the one on the left is connected to an archive database at Canada Revenue. So, you can see I'm pretty focussed. Hazel is watching my back. I don't need you or want you to worry about me anymore."

"Anymore."

"Not like this, hovering over me! It's been a year. I've officially survived."

"You should sue them. It's their fault you didn't obey the restrictions of your leave. They let it happen. And as a result, you're getting worse instead of better."

"Look!" said Wingate, becoming angry. "You swan in and out of here with your narcotic teas and weird salads saying you're here to *help* me, but I don't need that kind of help! I can boil a goddamn kettle, Michael. What I can't do right now is dot every *i* fast enough. Renald is still a captive and you're on me for not —"

"Hey, calm d —"

"No," said Wingate. "Why did you come here? To live somewhere for free? To make amends for being a shitty brother?"

"Jesus." Michael Wingate snatched the tea off the desk. "I came to help because you needed help and there was no one else. And if I'm a shitty brother, you're a shitty patient. Look at you."

"I have a job to do, OK? If you really want to help me, help me. Pull up a chair. Time is running out."

Michael was silent for a moment, and he looked angry and chastised. Then he put the teacup down and joined his brother at the table.

"Do you remember I told you about Leon Cutter?" James said.

"Yes."

"He had another name."

Gloria Whitman's home address in Clipper Falls was 11 Tennis Court. "Cute," Hazel said, craning her neck to find the street signs.

On the highway up, she put her flashers on, but no siren, and pushed down on the accelerator. She never got tired of motorists' reactions to the flashing lights: a brief panic followed by herky-jerky order. Tennis Court's stem road led to a circular street. You could go either way. She turned right and parked. The numbers on that side were in the fifties. She crossed the road and started at one.

Six houses in, she came to number eleven. A new-looking Mazda 5 was in the driveway – she noted the licence plate bracket said *Alamo/National*. She crept up to the gap between numbers nine and eleven and walked down a path. A small window midway along the side revealed flittings of shadow against a wall. There was movement in the back of the house.

A deck at the rear extended halfway into the backyard. Hazel pulled out her gun. Crouching down, she checked the yard. No dog. She went to the other side of the deck. From her vantage behind a wooden post, she could see the back door at ground level, and she could lift her head and see the sliding glass doors from the interior to the deck. In that room, a woman sat on a couch, bent forward over a coffee table and working on a laptop. Her mouth was busy: she held a cigarette in one corner of it while talking to one corner of her screen. Hazel watched her eyes scan up and then down and then up again. She crouched and leaned against the post. Was it Gloria? She hadn't seen her child-hood friend in at least forty years.

There was a sudden vibration in the post. She felt some-one's footsteps thudding in her shoulder.

When the thudding stopped, Hazel crab-walked to the back door and tried it: locked.

Her hands were shaking and sweating. A door shut inside the house and then nothing. She could either call for backup or kick in the door. She took two steps back and kicked in the door the way she'd been taught, with her foot sideways, right on the lock. "Coming in!" she shouted.

Silence.

She ducked her head to the right to look into the now-empty room and continued through the galley kitchen into the front hallway. "Gloria? I saw you through the window," she said. "It's Hazel Micallef. Come out."

She swept her Glock around to the stairs and then up at the second floor. She walked backward into the hall. "Who were you talking to, Gloria? She heard her voice echo upstairs. The first floor was clear. Through the dining room window, she confirmed the Mazda was still in the driveway. The house seemed empty now. A nice old house like this, you probably couldn't fart without making something creak. There was a thumping noise below her. Very soft.

Hazel kept her gun at the ready and slid back toward the kitchen. She knew what that sound was. She listened for its counterparts: a click and a hollow bonk, another click. A pause, as someone loaded wet laundry into the dryer. Then two hollow thuds in quick succession.

She heard footsteps ascend to a door under the stairs. Hazel stood in the open kitchen doorway, her gun drawn on a head-level bead.

The woman was singing. A *la-la* song, not something with words. Too bad. Not much of a soundtrack to end your freedom on. The basement door swung open and she stood there holding a suitcase with a newly lit cigarette between her lips.

Now Hazel was sore.

She cocked the gun.

"Hello, Gloria."

"Hello, Hazel."

"Put the suitcase down and go into the kitchen." She directed her with the end of the gun. "Take a seat."

Hazel waited until she complied, and then she took the old pewter flask out of her pocket and placed it onto the kitchen table in front of her.

] 28 [

Gloria's face drained of colour, making her features look cut in. She looked like an etching of herself. "I remember this," she said under her breath. She picked the flask up. "Where did you – ?"

"They found it with her bones."

"Whose?"

"Don't do that. You know whose bones."

Gloria Whitman – barefoot in grey sweats and a black T-shirt – took a drag on the cigarette and considered the flask. She'd kept her blonde hair and her nice shape; Hazel imagined she had as many younger lovers as she could handle. "Yes," she said. "I know."

Hazel sat beside her at the table. "You went back. Why?"

"I wanted to make sure she didn't tell my father. About stealing the cigarettes."

"And?"

Gloria flashed a look at Hazel that she couldn't inter-pret. Shame, or anger. "She'd gone back to the Pit. She was down there, smoking."

"How did you know to look for her there?"

"I didn't. I just retraced my steps and there she was."

"Waiting for you?"

"Smoking. I told her I was sorry about stealing the Luckys and I asked her if she'd keep it between us. She said, 'Why should I do that?' She stood up and came toward me."

"And? You defended yourself by – what? – hitting her on the head with a rock and shoving her over the edge?"

Tears began to run down Gloria's cheek. "No . . . no. I didn't mean to . . . I walked away from her! She followed me, calling me names, calling me 'white ghost.' You remem-ber, she was a lot bigger than me. When you and me were up there together, it was two against one. You could've taken her on your own." She searched Hazel's eyes for understanding. "But I couldn't. I tried to get away from her, but she caught up to me on the path and told me when my dad heard all the things I'd done, he'd probably disown me. I begged her. I offered her the flask, told her she could keep it. And then she . . . there was a . . ."

She couldn't continue.

Hazel put a hand on her arm. "It's OK . . . you're doing good. What happened?"

"*No*," Gloria said in a choked voice. She got up from the chair and stumbled to the sink, gagging. Hazel listened to her throw up. "I've lived with this for so long," she said after a moment. "Sometimes it doesn't feel real."

"What happened, Gloria?"

She remained hunched over the sink, her shoulders shaking. There was an empty water glass on the counter and Hazel rose to get it and fill it for her. She stood beside Gloria and ran the tap. There was no vomit in the sink. Gloria Whitman was no longer crying. She felt a hand on her shoulder and she froze.

"What happened next?" Gloria said in a quiet, calm voice. "What happened next is that there was one less Chink slut on the planet."

Hazel had no time to react. The blow drove her backwards into the kitchen table. She felt something hard explode against her forehead. The scent of iron filled her head.

"Nobody knows who Carol Lim was," Gloria Whitman said. Hazel heard a high-pitched squeal in her head. Out of the corner of her right eye, she saw a shiny white arc, like a piece of gleaming bone, and she reached up and pulled it out of her cheek. It was the handle of a mug.

Everything was moving in slow motion: her mind struggled with the information that Gloria had struck her and that there was blood steadily flowing down the side of her face. *What do I have to do right now?* she asked herself, trying to cut through the interference of pain and fear, and she brought her attention back to the room in time to see a knife clenched in Gloria's fist. She threw herself to the floor and rolled under the table, and Gloria slammed into it. The knife chunked into the wood above Hazel's head. She swung a leg out and hooked Gloria behind the knee and yanked. She heard the knee pop and Gloria flew backward like she'd slipped on a banana peel. Her head whacked the terra cotta floor. "God," Hazel panted, sliding out from under the table. She hoped she wasn't dead.

She wasn't. Somehow she was already trying to get to her feet. She wasn't too steady and by the time she was standing, Hazel was waiting for her with the Glock trained on a freckle between her eyes. "Give me one reason," she said. Gloria straightened her body. She'd had an ounce of pride knocked out of her, nothing more. "The instant I stop seeing both of your hands, I'll pull this trigger. Now go sit down in the living room. You can show me what you were doing on your computer."

There was blood all over the kitchen floor, drops and smears, all from Hazel's forehead and cheek. She didn't know how to stop it but there were other priorities right now. She moved Gloria out of the kitchen at the end of her gun. They went into the living room, which was done up in pretty yellows and blues. The couch was upholstered in a bright daisy print. Hazel pushed Gloria onto it and dripped onto the cushions and the cream-coloured shag rug. Dark, red spots. "What did you do?" Hazel said. She was beginning to feel dizzy. "Why did you go back?"

"I told you. To make sure she kept her mouth shut."

She stood up and kept the gun on Gloria. "Did you kill her?"

"I think the fall did." In her mind's eye, Hazel saw Gloria Whitman's head exploding. "You're a pretty sentimental person. You think people are all alike. They're not and the ones who aren't like us already know we're not like them. They think about it all the time, and they're doing something about it. Fucking themselves toward a majority. It's all about the numbers, Hazel. My father could count. Could yours?"

"Your father worked at local foster homes and nursing homes. He had a little circuit in Westmuir County."

"Daddy was busy. People loved him."

Hazel reached behind herself for a chair and tried not to take her eyes off Gloria. She spun the chair around and sat in it. "You really loved your dad, didn't you?"

"All girls love their daddies. And after Mama died, he was all I had. He threw himself into his work and forgot his suffering."

"How did your mother die?"

"I thought you wanted to know how *Carol* died. I went back and found her. 'One more nip before you go?' I asked her. Then she lost her footing."

"We've found the bones of almost two dozen boys in the fields at Dublin Home."

Gloria felt along her side of her head with a fingertip. It came away bloody. She smiled at it. "I looked over the edge and she was lying on a slanty rock face, her arms and legs pointing all over. She began to slip down between the cracks —"

"He came at night and drugged them in their beds and carried them out. Did to them whatever he felt like doing to them." Gloria listened impassively. Her face was still, her pupils tiny. "He killed them. And he hacked them apart. And burned their bodies in an incinerator. Anything that survived the fire, he scattered in the fields. He was a murderer. Did he teach you how to do it?"

Gloria gave her a cockeyed look. "Maybe I taught him."

"You're under arrest for the murder of Carol Lim. Do you understand? You have the right to retain and instruct council as soon as you wish. If you don't have your own lawyer, we will provide you with a toll-free telephone referral service."

"Our tax dollars at work," Gloria said. She seemed not the least perturbed by the situation she was in. For a moment, Hazel wondered if they were alone in the house.

"Anything you say can be used in court as evidence. Do you understand what I've said to you?"

"Oh, fuck off," Gloria replied, and Hazel cold-cocked her. She slumped against the back of the couch. Hazel cuffed her.

"Would you like to see a lawyer?" she said, completing the recitation of Gloria's rights over her insensate form. "We'll never get your dad for what he did, but we've got you." *How much blood can there be in a person's face?* she thought with a dreamy abstraction that she realized meant she was losing consciousness. She sat down on the couch beside Gloria, who was breathing the even, steady breaths of the unconscious. *How much blood can there be in your head?*

She dialled Wingate's home number. "What are you doing right now?"

"Michael and I are combing through data."

"Why?"

"What's going on? Did you find her?"

"I found her."

She heard his chair squeak back. "What's wrong?"

"Gloria tried to drink coffee out of my skull."

"What?"

"Never mind. I'm a little shaky, but I think I'm OK. I have her. She's asleep. Can you drive? How much of your brother's happy tea have you had?"

"None."

"Then get going. Head north on 33, flashers no sirens. I'll do the same."

"What did you do to Gloria Whitman?"

"Only what was necessary," she said.

It took two hours for Ray Greene to get the information he wanted and the warrant he needed to enter 2 Chamber Street. He had the stats on Mrs. Whitman: death certificate signed by her husband; no ashes, no urn in the Port Dundas columbarium; a certificate of cremation signed, by the director of the now-defunct crematorium, in a hand it took a half-hour to determine was Dale Whitman's and not Edwin Curry's, whoever that was.

The current owners objected to entry on the grounds that they were members of the local community *in good standing* and there was no nefarious activity going on in their old stone house. "We don't even have teenagers," the wife protested. Greene asked them politely to wait either at a neighbour's house or in the community policing van, where there was hot coffee and Peek Freans. Muttering to each other, the couple elected to visit friends across the road, friends whose combined income, the husband said loud enough for all to hear, exempted them from being bothered by the police.

When they were gone, Greene deployed Fraser and a local stonecutter named Fred Steptoe, who came in his truck and went into the house with a sledgehammer over his shoulder. Ray had never been in any of these old houses near the river, although he'd grown up in the town. His parents preferred to be on the outskirts, where they could farm a small plot and still take advantage of the nearby services. That was in the forties, the old house having long since been replaced by an ATV and Ski-Doo store.

This house was dark and unfriendly. Low ceilings, uneven floors. Musty smelling.

"Basement?" Fraser asked.

"If there's anything it would be down there." Ray opened the door to a ramshackle flight of wooden steps that led down into the dark.

Fraser took the lead.

"Cabinet of Dr. Caligari," Steptoe said.

A pull-string switched on the single bare bulb in the basement. The three men stood at the bottom of the stairs getting their bearings. No windows. A furnace, a storage area, and a discarded toilet. The corners of the room were blurred with dust and cobwebbing. "We need more light than this," said Greene, and Fraser snapped his flashlight on. The commodious space sprang to life where he pointed it: strands of old spiderwebs hung in the corners; a white fungus at the base of the wall glowed silver in the beam. In one of the walls there was a small larder door painted green with a lock on it. Steptoe said it would have been common in a house this old for there to be a root cellar. He'd seen a lot of them just like this one, a small, green, cross-braced door. "Always green," he said. "I've never understood that."

They walked the perimeter of the basement looking for broken or discoloured concrete. Fraser bent close to the floor and felt some of the cracks he found with his fingertips. With the end of the sledgehammer, Steptoe tapped the join between the walls and the floor. "Unlikely anyone would dig at the edge of the room. Too much risk of leaking. If what you think is down here is down here, I'm sure they were counting on the basement staying dry and undisturbed." He continued to tap, moving now in a spiral toward the centre of the room.

Fraser reached the green door. "Can you come break this lock?"

Steptoe inspected the combination lock and produced a long-shafted screwdriver from his back pocket. He put the shaft through the steel shackle, torqued it, and snapped the lock open.

"Handy," said Fraser. He opened the door all the way. It was solid wood, two inches thick. "Holy shit," he said. "Look at this."

The back of the door was pocked with black gashes about an inch in length. Fraser looked closer and saw they were narrow openings in the wood, about a millimetre wide at the top and pointy at the bottom. He ran his finger down one.

"Wow . . . someone was in here with a knife. They stabbed the door about a hundred times."

Ray came over. "You think they were locked in there?"

"Why with a knife?" Fraser asked.

They stepped into the root cellar. A couple of empty vegetable crates lay on the floor with their weathered paper labels drooping. The few shelves were all but empty. A bottle of something in a murky liquid sat with an air of menace on a top shelf, an old paint tray to its left. Fraser passed the bottle to Greene, who set it down carefully.

When Fraser pulled the paint tray down, he almost dropped it – it was incredibly heavy. He set it down on the floor and shone his light on it.

"Oh, yeah," said Greene. "Concrete." A wooden paint stick was stuck fast in about two inches of it. Ray tilted his head and read the faded pink stamp on the stick: MAIN STREET HARDWARE *Proudly representing Canadian Paint Co. Tel: WE 6-9521.*

Steptoe's hammer had been going *tok tok tok* all around the basement. In the root cellar it went *tok tok tok* and then it went *tonk.* He tapped again. The floor made the sound again. "Could be hollow here. Might just be pipes," he said. "You want me to break it?"

Greene's glare said *What are you waiting for?*

Steptoe swung the hammer.

] 29 [

In 1984, all OPS cruisers were fitted with reinforced separators to keep cops safe from their prisoners. In all the time since, Hazel almost always kept the heavy Plexiglas window between back and front open, mainly for ventilation.

She wasn't taking any chances now, though. Gloria, although groggy and in agony, had woken. Hazel piloted her soundlessly into the back seat and then closed and locked the separator. She lowered herself into the driver's seat, holding her breath and then breathing, until she was sitting behind the wheel. Her acrobatics were beginning to have consequences and her lower back was seizing. She wondered how fast Wingate could drive. He was already not just in over his head — his feet were planted in the muck, too, so it didn't matter now. They had to get Renald back. They had to bring boys who had been in the dark back into the light and name their killer. In the rear-view mirror, the murderer's daughter stared uninterestedly out the window. Her face had swollen up. The gun had split her left cheek against the bone, and her lips as well. Her blonde hair on one side was sticky with blood. *Try to get that colour at the Betty French Hair Emporium*, Hazel thought. Gloria turned to look at Hazel in the mirror with dead eyes.

The Plexiglas barrier was soundproof. To talk, Hazel had to push a button. "Are there others?" Dead eyes. "Did he teach you? Your father?" Gloria's mouth remained sealed in a thin line. Her eyes said nothing.

Hazel pulled her gaze back to the highway. Her pulse was irregular and she'd had a few palpitations: heavy thuds in her chest, as if her heart were falling down the stairs. Her temple throbbed where Gloria had stuck her, and the wooziness ebbed and flowed. She grabbed a bunch of napkins out of the glove compartment and held them against the wound. The bleeding had slowed to a trickle. Her hair was a sticky mess. The combined smell of blood and sweat made her feel sick. She was dizzy. "How did your mother die, Gloria? How old were you?"

"*We* were nine," Gloria said. "You were at my mother's funeral service."

"Yes. You know, I'd forgotten there was no casket."

"She was cremated. Dust to dust." Gloria leaned into the barrier and Hazel shifted to her left instinctively, as if it didn't matter that Gloria was cuffed behind glass. There's no evidence linking me to anything. A judge will set me free in two minutes."

"I won't let that happen."

Gloria took a deep breath and let it out. "Oh, Hazel. Such a goodie."

"Did your father show you how to kill?"

"What happened to you and Andrew?"

"Did your father teach you to kill?"

"Only when I was old enough," she said.

Hazel stabbed the talk button and her cell rang at the same time, startling her. She flipped it open. "We found her," Ray Greene said in her ear. Hazel pushed the button again, bringing Gloria Whitman back into the conversation. She put her cell on speaker.

"Oh yeah, where was she?"

"Buried under the floor. Inside a root cellar. Stab marks all over the door."

"Stab marks?"

"On the inside of the door. Looks like she was shut in there with a knife. Maybe to put herself out of her own misery if it got to be too much." Hazel watched Gloria's reaction. There was none. She wore the countenance of someone sitting on a bench in the park. Ray continued, "Fraser said he imagined when she finally died, Whitman just dug the hole and rolled her into it. He fitted a plank of plywood over her and poured two inches of concrete on top. Done."

"What's left?"

"Not a lot. Acidic soil. That'll break down bones in less than forty years. But there's teeth, a jawbone, and some of the pelvis. There's enough. Where are you?"

"Bringing in Gloria Whitman."

There was a brief silence on his end. "Good for you, Hazel. Nice collar." He hung up.

"What did your mother die of?"

"Her imperfections," Gloria said. "She cut my balls off in her womb."

"*What?*"

"My father thought I was perfect. 'My issue goes through you alone,' he told me. No siblings, no half-siblings. He said he hoped I'd have a hundred children. My mother . . . he put her down."

Hazel shuddered at the phrasing. "You knew she was locked up in there. Her screams must've . . . You helped him kill her."

"We kept it in the family. I helped him a couple of other times, too."

Hazel thought about turning her off again. Gloria's face in the mirror had begun to glow. She was flushing. She remembered that look from when they were kids: wide-eyed and greedy. Just as she was seeing her in the rear-view, so had she seen Gloria in mirrors throughout their youth, hungrily grazing her own face with her eyes. It hadn't changed in all these decades: a psychopath's intense love for the beloved. Dale Whitman was the beloved; that was who she preened for in the mirror, he the father-husband, she the mirror-wife.

"Once he brought a boy home," she said. "A black boy with a funny name. Nobody wanted him. They kept trying to get some couple to take him, but nobody would. My dad gave him a needle and brought him home in the middle of the night. He was sleepy, but he was awake. He smiled at me."

"Black?" Hazel asked.

"Brown, whatever. Not white."

"Charles Shearing."

Gloria shoved herself forward and pressed her face to the Plexiglas beside Hazel's head. "Maybe Charlie."

"Confess your part in all of this and maybe I can keep your father's name out of the news. Preserve his reputation. You could give Carol's mother some closure."

"And why would I want to do that?"

Dead eyes.

Wingate sped north. Hazel hadn't sounded very good on the phone. When they talked to each other these days, it was by cell, not radio. Who was she going to call when he was gone, he wondered.

Now he was driving up the 41 at 145 kilometres an hour to intercept her. She told him she'd lost "some" blood.

His phone rang: Michael. He put the call on speaker.

"I found Cutter," Michael said. "He came to Charterhouse as Couture and Dublin Place –"

"Home –"

"As Couture, and then when he leaves, he's still Couture. No name change, like you say."

"I've been staring at my notes on Cutter. They're on a yellow legal pad. You see them?"

"This collection of scribbled symbols?"

"Yeah. Look it over. You're probably the only person on the planet who can read my handwriting. Where is he? What's his next move? Maybe we can cut him off before he makes any more rash decisions with one of our own."

"I don't know. Where are you now?"

"Driving as fast as I can, north."

"Should you call an ambulance? Is she really hurt?"

"She's made of some kind of material you can't get any-more," Wingate said. "She'll be fine."

Hazel passed the sign for Caplin – forty kilometres to go – and she was seeing things. Flashes of light in her field of vision, tiny pale stars that were hollow in the middle. "You don't look so good," Gloria said into the back seat micro-phone. "Maybe you should pull over."

"You're pretty blasé for someone who's going to spend the rest of her life behind bars."

"I'm beginning to wonder if either of us is going to make it back to Port Dundas. To judge by your driving. You should get a couple of corks for those holes in your head."

She'd soaked through the wad of napkins. Maybe it was blood loss, this feeling she had of becoming lighter and lighter even as the road elongated in front of her. She heard Gloria at a distance say, "Oh shit —" and then Hazel saw the side of the road coming toward her, and beyond it, flashing lights. Broken, half-mad James Wingate to the rescue.

James Wingate marched Gloria Whitman into the back of the station house. Ray Greene came out of his office, and then most of his colleagues in the pen stood up and watched him emerge from the rear corridor, one hand holding onto the cuffs behind Gloria's back. No one said a word when he took her past Hazel's office and down the hallway to the cells.

"I want all hands on deck at four o'clock," Ray said returning to his office. "By then, we better have something on the whereabouts of Melvin Renald. Detective Inspector Micallef will brief us on progress in the case. I'm clearing overtime for anyone who wants it."

Greene closed himself in his office and called the reporters he'd promised the rest of the scoop to. It paid to keep a couple of decent journalists on your side, to ensure a proper flow of information. To Ray Greene, the press was an extension of the police, if used properly.

"Headline," Ray said to each of the reporters in turn. *"Family Murder Spree Solved.* Lead: *Port Dundas OPS say they have identified the culprit in the murders of more than twenty young men at the Dublin Home for Boys. The murders, which took place over a ten-year period from 1951 to 1960, are believed to have been committed by a former Port Dundas citizen, Dr. Dale Whitman, now deceased. According to police, the doctor's daughter, Gloria Whitman, was also involved. Today the Port Dundas detachment of the OPS announced the arrest of Ms. Whitman on first-degree murder charges in connection with the 1957 disappearance of local girl Carol Lim. Lim's body was discovered yesterday at the site of the Gateway Plaza, immediately after a groundbreaking ceremony meant to inaugurate construction. We believe that Miss Lim was murdered."* He listened for typing. "You can write the rest yourself."

Hazel accepted a total of nine stitches in the two gashes in her face, no anesthetic, but she wouldn't take a gauze bandage around her head, nor a painkiller. One of the paramedics that attended to her was Mira, who'd come to the house, and she gave Hazel a hairy eyeball. "You're a handful, too," she said. "As bad as your mother."

"No," Hazel said. "She's as bad as I am."

She went to lie down in her office. The full briefing was scheduled for four o'clock. Her head was swimming with pain and information, much of which was settling now as hard fact.

She closed her eyes and listened to the life of the station house. There was a calm that came before announcing a dreadful truth. She listened to Melanie Cartwright's printer spitting out sheets of paper. Briefing materials. The matter out of which the story gets stitched together.

She went back in her mind to the day she and Gloria had taken their walk up the bluff. She saw the sky again, its zippers of white cloud. Felt the twigs underfoot and smelled the sunbaked leaves on the ground. She walked along the path that followed the edge of the bluff to the Lion's Paw and she encountered Carol Lim there, standing looking out over the country below them. She said nothing to Hazel, but handed her the battered pewter flask and began to climb down. Hazel went to the edge and watched her as she gingerly picked her way down the rock face. When she was partway down, she slipped one leg, and then the other, into a space between boulders as big as cars, and disappeared into the dark. Then a bell chimed and she woke up. It was ten to four.

Hazel stood at the back of the pen and called for quiet. The room settled. She thanked everyone. "Now, I have a number of important announcements to make. First, as you know by now, the body found in the rubble of the Lion's Paw has been positively identified as Carol Lim. She vanished in October of 1957 and was never found, although it was until now impossible to prove that she was dead. As a department, we have offered our deepest condolences to the extended Lim family, who have waited a long time for an answer."

"What happened to your head, Hazel?" came a voice from the room.

She touched her stitches with a finger. "Please save your questions until later. You will be aware of an ongoing – albeit until recently stalled – investigation by the OPS concerning unidentified remains found on the grounds of Tournament Acres. Now that the crime site has been reopened by our friends at the RCMP, you can expect to be sent back out there with finer-toothed combs.

"We will be releasing the names of boys who are shown to have been taken in at Dublin Home, but whose names never appear afterward in any public record. Among those names, we believe, will be the names of the murdered children, and we are going to ask you to contribute to finding relations of these boys, no matter how distant, so they can give their remains proper burials.

"Today we have arrested Gloria Whitman, sixty-four, originally from Port Dundas, and charged her with first-degree murder in the death of Carol Lim. We believe that her father, a well-known physician and prominent member of the community, is the person who orchestrated the abductions and murders of boys at Dublin Home."

Murmurs arose in the pen like a shudder. Hazel called for quiet again, but the unrest was spreading. Some officers had risen at their desks and were looking in the same direction: the front of the station house. Right in front of Hazel, at the back of the pen, Constable Eileen Bail put her hand on her holster.

"What's going on?" Hazel said. Half her officers were standing and blocking her view. She heard Sean Macdonald's voice: "Drop your weapon!"

Hazel shoved her way forward and got to the front counter as Leon Cutter came through the front door of the station house, pushing Sergeant Melvin Renald in front of him with a pistol against his temple. The sergeant looked enervated; his face was dirty and his eyes sunken, as if he'd been kept in the dark.

"I'm keeping my word," Cutter said. "Here's your boy."

He shoved Renald toward the arms of his colleagues.

"Now give me our killer," he said.

] 30 [

Wednesday, October 31, afternoon

The day went by in a blur to Detective Sergeant James Wingate. The sight of Hazel with the side of her face gashed open had set his nerves jangling, and as soon as Gloria Whitman was locked up behind bars, he left the station house and drove back to his apartment with his head blaring. Michael came out of the office, surprised to see his brother back, and then his look turned from one of surprise to alarm. James looked like he was going to collapse.

Michael took him into the bedroom and removed his jacket and shoes. "You look like shit," he said.

James lay there breathing slowly, but not slowly enough. "I just locked up Gloria Whitman," he said, smiling weakly. "What have you got to show for your afternoon?"

"Something that is going to blow your mind, actually.

But I'm not telling you anything until you have a Xanax in your system. You're coming apart." He went into the bathroom to fetch the pill.

They gave Renald water and an OPS jacket to keep warm. He shivered and hacked into his fist. "You fucking animal," Hazel said to Cutter. "Was this really necessary?"

"Put him somewhere safe, before I change my mind," Cutter replied. He kept his gun trained on a single person: Macdonald. The rest of the detachment had their guns trained on Cutter. Hazel put Melvin Renald in her office.

"You're OK now, Mel. You're home." She took him inside and left him on her couch. He looked shell-shocked. "You'll be safe in here, OK?"

Back in the pen, Ray was trying to talk Cutter down. "You're holding a gun on an officer *in* a police station. You must know every unit in the area is racing toward us. Don't let this end badly, Leon."

"What are you going to do for me? For us?" Cutter asked, the gun shaking at Macdonald.

"I can assure you that justice – as much as it is possible – will be our goal for you. But you can't get it this way. You have to surrender."

"We don't need the OPS to get us justice. Where were you in 1956, when he took three of us in one month alone? How come nobody knew?"

"It was a different time," Ray said. In the distance, the shrill whine of sirens was forming. "Come on, Cutter. Put the gun down."

"Give me the bones," he said.

"I can't. Every effort will be made to repatriate the bones to family members and if that fails, then a dignified burial."

"What family members do Deasún and Shearing have?" he asked before spitting out the answer: "None!"

"Eloy Maracle is back with his brother. The same is possible for all of these missing dead."

"If you won't give me the bones," said Cutter, "then give us the woman who's locked up in that cell back there."

"How do you know who's locked up or not locked up here?"

"News travels fast. Give her to us and we'll see what we can do with *her* bloodline. That's the kind of justice we can accept. Symbolic justice." The words *end his line* rang in Hazel's head, but they were cut off by sirens. A white light flashed through the room. Tires screeched and doors slammed.

"They're coming," said Greene, imploring Cutter.

"WE HAVE THE BUILDING SURROUNDED." A giant voice shook the station house. "LOWER YOUR WEAPONS AND EXIT THE BUILDING WITH YOUR HANDS UP."

Hazel said: "They're waiting for you, Leon. Don't make a mistake."

The hubbub on the other side of the room intensified. Someone was coming in through the rear parking lot door. It was Wingate. But not James. Michael Wingate.

"Sorry to interrupt! Can I come in?" He was crouched down, inching toward them and holding a piece of paper high in the air. "He was in Dublin Home for seven years!" he said.

"Who?" said Hazel. "Where is your brother? What are you doing here?"

"Ronald Melvin. He was born Ronald Melvin!" Wingate said.

She snatched the paper from James's brother. Cutter began to laugh. She scanned the information. It was a legal name change record. In 1977, Ronald Melvin had changed his name to Melvin Renald and joined the academy. Her jaw locked in a half-open position. "Oh, shit," she said. She spun to see her office door was already wide open.

"Ten-minute head start," Cutter said, placing his gun on the countertop. Macdonald leaped over and cuffed him.

Hazel ran down the corridor to the cells. Gloria was gone.

"THIS IS SUPERINTENDENT MARTIN SCOTT OF THE RCMP. WE WANT TO NEGOTIATE A PEACEFUL END TO THIS SITUATION."

Hazel ran out the front of the station house waving her hands. "Find Renald!" she yelled. Beside his car, Scott looked at her, perplexed. "He's been working with Cutter the whole fucking time. He has my prisoner!" Greene and Fraser ran past her.

"We're going to fan out," Ray said to her. "Bail, Macdonald, Wilton, and Windemere are already on the road."

"Call Victoria Torrance!" she shouted.

"Already did!" His cruiser was parked in front. He and Fraser jumped into it. Hazel ran into the road and waved Superintendent Scott into his cruiser.

"Get me to Tournament Acres," she said.

Martin Scott drove his cruiser at 165 kilometres an hour. "By permission of Her Majesty the Queen," he said. Hazel sat in the passenger seat holding on to the dashboard. The road sped by under them. "Why do you think he's gone back to the home?" he asked her.

"You didn't hear Cutter. They're after poetic justice now. Dublin Home's got to be the backdrop."

"I can go faster."

"This is fast enough," she said.

He put on the cruise control and focused on weaving in and out of lanes. Normally, such wild driving would have made her sick, but she trusted Scott, and as fast as he could go was the speed she wanted to go. She wondered where Wingate was if he'd had to send Michael. He was going to get another commendation if she had anything to do with it.

"Who killed the Fremonts? Are you going to tell me it was Willan?"

"He didn't do the killing. Bellefeuille did."

"Givens?"

"Same."

"Willan had these people *executed*?"

"He claims Bellefeuille was acting on his own. You should hear what Bellefeuille claims."

The mileage signs for Dublin ticked down. "So, are you married?" he asked her at the ten-kilometre sign.

"Divorced," she said. "You?"

"Inevitably." He turned onto Concession Road 7. They stopped speaking until the old boys' home came into view. Hazel saw Renald's cruiser parked under the gnarled apple trees.

"Cover me," she said, getting out of the car.

"Can we have a drink afterward?" he asked her, taking the safety off his sidearm.

"Maybe you *are* going too fast." She moved forward lightly on the tips of her toes and came into line with the door of the home. The plywood barricade had been prised off and it was open a crack. Scott trailed behind her at fifty paces. She waved to him to stay farther back.

The foyer of the abandoned building was still lit with late-day sun, and Hazel stepped inside with her gun drawn. Immediately, she saw Renald on the upper landing with his arm around Gloria Whitman's throat. He pulled her away and they disappeared through one of the doors to the upstairs dorms.

"Mel!" she shouted. "We have Leon. This was all his idea. I don't know what he told you, but you are a police officer *first*!" Another door closed distantly. She began up the stairs. When she got to the landing, Martin Scott was standing inside the front door. She went into the first dorm room and walked through it to the door leading to the one beyond.

"Sergeant Renald?" she called. "This isn't you. You believe in justice. You've spent thirty years in the force."

"Waiting for my chance," he said, but she couldn't tell which of the other rooms he was in. "Like Lionel. Like Rex. Cutter always said we were going to need the law if the truth was ever going to be known! About what happened to us." Hazel put her hand on the doorknob.

"Let her go," she said.

"Is that what you would do?"

She felt the vibration of his voice in her palm and she threw open the door. He was standing silhouetted against the back window, with Gloria Whitman in front of him, his arm around her midsection. When he saw Hazel, he shoved Gloria away and turned his gun on his colleague.

"Shoot him!" Gloria said. "The sick fuck!"

Hazel ignored her. "It's over," she said to Renald.

"Get your gun off me and put it on her," he told her. She didn't. "She's just going to go free?"

"No. She's going to jail."

"It's you or her," Renald said. "Make a statement, Hazel. Shoot her."

"Why?"

"Full circle." He wagged the gun at her. "Justice comes and has its fill. You end the killer's line, just like he tried to end ours."

"He's already dead, Melvin."

"Not so," he replied. "He lives on."

She put her gun on the floor.

He looked disappointed. "Well," he said, "they must be on their way. Time's a-wasting."

"Drop it," Martin Scott said from the other doorway.

"Not a chance," said Renald, and he spun and fired a single bullet through Gloria Whitman's forehead. Hazel lunged for him and Scott held fire. She knocked Melvin Renald to the ground and he simply let go of the gun. Gloria lay on her side, one eye open and one closed. She looked surprised.

On Main Street there were children dressed as cartoon characters and spacemen and all manner of evil spirits. The scene was cheerful and dark at the same time. So much fake blood. Hazel walked in the direction of the Kilmartin Bridge.

Herbert Lim Grocery had long ago changed hands. It was called Kilmartin Convenience now, and a neon sign in the window said INTERNET. Buzz Lightyear and a gorilla

came out of the shop and a large peanut went in. She listened for a moment to all the happy chatter.

Mrs. Lim still owned the building and lived in the apartment above it. Hazel had been here a few months ago, just
to check in. Mrs. Lim had offered her tea and gingersnaps,
and they'd spent an hour together. She'd given up on a
happy life, she told Hazel. Being alive was almost enough
after the disappearance of her daughter. Almost.

It would be all over the papers tomorrow, even the big
ones. Hazel opened the gate and climbed the stairs. She
rang the doorbell and after a brief wait Mrs. Lim answered.
She moved slowly; she was brittle and bird-like. "Hazel."

"I've come to bring you some news."

Mrs. Lim blinked a couple of times. "I see. Are you
coming in?"

"Yes."

This time no tea was offered. Hazel sat at the kitchen
table trying to think of how to say it. Mrs. Lim watched
her with glassy eyes, her hand a fist over her mouth. "You
found her," she said.

Hazel couldn't look up. "Yes."

"I want to bury her."

"You'll be able to do that soon, Mrs. Lim. I'm sorry to
bring such sad news."

"Thank you," the old woman said. "I prayed for this,
that god would let me know in my lifetime. Yes, thank you.
It is good news."

"Mrs. Lim –"

"Now I know she is dead I will stop thinking about the life she had in my dreams. The children she had. She was happy, but I was alone. I am glad I'll be able to put flowers on her grave."

Hazel suddenly covered her mouth. Mrs. Lim put her hand on Hazel's arm and stroked it. She felt deeply embarrassed to cry, and she tried to apologize, but Mrs. Lim stopped her by squeezing her arm hard. "You have never forgotten her," she said. "You didn't know her very well, but you have always acted as her friend."

"The message wasn't from her," Hazel said.

"No, dear. It wasn't."

Hazel tried to grapple with the enormity of Mrs. Lim's kindness. "Part of me still really believed she was alive."

"You were a good girl, Hazel. And you are a good and compassionate woman. Thank you for coming to see me."

Hazel walked back to her car among the older kids, the ones who'd put little or no effort into their costumes. Most of them were no older than she and Gloria had been when Carol disappeared. At that age, Hazel had not yet developed a grounded belief in human evil. When you're fourteen, death is abstract. A vague and distant place. She'd been happy to troop in these streets with her bag full of candy. When she got too old for it, she took Alan, whose preferred costume – even when it was too small to wear any longer – was a skunk. For a while, before he left home, Hazel had called him Stink. Affectionately and accurately.

She went back to the station house but didn't go in. She got into her car and drove back to Pember Lake. Her mother seemed to be living in 2007 when she arrived home. Tiny mercies, Hazel thought. She made a quick plate of scrambled eggs for them both and they ate together in a companionable silence. "Do you remember Carol Lim?" Hazel asked.

"I still think about her."

"We found her body. Yesterday."

Emily put her fork down on her plate. "No end of bad news. Can't do anything about it."

"We got the person who killed her."

"Well, I'm glad," Emily said with a distracted air. She pushed a couple of curds of egg around her plate.

Hazel changed the subject. "I was thinking we might have Martha and Emilia here this year for Christmas. Would you like that?"

"If you do the cooking," her mother said. "And the cleaning up. And will it be a dreary, dry Christmas?"

"I don't know what the weather will be like."

"I mean will there be liquor?"

Hazel laughed. "If we don't top you up sooner or later, you won't stay so beautifully preserved."

———

That night, after her mother had gone to bed, Hazel went to the end of the second floor hall and pulled down the attic stair. She tested its solidity and climbed up. At the top, the light switch was where she remembered it. Attics were where things you couldn't let go of spent their decades hidden and misremembered.

A warm, orange light flooded the cramped space filled with boxes and a dress form and paintings everyone had stopped liking. Blocking the only window in the place were bankers boxes, piled three deep. Both she and her mother were meticulous about such things as packed boxes. Not only did every one have written on it a summary of its contents, but somewhere up here there was also a manifest that collected the details in one place. Emily could file with the best of them from her years in public service.

Hazel began reading lids and moving boxes off their piles. There were nine of them on the floor behind her when she found the box marked, simply, ALAN. She brought it over to where the light was strongest. Inside were some of the books he'd left behind, along with pads full of his drawings, several 45s, a few hockey cards, his high-school diploma, and a handful of postcards he'd sent from travels in Thailand and Cambodia. That was his life: things in a box. She thought of the plastic bin containing Carol Lim's rotted belongings.

Under this pile of oddments, at the bottom, Hazel found the white inventory box Alan had taken her to see that Christmas Day. She took it out, feeling its weight, and rested it on her lap. The lid slid up off with the sound of a hollow kiss. Inside, catching the light in their angled faces, the silver hearts were as bright as the day they'd been struck.